VOLUME 3 | 2022

MONKEY

EDITORS
Ted Goossen
Motoyuki Shibata

MANAGING EDITOR
Meg Taylor

CONTRIBUTING EDITOR
Roland Kelts

MARKETING MANAGER
Tiff Ferentini

ART DIRECTION & DESIGN
The Office of Gilbert Li

DIGITAL PRODUCTION
Bookmobile

WEBSITE
Kaori Drome

COVER
© Akino Kondoh

INSIDE COVERS
© Konor Abrahams / TOOGL

ISBN: 978-1-7376253-3-9 (print)
ISBN: 978-1-7376253-4-6 (ebook)
ISBN: 978-4-88418-593-0 (Japan)

Published annually by
MONKEY New Writing from Japan,
a nonprofit corporation.

MONKEY New Writing from Japan
422 East End Ave.
Pittsburgh, PA 15221 USA

Distributed by Ingram in the U.S.
and Kinokuniya in Japan.

Printed in Japan by Shinano.

MONKEY New Writing from Japan
benefits from close collaboration with
MONKEY, a Japanese literary journal
published by Switch Publishing.

We gratefully acknowledge the
generous support of Kōji Yanai.

Subscribe, shop online, and
sign up for our newsletter at
monkeymagazine.org

THE MONKEY SPEAKS

Yet again this year, our writers and translators have received international recognition. Aoko Matsuda's *Where the Wild Ladies Are*, translated by Polly Barton, won a World Fantasy Award in the best collection category; Mieko Kawakami's *Heaven,* translated by Sam Bett and David Boyd, was shortlisted for the International Booker Prize; and Haruki Murakami gleaned another international honor by winning the Prix mondial Cino Del Duca.

In this issue we welcome new writers (Kaori Fujino and Natsuko Kuroda), new translators (Chris Corker, Gitte Hansen, Kendall Heitzman, Laurel Taylor, and Asa Yoneda), and well-established poets (Keijirō Suga and Mutsuo Takahashi). We are also happy to introduce the legendary Midori Osaki.

While our regular contributors—both writers and translators—appear in almost every volume, we're equally committed to introducing new voices, so it's a real balancing act! We can say with confidence that *MONKEY* delivers new writing from Japan at its best, translated by some of the leading practitioners of literary translation. And let's not forget the contributions from American and Canadian friends of *MONKEY*: a poem and story from Stuart Dybek and stories from Matthew Sharpe and Eli K.P. William.

Volume 3 celebrates "crossings." Transitioning out of the pandemic, we are inspired by stories of transformation and the joyful play of influences back and forth between Japanese and Western literatures. Indeed, this is what we've been up to from the very beginning: crossing borders of geography, language, culture, gender, politics, you name it! The pieces in this volume manage to cross borders in new, mindbending ways, starting with a pictorial exploration of a prehistoric cave by Satoshi Kitamura and ending with Kyōhei Sakaguchi's story set in a strange country whose geography and population keep shifting.

No passport necessary, no Covid tests required. Happy crossings!

Ted Goossen
Motoyuki Shibata
Meg Taylor

VOLUME 3 | 2022

MONKEY

Crossings: A Monkey's Dozen

© Akino Kondoh

Mieko Kawakami

Upon Seeing the Evening Sky

translated by Hitomi Yoshio

I USUALLY WORK IN A STUDIO about seven minutes by bicycle from my home. It's close to my son's school, so I drop him off in the morning before starting my day. As I write this, we are in the middle of a state of emergency, and many of our routines and habits have been upended by the pandemic. Now I try to work on a laptop, sitting at the kitchen table alongside my son who is attending classes online, but so far this has not been going well. My husband is also a writer, which means the three of us are home all the time. Our compassion for each other is gradually wearing thin, as the comfortable distance between us—made possible in the past by the time we spent apart—disappears. Naturally, it is difficult for me to write as I normally do. This is not so much a matter of feeling as it is a matter of body. Details such as the size of my computer screen or the distance between my chair and desk can have unexpected consequences. Within an hour, my arms and shoulders begin to ache, and my writing feels off-balance. Only in its absence have I learned to appreciate the harmony that had developed between my body and my habits.

Before the pandemic I used to pick up my son and return home at the end of the day. I would ride my bike with my son on the back seat, in twilight. Stopping at a traffic light or waiting at the railroad crossing, I always look toward the western sky. Sometimes there is not a cloud in the sky, while other times a spectacular sunset unfolds before me. There are ordinary sunsets too, of course. But what they all have in common is that they never fail to grab my heart. Beauty becomes indistinguishable from that which cannot be retrieved—or perhaps from loneliness itself—and it takes my breath away.

Last year, during early summer, my grandmother died. She had been like a mother to me. Since my childhood, I feared the inevitable separation that would one day come between us. It was an extreme sort of fear. When I imagined that moment, I would cry and cry. *Don't cry, don't cry,* she would say with a smile. As I sat in the hospital room watching her gradually wither away (that's literally how it felt, since she died of old age), I had a strange sensation that somehow a long time had passed, and I was witnessing what I had feared for so long. For a few months after my grandmother was gone, I felt light-headed doing chores around the house, riding my bike, or sleeping. "Feeling foggy . . ." I often said to myself, as if my body had lost its center.

The sky at dusk began to remind me of my grandmother, no matter what kind of sky it was. A faint trace of cloud, a spectacular shiver-inducing mackerel sky, a deep rose-colored brightness that was out of this world . . . whatever shape it took, I would think of my grandmother the moment I looked up. Why was that? We had never watched the sunset together, nor do I have any memories of talking with her about the sky, the clouds, or the beauty of nature. Still, I thought of her. It was as if the sunset sky and clouds—the things that grab my heart, not her face or form—had come to embody my grandmother. Perhaps this is what remembering is really all about. Our memories are mysterious. There are so many things we can recall—the color of a landscape, for example, or the shape of something we have seen— but how they "remain" in memory is ambiguous. When discrete facts join together to reach a certain density in our memories, then boundaries loosen and everything flows and blends together, untangling and spreading the colors before fading away like a sunset. Perhaps we all end up like that. Why does the evening sky—the clouds and the colors and the passage of time—seem to resemble our memories so closely? Lingering at the railroad crossing, watching the sky burn, I tell my son, "The sunset reminds me of Granny Mitsuko." He, too, watches the sky in silence.

Ten days have passed since I began this essay. I'm starting to get a little accustomed to life during this seemingly endless shutdown. A different kind of harmony is beginning to emerge. How to divide time, a change of mindset, a new and more positive way of thinking . . . these are the things we are figuring out.

The other day, my son and I took a walk at the end of the day for the first time in a long while. The sunset was so vivid we could almost touch it. I thought to myself—there's never been a world without a sky. The same was true of the ground, the sea, the light. No matter what happens on this earth, no matter how foolishly human beings act, the sky will always be there. A deep connection must exist between the sky and what remains of those we will never meet again. My son and I watched the evening sky in silence. 🐒

Makoto Takayanagi

———

The Graffiti

translated by Michael Emmerich

IT BEGAN WITH a bit of graffiti.

The vestiges of a long, restless night lay capsized for hours on the city floor, even as dawn approached, coating everything in the velvet lethargy of the slugabed. The moment the first gleam of sunlight trickled in, gently stirring the folds of a shallow sleep—that was when the graffiti appeared. Aside from its glistening wetness, which seemed almost intentionally to mark its presence, it was just an ordinary scribble.

Soon, though, we realized it could not be covered over. Before the paint had time to dry, the same graffiti would reappear, traced by an unseen hand. Indeed, each time anyone attempted to erase it, the graffiti would enlarge its territory, unfurling in ever more intricate designs. And whenever you looked, it always had that same fresh-painted sheen.

You could not *read* the graffiti.

It was not written in the Roman alphabet, or in kanji. Neither was it Hangul or Sanskrit—that much was clear to all. The voices that ventured to suggest the strokes must be Arabic, or ancient runes, were soon quelled by the proliferating silences on the wall. Ripples of doubt began to spread as to whether the marks were writing at all.

If just one of the city's residents could have grasped the meaning the graffiti exuded, surely it would have remained on that wall forever. Because graffiti depends upon this relationship, between the one who sends the message and the other who perhaps unknowingly accepts it, as when, looking up, you notice a word on a bathroom wall.

The graffiti was written in a script that did not exist.

Amateur researchers scoured every book in the city library, but their efforts afforded not even a brief respite from our collective bepuzzlement. Experts in all the world's writing systems, specialists in every language, scholars of ancient civilizations were hastily summoned from larger cities in the region to engage in a series of lightning-quick debates, but none yielded more than a burst of midsummer rain.

By the time it hit us, one morning, that we had no prospect of identifying those marks or their provenance, or who had traced them, or why—that we must assume they were in a script that *had not yet been written*—the situation had grown more unmanageable than an untamed horse in rut. Every wall in the city (including things that merely saw themselves as walls) was covered entirely in graffiti.

At least then the graffiti was only on walls.

The day after the simoom swept through, we woke to a strangely washed-out landscape. Nothing had changed, not the tiniest detail, yet somehow the city felt distant and unfamiliar, like a painted backdrop in the theater. All the writing in the city, everything, had been replaced overnight by those illegible forms. Every billboard, every street sign, even the nameplates on our houses.

There was no sense in writing the words again. Even if you fixed a billboard or replaced a nameplate, by the next morning your work would have been undone. We quickly decided it wasn't worth the trouble. Writing is just writing, we told ourselves, they're just *signs*—we should bundle them up like a stack of old letters and return them to the sender.

The situation began to affect us directly.

The city seemed lost in a daydream, slumbering on and on. Or rather, the city had been translated, just as it was, into a dream. And somewhere in this dream city we had made a wrong turn. We would try to strike up a conversation with someone (a lover, a neighbor, one's spouse) about something trivial (a cat's pregnancy, a lover's mole, the training of dolphins). But our tongues would do their own thing, sending out the weirdest words.

We had no idea what they meant. Neither, of course, could we understand each other—not a bit. We used our own words in our heads when we were thinking, we were certain of that, but the moment we tried to communicate our thoughts to someone else,

incomprehensible babble that had not previously risen into our consciousness would explode rapid-fire from the tips of our tongues. In no time, the city was awash with unfamiliar clusters of sounds.

We threw ourselves into silence.

Determined at least to try and resist, we staunchly refused to speak. We had our pride. Speechlessness filled the world; silence ruled the city. There was never any hullabaloo, just the scritching and scratching of pens on paper when a small group gathered in secret to pass notes back and forth, like a melody erupting from deep in our hearts to be borne off by the wind.

The clear scent of sweet osmanthus hung in the air the day our pens betrayed us. Until then, our handwriting had been docile enough; now, suddenly, the lines we traced across the paper began writhing like worms. Our hands skittered off, directed by some other power. The patterns that emerged would change, as if they harbored a life of their own, yet with no sense, there, of any will to communicate.

Books were the last bastion.

Before, we had never given books a second thought; now it was impossible to endure without them. It didn't matter what they were—any printed matter would do. We battled for books, drowned ourselves in type. Even during sex we would not let them go. Soon, however, we began to abandon our reading, to spend more time lost in reverie, staring into the distance with the look in our eyes of one exploring the folds of her most secret memories as they faded away.

In any event, by then the pages' margins were so crammed with illegible notes scrawled by previous readers (comments, annotations?) that the texts themselves were all but overwhelmed. It was only a matter of time until it became more difficult and time consuming to decipher the original printed text than to catalogue the ancient artifacts at an excavation site.

The invasion has reached our dreams.

Many among us have begun muttering those weird words in our sleep. Perhaps as we slumber, night after night, we travel in that language. We make a conscious effort not to reflect on what is happening, not to recognize that, soon, thinking in this language will come naturally, that we will manipulate its words with facility in flawless conversation.

We can no longer tell whether this consciousness itself has been stitched together in our old language, or if instead it is the new tongue that has come to rule our lives. Indeed, of late we have often felt stirring within us a sense that perhaps, in reality, we have been embedded in this language ever since we were born. 🐵

From the modern Japanese
translation by Seikō Itō

TADANORI
A Noh Play

translated and with an introduction
by Jay Rubin

WASTED TALENT:
AN INTRODUCTION

ONE OF SIXTEEN WARRIOR GHOST PLAYS written by Zeami (1363–1443) in an essentially narrative mode, *Tadanori* recounts episodes from the life of Taira no Tadanori (1144–1184) as depicted in the fourteenth-century epic *The Tale of the Heike*. We see Tadanori as a warrior cut down on the battlefield but also as a poet whose death was a terrible waste of literary talent. Ironically, the only example of Tadanori's poetry quoted in the play—taken from *The Tale of the Heike*—may not have been written by Tadanori at all, but it is quoted in full three times for its symbolic value. Its title is "A Journey's Lodging":

> Traveling, and comes the dark:
> If I should lodge beneath this tree,
> Cherry blossoms will be my host tonight!

According to the Noh scholar Keiichirō Tashiro, the poem may be read as an allegory for the fall of the Taira (benighted in their journey) and for Tadanori's determination to "lodge" himself in poetry (symbolized by cherry blossoms) rather than entrust his posthumous fame to military exploits. What matters finally is Tadanori's (and Zeami's) commitment to the life of song. He remains mired in the "sin" of attachment to his art and his wish for fame, unwilling to trade the Way of Poetry for the nothingness of Buddhist detachment.

This translation of novelist Seikō Itō's modern Japanese rendering of Zeami's text first appeared in the April 2021 issue of the magazine *Shinchō*, where it benefitted greatly from the attention of Maho Adachi and other members of the editorial staff.

AS WITH MANY NOH PLAYS, *Tadanori* begins when a traveling priest addresses the audience as our guide to the supernatural world, but we quickly learn that, unlike the typical generic holy man, he has deep ties with the protagonist.

TADANORI

WEARY EVEN OF BLOSSOMS, we have entered the priesthood.

Weary even of blossoms, we have renounced the world and its aesthetic pleasures.

Though dark clouds may obscure the moon, that means nothing to us.

So sing the itinerant priests who appear before us, and one of them turns to speak: "I am one who formerly served the poet known as Shunzei, Lord Fujiwara no Toshinari. After Toshinari passed away, I cut the cord that bound my topknot and donned this priestly garb. Never having seen the West Country, I determined that I would make a pilgrimage to the west now in spring."

The priests sing of the landmarks on their journey: "We head for the Seinan detached palace in Toba, pass Yamazaki where the mountains separate us from the capital, need not tarry at the barrier gate which remains only in name, find no comfort in the ceaseless cares of the road, while our troubles mount in dealing with life's real challenges, then cross the murky waters of the Akuta River and make our way through the bamboo-grass thicket of Ina."

We pass Koya Pond, clear to the bottom, in which the moon's reflection seems to lodge. We have no choice but to hear the wind blowing through the reeds, making sounds reminiscent of the world we as priests wish to ignore, pass Mount Arima, where we dream of the inescapable travails of the world, waking to the far-off bell of Shitennō Temple in Naniwa, on to the shore at Naruo where skiffs can be seen far out on the waves, yes, far out to sea many skiffs.

"So swiftly have we traveled that already we have arrived at this place called something like the Suma shore in the Province of Tsu. Here, on this beach, I see a lone cherry tree. Could this be the young cherry I have heard so much about? I wish to approach it for a closer look."

"Yes, let us do so," say the other itinerant priests.

At that point an aged fisherman appears.

"Ah, yes, undaunted by the cruel labor I must do to make my way through the world here in Suma, I dip brine from the sea, and when not dipping brine, I haul kindling for the salt fires without a moment to dry these sopping wet robes I am long used to wearing back and forth between hill and shore for my life by the sea here in Suma."

Still more the old man mutters: "The calls of the fishermen to each other never cease, and the constant cries of the plovers sound faintly in the distance."

He continues: "Well known is the loneliness of life on the Suma shore. As the poet Ariwara no Yukihira wrote: 'Should there be one who asks how I am doing here, tell him I live sadly, wet with tears, dripping brine for the salt fires.' Truly, is there anything here that does not call forth loneliness?—the skiffs of the fishermen, the smoke of the salt fires, the wind in the pines."

And the old man tells of the cherry blossoms: "A single cherry tree stands below the hill here in Suma, planted in memory of one who passed away. Just now happens to be the season when the spring cherries bloom, and though I am but a passing stranger where an offering would be concerned, each time I drag my way home, returning from the mountain, I shall break off a blossom and add it to my firewood, making an offering on my way."

Then the traveling priest addresses the old man.

"Pardon me, aged sir, are you a person from the nearby hamlet?"

"Yes, I am indeed a fisherman from this shore."

"If you are a fisherman, you must live on the shore, but you have come out now to the hills, so are you not then what they call a hill person?"

"Are the shore people, then, to leave the brine they have dipped as-is, unburnt?"

"No, no, you are correct. Smoke rises on the evening shore from the salt-making fires."

"So that the fires will burn without ceasing, we hurry to the hills to gather wood for the salt burning."

"Roads to sea and mountain differ, but both lead away from the village."

"Where rarely sound the voices of people on the Suma shore."

"In the mountain hamlet close behind the shore,"

"Is what we call firewood and so..."

"Because there is firewood, the ones who go back and forth to fetch wood for salt burning..."

"...are sea folk, that is. How foolish your question, Reverend Sir!"

The old man continues, as though singing.

Truly, the Suma shore is different from other places. By which is meant that harsh for blossoms are the strong winds that blow through the peaks and the winds that blow down from the mountains, their sounds loathed, but the young cherry tree of Suma is not at all distant from the sea; the shore breezes reach here and scatter the mountain cherries.

Whereupon the traveling priest says, "The sun has already set, you see. Please be so good as to provide us with a night's lodging."

"How lacking you are in poetic sensibility! Could there be any better lodging than beneath these blossoms?"

"Surely, this would be a lodge beneath the blossoms, but then who would be our host?"

"This poem appears in *The Tale of the Heike*:

Traveling, and comes the dark:
If I should lodge beneath this tree,
Cherry blossoms will be my host tonight!

"But the poet himself lies here beneath the moss. Moved to pity, even simple sea folk such as I often stop by here to pray for him. Passing strangers though you priests may be, why do you not also say a prayer for him? How thoughtless you are!"

"Surely it was the Lord of Satsuma who sang:

Traveling, and comes the dark:
If I should lodge beneath this tree,
Cherry blossoms will be my host tonight!"

"Yes, the warrior known as Tadanori, who fell here in the battle of Ichi-no-tani. And so a person with ties to him planted a cherry tree to mark the spot."

"How strange that we should have met like this! So, then, as Toshinari's..."

"...friend in poetry, one who shared deep ties with him..."

"...will host the lodging..."

"...where you stay tonight."

Listen, then, to Buddha's *Law Alone* (Tada Nori) and take your seat upon the lotus pedestal amid the blossoms of the Pure Land.

The old man replies, "How thankful I am! Hearing voices raised in prayer, I can be reborn a Buddha! What joy this gives me!"

The itinerant priest thinks to himself, How strange! This old man seems happy to take my chanted prayers as meant for himself. How can this be? Then the old man says,

"I came here to receive the power of your prayers, Reverend Sir."

So, then, sleep this evening beneath the blossoms, he says, and wait for an oracle in your dreams while I bring a message to the capital.

And as if lodging in the shadows of the blossoms, he has mysteriously vanished, gone who knows where like a rootless plant.

Kyōgen interlude

AT WHICH POINT there appears a man from Suma.

"I who appear before you now am one who dwells on the Suma shore. I have not left my house for a long time, and so today, in search of healing comfort, I will go out to see the young cherry tree. Oh, here there is a priest I have never seen before. Pray tell, Your Reverence, why might you be resting here? Where have you come from and where are you going?"

"We are priests from the capital. Are you a resident of this area?"

"Yes, I am one who lives here."

"If so, please draw closer. I have something I wish to ask you."

"I shall do so."

The man approaches and sits down.

"So, then, what might you wish to ask?"

"Pardon me for this unexpected request, but could you please tell me any tales you might know about this young cherry tree and about how Tadanori met his death?"

"Your request is indeed unexpected. True, I do live in this area, but I know little about such things. Still, I will tell you what I have heard."

"I would be grateful for that."

"Well, then, in the entire House of Taira, I am told, it was the great general known as Tadanori, Lord of Satsuma, who most excelled in both the literary and military arts. Thus, he said to Lord Toshinari, the poet Shunzei, if you are choosing poems for the next imperial anthology, the *Senzaishū*, I wish to be included among the poets, for I am, first, a practitioner of the Way of Poetry. Though Tadanori said this, because the entire Taira House was under imperial censure at the time, Shunzei could only reply, 'Your request can probably not be fulfilled.'"

The man continues:

"But Tadanori was not ready to abandon hope. On his way down here from the capital, he turned his horse back at Yamazaki and called upon Lord Toshinari once again, showing him the many poems that he had brought along. 'If any of these should be suitable,' he said, 'please choose them for

inclusion.' And with that, they say, he departed once again."

The traveling priest is listening intently.

"Because of this, it is said, when Lord Toshinari was choosing poems for the *Senzaishū* during the time of the Cloistered Emperor Go-Shirakawa, he did include one poem of Tananori's but labeled it 'Poet Unknown.'"

The man continues with a description of Tadanori's last battle.

"Now let me tell you how Tadanori met his end in this place. The Heike established their camp here, making the east side the front of a castle to protect the forest of Ikuta, setting the rear in Ichi-no-tani to the west, and guarding the three leagues between them with many troops. The Genji divided their more than sixty thousand mounted warriors into two wings, attacking the Heike fortress from both sides and easily breaking through. Many Heike men were either cut down in battle or fled in disarray to their boats."

He goes on to describe Tadanori himself.

"Amidst all this, Tadanori was a general on the west end. With his camp already crushed, there was no more he could do but quietly flee in defeat, mixing in with the fleeing common soldiers, but Okabe no Rokuyata Tadazumi, a warrior from Musashi Province, spied a high-ranking enemy general and pursued him, cutting him down with the aid of a fellow Genji warrior. Both enemies and allies are said to have shed tears at the sight, crying, 'Oh, Tadanori has been killed! What a heartbreaking end for such a marvelous general, so gifted in both the literary and military arts!' And as for this young cherry tree, some say it was planted after his death, and others say it has always been there, but I do not know which is true."

Having told the traveling priest this much, the man turned toward him and said,

"This is what I have heard, but I am curious why you have asked about these matters."

"Thank you for your painstaking account. I have asked for this very reason: I am one who used to serve Lord Toshinari, but after he died, I became—as you can see—a monk. An old man was here before you came along, and when we traded remarks, he told me the full story of the young cherry tree as you have done, and about Tadanori's fate as if it were his own. No sooner had he finished asking me to convey his words to the capital than he disappeared in the shadow of the blossoms."

The man replies,

"How strange what you have told me! First of all, I can't believe there is an old man like that in these environs. He must surely be the ghost of Tadanori himself! I say this because you, Reverend Sir, tell me you once served Lord Toshinari. I believe that Tadanori appeared and traded words with you because of that bond. If you believe so, too, I ask you to stay here a while and chant a holy sutra in his memory."

The traveling priest replies, "Let me do so, then, staying on here and chanting a holy sutra in his memory."

"Please do let me know if you have any further use of my services."

"I will be sure to ask you."

"I understand, Your Reverence."

THE PRIEST then goes to sleep.

Spreading one sleeve on the ground, I sleep alone with grass for my pillow, spreading one sleeve on the ground, I sleep alone with grass for my pillow. Surely my dream journey will be lonely, too. I fall asleep on my journey here beneath the night cherry on this hill by the shore, where the moon is lost to sight behind the hill. The night deepens, and along with it my heart as strong winds sweep the shore.

A figure appears in the night.

"I feel only shame, returning once again to this place where I died, to reveal myself in your dream. I woke from my sleep in the other world, but my heart still lingers in the past, and so I have come to you as a ghost to tell my tale as in that rainy night scene in *The Tale of Genji*. This world of ours is full of obsessions and delusions at the best of times, but what most keeps me sinfully clinging to this place, despite the timeless honor of having had my poem chosen for inclusion in the *Senzaishū,* is the bitter knowledge that, denounced as a Heike rebel against the throne, I had my work labeled Poet Unknown. Now even Toshinari, who chose my poem, has departed this world, but because you used to serve him, I have come into your dream like this, O monk, to ask you to tell my story to his heir, Lord Teika, and plead with him to put my name on my poem, if possible. Hear me, O Suma shore winds, and blow gently so as not to wake him from his dream!"

Yes, truly, the priest replies in his dream, to have been born into a house that appreciates poetry, to have followed that Way oneself, to have given one's heart to such a world that our country has possessed since its earliest days, is the very finest thing that a person can do.

"And above all, Tadanori is one who achieved fame in both the literary and military arts."

Then came the reign of Cloistered Emperor Go-Shirakawa when Lord Fujiwara no Toshinari, a man of the third court rank who lived on Gojō in Kyoto, was chosen to compile the seventh imperially commissioned poetry anthology, the *Senzaishū.*

Tadanori continues his story.

"It was autumn in the second year of Juei when the Heike withdrew from the capital and I had much to do, so much to do, but in my heart there bloomed the flower of poetry, and so when we came to the Fox River, all I could think of were the orchids and chrysanthemums that Chinese poetry associates with foxes. There I turned back toward the capital and went to the home of Lord Toshinari, whom I begged to choose my poems. My hope fulfilled, I returned to the Way of the Bow and Arrow, sailing first to Kyushu in the west, then back here to the Suma shore, where the shining Prince Genji had lived in exile. How foolish of me not to realize that a Minamoto place could not be good for the Taira!"

Here was fought the battle of Ichi-no-tani, and when it seemed that our time had come, we all boarded our ships and put out to sea.

"I, too, galloped to the water's edge, thinking I would board a ship, but I looked back to see six or seven mounted warriors pursuing me, their leader proclaiming, 'I am none other than Okabe no Rokuyata Tadazumi, man of Musashi Province!' Exactly what I was hoping for. I yanked on my horse's reins and turned back, grappling immediately with Rokuyata. We crashed to the ground between our horses and I held Rokuyata down, drawing my blade, when—"

One of Rokuyata's men circled around behind Tadanori, who was on top, and hacked off his right arm. Tadanori grabbed Rokuyata with his left hand and thrust him away. Knowing his time had come, he said, "Stand back, everyone! I shall pray toward the Pure Land in the west," and he intoned, "KŌMYŌ HENJŌ JIPPŌ SEKAI, NENBUTSU SHUJŌ SESSHU FUSHA / The light of Amida Buddha illuminates all things everywhere; He will abandon none who call His name."

These words of prayer were hardly out of Tadanori's mouth when Rokuyata drew his sword and mercilessly cut Tadanori's head off.

"At that moment, Rokuyata thought in his heart—"
Oh, how pitiful to look upon his corpse! Still young, he would surely have had many long years left before him, and one can see from the brocade warrior's robe beneath his armor, as colorful as autumn leaves this unsettled autumn day when rains come and go beneath the thinly overcast sky, that he was no ordinary mortal but rather a son of noble birth. Wishing to know his name, Rokuyata was amazed to find in the man's quiver an arrow with a poem-slip attached. He saw it bore the title "A Journey's Lodging," beneath which was the verse—

Traveling, and comes the dark:
If I should lodge beneath this tree,
Cherry blossoms will be my host tonight!

And below the verse, the poet's signature: Tadanori.

So, then, there can be no doubt that he was the Lord of Satsuma whose name the storm winds cried aloud: Tadanori! How heartbreaking!

"Because you came beneath the blossoms of this cherry tree, O priest, I made the sun go down and kept you here in order to tell you my story this way. Surely you can have no doubt now that this has been my story. They say the flower returns to its root. It is the same with me. Please pray for me when I am gone."

You lodged beneath this tree on your journey, and the blossoms have, indeed, been your host. 🐵

Note from the translator: The date November 25, 1970 will always have special significance for me. I was eating breakfast in the narrow kitchen of my Cambridge apartment, getting ready to drive to the hospital to bring my wife and newborn son home, when I heard a report on the radio that the novelist Yukio Mishima had disemboweled himself in the name of the emperor and then been beheaded by one of his followers—in a bizarre imitation of a traditional ritual suicide. The conjunction of new life and grisly death was almost too much for me to comprehend. The memory of my eagerness to bring my wife and baby home must always coincide with a mental image of Mishima's severed head—a head that had been so full of creative intelligence and passion.

The date took on added significance for me some years later when I translated a heartfelt speech on individualism delivered on November 25, 1914 by the great Meiji novelist Sōseki Natsume. Sōseki spoke at Gakushūin, the Peers School, which Mishima later attended. The director of the school had been General Maresuke Nogi until 1912, when he chose to follow the Meiji Emperor in death by committing *seppuku* (more commonly known as *harakiri* in the West).

This perhaps exhausts the coincidences, but the collision of life and death, of personal fulfillment and self-immolation, of immense creative energy and physical dismemberment that I associate with that one point on the calendar are exactly what come to mind whenever I read Zeami's great warrior ghost play *Tadanori*.

Of the numerous warrior deaths recounted on the Noh stage, Tadanori's was one of the most gruesome. Both his head and arm were chopped off in battle. Beheading was a relatively common event in medieval Japanese warfare, and so what has caught the imagination of later generations is the severed arm. A funerary mound and shrine have been erected at the site for Tadanori, with a large wooden right arm, as Royall Tyler noted in his *Japanese Nō Dramas.* That startling image comes less from the play than from the prose narrative *The Tale of the Heike,* which inspired the play. Everything in Zeami's version of the story, though, throws the emphasis on the horrid

waste represented by the severed head. For the bulk of the play is dedicated to showing us that Tadanori's is no ordinary warrior's head but one that in life, like Mishima's, had been full of literature—to the point of obsession.

"To have been born into a house that loves poetry, to have followed that Way oneself, to have given one's heart to such a world that our country has possessed since its earliest days," we are told, "is the very finest thing a person can do." The Taira were hardly a house of poetry. Indeed, for the most part they were tyrants and murderers, but it is the artistic side of the Taira legacy that is of most interest to Zeami, a man who lived for art.

In closing, let me note that the son I brought home from the hospital on November 25, 1970 is now a professional musician. Not lucky enough to have been born into a house of poetry, he nevertheless went on to live a life of song, which may well be, as *Tadanori* tells us, "the very finest thing a person can do."

Kaori Fujino

———————

Someday with the One, the Perfect Bag

translated by Laurel Taylor

NONE OF NAGANUMA'S COWORKERS knew much about her until the day she went missing. Not because they were coldly indifferent but rather because they practiced the warm indifference of not wanting to ride roughshod over someone's privacy, of wanting to let someone get on with their work, of wanting to maintain a measure of mutual politeness and decorum. People refrained from expressing concern, even after several days of unexplained absences. Someone in general affairs rang Naganuma's cell phone every day, but only because it was their job to inquire. Eventually, however, her parents were contacted, and when they expressed shock and rushed to Tokyo, people were forced to conclude Naganuma was missing—the news spread through the office like blood pumping through a body until everyone knew. That she was missing. This became the most noteworthy thing about her.

A policeman came. The company was a large e-commerce vendor, so most of the employees were temps. Naganuma was a temp, as was the woman in general affairs who had been calling her every day. Every single temp in the company was a woman. Who had been friends with Naganuma? Was she seeing anyone? He began his investigation by questioning the other temps, particularly those who worked in Naganuma's department. These women proffered uniformly uncomfortable smiles. Not one of them could give concrete details. Was anyone here close to her? No one could give a name. So Naganuma . . . wasn't the friendly sort? The temps said no—she wasn't mean or weird, she was normal and she did her work. At this point, a full-time employee, their boss, interceded: Ms. Naganuma was a customer service representative in the call center. Of course some of the workers on this floor handle inquiries by email. Yes, that's right, even now we get a large number of orders by phone, and some people prefer to get their questions answered by phone. Yes, exactly, we get so many calls that our staff don't have much time to talk to each other. And of course for many of our temps this job is only a placeholder. Not much time to form deep relationships. One of the temps, hearing this explanation, was inclined to agree. She was still young and had vague dreams of one day being hired as a salaried employee at some other company, of having a future protected by a company pension, social security, work benefits, bonuses, and paid vacation. A different temp resented the assumption that most of them would be here only a few months. She had been a temp at this company for over twenty years, paying into the national pension plan and unemployment insurance the whole time. So you're saying my whole life is just a placeholder? But neither woman said anything. The other women were silent, too.

The policeman changed his approach. Did Ms. Naganuma have any financial difficulties? This wasn't a baseless question. Naganuma's bank balance was basically zero. Her pension and insurance payments were behind, and she hadn't paid her last month's rent. She blew a lot of money on designer handbags, didn't she? This question missed the mark slightly. While Naganuma's one-room apartment had been buried under a mountain of bags, only a few of them had designer labels. Aside from the bags, the only things in her room were the bare necessities. No television, no washing machine. Not a single book. The only furniture was a low folding table and her bed. A laptop rested on the table. The refrigerator was tiny. A rice cooker atop it. The microwave sat on the floor. Her dishes consisted of one mug, two plates, and one small jar, all kept in the kitchen cabinets. Her clothes were in the built-in closet. A single glance was enough to see they were cheap—three shirts and three sweaters, two pairs of slacks, a cardigan, a scant number of undergarments tucked in a little hamper. No accessories. Only one pair of shoes. And then the bags. Spread like puzzle pieces across the floor with only a narrow trail passing through, and even more hanging from rows of tension rods across the ceiling, obstructing the overhead light. The closet was so stuffed with bags it couldn't be closed. There were bags under the bed and bags on top of it. They were piled on the microwave, hanging from the kitchen cabinets, stuffed inside the cupboards under the sink, even lined in tight rows on top of the two-burner range, which showed no other signs of use.

Unlike Naganuma's room—a cave untouched by man—the floor where the customer service reps were jammed together was a vast plain of desks ranged in orderly rows, divided by simple partitions. Everywhere

the sound of typing and the incessant ringing of telephones and fax machines. Well, can you tell me anything else about Ms. Naganuma, anything at all? The policeman asked, not really expecting anything. But a hand slowly rose from somewhere in the center of the plain, like a blade of grass that had grown a little too long. Naganuma loves bags. She told me so. She came to work every day with a different bag.

I see. The policeman nodded. So that's why she spent so much?

It's not that she was spending. Another hand went up. That's right. That's right. The temps ceased raising their hands—in the silences between the ringing of telephones and faxes, voices rose. Naganuma was *searching*. Yeah, that's it. That's what she said, that she was searching. I heard her say that, too. I remember now, she was looking for *it*. I knew it, I thought that might be it. So that means she found it? Maybe. Maybe. I bet she did. Oh, I'm so glad for her.

Wait just a minute, what are you talking about? The policeman interjected. What was Ms. Naganuma searching for?

A few seconds passed. The clamor of demanding phone calls and faxes and obliging mechanical responses rolled in like waves. Thank you for your call, this is Tamura speaking, Thank you for your call, this is Hayashida speaking, Thank you for your call, Thank you for your call, speaking, this is Yoshimoto, this is Tominaga, this is Tanabe, this is Itō, this is Kurata speaking.

Well, a bag, of course. A voice came from the depths of the plain, so distant the policeman couldn't tell who was speaking. The one, the perfect bag.

Yeah, she used to say if only she had that one. As before, several voices joined the clamor. The one, the only bag she'd ever want or need. Sooner or later she hoped she'd find it. She said she wanted to meet it. She said she dreamed about owning it. She said if she found that perfect bag, she'd fill it with whatever it could hold and then go somewhere, anywhere. Somewhere she needed to go, somewhere she didn't need to go. Somewhere near, somewhere far.

The policeman took notes. A page flipped. So you're saying, he repeated, there's a possibility that

Ms. Naganuma found that one perfect bag and went to some far-off place. Do I have that right?

Yes. The temp women nodded, as though a breeze was passing through the grasslands.

Understood. Then we'll begin our investigation there. Thank you for your help. So saying, the policeman left. Okay, as you were. So saying, their boss left the customer service floor.

Six months passed without a trace of Naganuma. Her parents decided to empty her apartment. We'll be coming by to thank you all. Twenty minutes after general affairs received this call, the Naganumas appeared, accompanied by professional movers. The full-time manager expected he'd have to say something along the lines of *My condolences*, but words deserted him. In an unending stream, the movers trotted in one cardboard box after another, stacking them high against the walls of the lobby. The Naganumas bowed and requested a meeting with their daughter's coworkers. A temp worker from general affairs, who had accompanied her boss down to the lobby, ushered the Naganumas into the elevator. All the while more boxes piled up. The lobby was all glass and light—a fact the employees took pride in— but it grew darker and darker. As though they were building a barricade against an oncoming siege. The manager hurried after the Naganumas and the temp, though he looked over his shoulder again and again. What's all that? he asked, trying to maintain a smile. Those are all our daughter's bags, Mr. Naganuma muttered.

As always, the customer service floor was deluged with demanding phone calls and ringing fax machines, clacking keyboards, and the reps' responses. Everyone, I'm Naganuma's mother. Mrs. Naganuma began in a quavering voice. She tried to speak as loudly as she could, to make her voice carry across the room, but it cracked at having to speak before so many people, leaking out like a threadbare sigh—it barely reached the third row. The temps who did hear her—aside from those on the phone or those whose phones had just started ringing—paused in their work and focused on Mrs. Naganuma. Everyone, thank you for looking after our daughter. We're sorry she caused you all so much trouble. I really had no idea, but you could tell just from looking at her little apartment how much my daughter loved bags. We've brought every last bag here. We hope you can put them to use. I think that's what she would have wanted. The Naganumas stood side by side and bowed deeply to the customer service reps.

Scattered applause across the floor.

Well then, said the temp from general affairs, picking up where the Naganumas left off, the bags are in the first-floor lobby. On your way home tonight, you can open up the boxes and take whichever bag you'd like. A few temps replied in the affirmative, their voices oddly out of step with each other. One woman raised a hand. I'll send an email around to everyone, too. Again a few affirmatives, again oddly disjointed.

Well. Okay then. The full-time manager clapped his hands. On with your work.

When the work day came to a close, the temps went down to the lobby and solemnly, silently, took down the stacked boxes, peeling back the packing tape and extracting the contents. Once emptied, some of the boxes were resealed and set in lines to use as impromptu plinths for the bags. The rest of the boxes were flattened, stacked, tied in bundles with plastic twine, and set off in a corner. The work continued with the utmost skill and efficiency. Not only the customer service reps were involved but also the women from distribution—it wasn't uncommon for extra personnel to be exchanged between customer service and distribution, so the majority of the women attached to the call center knew how to handle cardboard boxes. Not to mention the contents were bags. Naturally, distribution center employees were tasked with carefully packaging and sending products to customers, and most of those products were things that needed to be handled carefully, like pottery or foods packaged in glass bottles. In comparison, bags were light and difficult to chip or break, and moreover these weren't company goods but rather things that would be theirs, so the temps were able to dispatch the unpacking with speedy aplomb.

But no matter how capable, the women simply couldn't open every box in a single day. And the workday had already finished. They stopped after thirty minutes. Only a fraction of the boxes had been opened. The temp workers looked at the bags they'd personally lined up. Bags of all different sizes, uses, and materials. Flimsy cotton eco-bags, hard leather handbags that could probably hold nothing more than a wallet and a smartphone, heavy leather tote bags festooned with designer logos, large rugged backpacks. One woman picked up a round basket woven of thick paper strips. She slipped it on her shoulder and nodded. I'll take this. It fits on my shoulder, and it seems like it'll hold a lot. Another woman: Can I have this one? I've always wanted one. She picked up a tiny nylon pochette. I think I'd like this one. A different woman, peeking through from the back, pointed at a rip-stop nylon eco-bag, thin but sturdy, made by an outdoor clothing brand. It was designed to be folded up, so she crumpled it into a ball the size of her fist and stuffed it in her jacket pocket.

Several other women chose their bags just as easily. Of course many couldn't decide. Someone said, Looks like my bag isn't in this bunch. Thus bag selection carried over to the next day.

That day, the temps who'd already obtained one of Naganuma's bags came to work not with their usual purses or rucksacks but with Naganuma's. The company didn't have a dress code for part-timers, but even so, the temps looked somehow peculiar to their salaried managers. The round basket, for instance, was a little too summery, as though meant for an outing or a picnic, but the woman who carried it seemed untroubled, though she wore a white blouse, gray slacks, and black pumps, which made the mismatch even more bizarre. And though everything they needed for work was already in the office and there was no need to bring anything from home, a nylon pochette still seemed too small for a daily commute, while a wrinkled eco-bag seemed too casual, verging on improper.

But the managers said nothing. They had no idea what would be considered sexual harassment these days. And there was no reason for them to mind what the temps used as bags. The larger question was when the huge pile of boxes in the lobby would be cleared away.

Just as on the day before, several women found their bags, took them home, and came to work with them the next day. Every day, more temps appeared with Naganuma's bags. Sakaguchi, who picked up her one-year-old grandbaby from daycare every day because her daughter couldn't get off work in time and spent even her days off feeding and bathing and looking after that child, leaving no time for herself, found a limited-edition backpack from a high-end outdoor clothing brand, now available only through internet auctions at an obscene price. Naitō, who found a full-time job fresh out of college but didn't even last a month and then wound up as a temp here, found a tote bag made of thick canvas with a leather handle. Komatsu, who considered this job a stepping-stone until she could make it as a novelist, found a beautiful little rucksack made of glossy purple nylon. Hoshino, who once a month played bass for an all-girl rock band and produced such thunderous music from her fingertips that she dazzled her audience into blinding white bliss, found a small black formal bag perfect for all sorts of family occasions. Kuze, who had started working at the company because she wanted someplace where she wouldn't have to explain she was trans, found a little basket woven from chocolate vines. Tanaka, who was working toward her Labor and Social Security Attorney qualifications so she could switch jobs, found a tote bag with a logo from some Scandinavian supermarket chain embroidered on the front. Kinoshita, who was working on her qualifications to become a Hazardous Materials Officer, found a clutch decorated with rows of chunky plastic beads. Park, who was aiming for her web analyst qualifications, found a high-end flagship bag, two years out of style. Adachi, who aspired to be a sommelier, found a satchel made of rip-stop nylon. Ikei, whose parents took care of her, who earned only ¥80,000 or ¥90,000 a month from this job but received an allowance of ¥200,000 a month from her wealthy family, found a messenger bag made of Cordura nylon. Tachibana, who took on as many temp jobs as possible and lived with her parents and so managed to earn ¥160,000 a month, but indiscriminately purchased everything from the bargain bin, and in spite of being such a cheapskate still had nothing in her bank account, found a fairly nice leather Boston bag with a shoulder strap. Sasaki, who pinched every yen and sent home ¥35,000 to her parents each month, found a one-of-a-kind tote bag made by an artist who pasted together antique fabric scraps. Suga, who still had ¥2.3 million left on her college loans, found a limited-edition shoulder bag, the result of a collaboration between a mid-level brand and a boutique fashion shop. Igarashi, who was in the middle of paying off a ¥28 million loan on a condo with her husband—even though it was only his name on the deed—found a provocative high-end purse that looked like a giant upended hat. Shimatani, who was currently undergoing fertility treatments, found a Cordura nylon bag from an outdoor brand—it had a detachable shoulder strap so it doubled as a pouch. Takeyama, who'd spent the last decade wondering whether she should have a child, found a duffle bag currently popular among high school students, and Hidaka, who was pregnant and whose stomach was growing bigger by the day but didn't qualify for maternity leave because she was a temp and was counting down the days until she had to quit, found a wide shallow tote bag in a daring floral pattern. Sawa, who'd been forced to quit her previous job when she gave birth and, once her child was in elementary school, interviewed at thirteen different places before finally being hired, found a woven raffia pochette. Hatta, whose parents and siblings all worked full time and so was the one who had to take care of her grandmother, found a polyester rucksack waterproofed with a resin polyurethane coating. Isojima, who collected insects as a hobby, found a leather briefcase designed to be worn three ways—as a cross-body bag, as a rucksack, or held in the hand. Ogasawara, who spent her free time going to jury trials, found a designer handbag shaped like a lemon wedge that had recently debuted with a New York fashion label. Kasuga, who watched anime and American sitcoms and feverishly wrote fan fiction, found a huge backpack that was *just* small enough to be a carry-on, even on budget airlines. Suzumura, who always carried a second book in case she finished reading her first and kept *another* book on top of that just in case she didn't like the first two, found a rucksack printed with stars. Miyano, who abused her husband, found a tote bag printed with a German art museum logo.

Yet still there were unopened boxes. Even after the overwhelming majority of temps from customer service and distribution had found their own bags, there were still more. Women from general affairs and from editorial and from quality control came and found their own bags. They were the last of the temps. Yet still there was no end to the bags. The full-time managerial staff grew more and more despondent as they wondered when, if ever, the last of the boxes would finally be cleared out. Could Naganuma really have fit all those bags into her one-room apartment? Surely not. And even if she bought nothing but bags, she couldn't possibly have bought that many on her salary. A few full-time workers were women, but only a few, and they had been doing their polite best not to look through the rows of bags or open the boxes that remained.

None of the temps suggested taking a second bag. Because each knew that the bag she had found was her one, her perfect bag, and it would be with her the rest of her life. More than half of them had already thrown out their old purses and tote bags. The women from the company they outsourced janitorial services to—who were also temps after all—were invited to look at the bags; management wasn't consulted. Instead a temp from general affairs directed everything, systematically ushering the cleaning women to the bags. A not insignificant number of janitorial temps were unable to find a bag on the first try. They came to look at the bags every time they visited the building. None gave up until she found her own bag. And the women who couldn't find their bags looked up at the mountain of boxes as though in supplication, not quite able to mask their expectations. Eager to reward their devotion, the women from customer service and distribution, as well as those from editorial, general affairs, and quality control who had been taught how to handle the cardboard boxes, put themselves to work opening them. After the workday finished, anyone who had time, even just a few minutes, stopped in the lobby and silently lined up bags. Even delivery women who came and went qualified for their own perfect bags. While waiting for a signature from general affairs, these delivery women, also temps, twisted around to gaze at the lines of bags.

Noticing this, women from general affairs urged them to go closer. Each woman wordlessly took a bag of her own and clutched it to her chest.

Someone in general affairs discovered a sheaf of resumes from past temps. Even during work hours the women now brazenly searched for homes for the bags. The resumes were digitally converted and passed to customer service. There the reps divided the data among themselves and, during breaks between their duties, contacted old phone numbers and email addresses. If the number or email didn't work, they questioned whoever did answer to see if they knew the woman, and if *that* didn't work, they scoured social media until every last former temp had been found. All the while, the boxes were still being opened; women in editorial and quality control systematically took photos of every bag that emerged. The image files were sent to customer service, and they posted the photos to a website, numbering each bag. They passed the link to those women who no longer worked at the company, and through their computers, through their smartphones, each woman avidly hunted for her fated, her perfect bag. No one worried that more than one woman would want the same bag, and sure enough, such a thing never happened. Once a bag found its owner, the women in distribution packed it up and handed it off to the delivery women alongside normal company mail. All of their packaging was made for company products, and the delivery fees were paid by the company. Sooner or later the managers would discover what they were doing, and it would certainly be a problem, but none of them worried about that.

One morning, the full-time managerial staff noticed the lobby bathed in warm sunlight and found themselves as euphoric as songbirds set free in a greenhouse. They soon realized this was because the cardboard boxes had at long last disappeared from the lobby. There were, however, a few bags left in a modest line in the corner. They sat atop the pile of broken-down cardboard boxes, each awaiting its fated owner. The women who were full-time employees walked up one by one as though captivated and, without hesitation, chose a bag.

Thus each of Naganuma's bags finally passed to the woman best suited to it.

The workday had just started. In spite of the early hour, on the customer service floor, machines were already beginning to ring like birds calling to one another, phones with orders or complaints and faxes with completed order forms. The birds called loud and long, and though from time to time they fell silent, the calls soon returned. As though in a dream, the managerial staff went to the customer service floor. No one was there. Not a single one of the temps usually packed into the space had shown up for work. The managerial staff hurried to check distribution and quality control, general affairs and editorial. No one was there, either. In fact, the women who worked full-time, who had been there just a moment ago, had also disappeared. The bags they'd brought to work that morning sat like puddles here and there throughout the empty offices, their contents missing.

Why was it that Naganuma disappeared, again? The men said nothing, each of them wondering only in their hearts. In silence, yet almost all at once, they remembered. That's right, she found her one, her perfect bag, and she took it with her to some far-off place.

One of the men said, So that means that the other women, the other ladies who work here . . . But there's one thing I don't understand, said another. I watched it all, and even though there were all those bags, there wasn't a single one made by our company. I checked so I know. So I guess that means she never tried one of *our* bags when she was searching for her own perfect bag. Of course we don't offer that many styles, but we hired some professor of ergonomics to develop them, they're supposed to be good.

Naturally, the men turned toward quality control. Their own company's bags were there. The target demographic was middle-aged and older women, so the bags had to be light. They had to be shoulder bags so both hands could be free. On the front of each bag was a large pocket with a metal fastener, meant to make valuables easier to access. The main compartment had also been carefully designed: a few slots for pens, a pocket for small items, and all of it lined with a bright kerria gold fabric to make it easier to see inside. The outer fabric was a glossy nylon printed with large roses available in two colors: faded vermillion or purple tinged with beige.

Each salaried man slowly picked up a bag, adjusted the shoulder strap to a size that suited him, and hung the bag across his body. None of them knew if this was his one, his fated, the perfect bag of a lifetime. They heard the ceaseless back-and-forth birdsong from the customer service floor drifting down to the dusty quality control room, its windows blocked by shelving. The men stood listening, waiting for a desire for some distant place to sweep over them. But there was already a place they'd been longing to go, even before they put on their bags. The lobby. They'd tasted it already, like joyful birds bathed in sunlight— and they wanted it once more. Beneath musty, dim lighting, dreaming their dream, for a little longer, they stood in silence. 🐵

Sachiko Kishimoto

———

I Don't Remember

translated by Ted Goossen

I SOMETIMES FEEL that there must be a second me out there. That there's one me who sits here and thinks, and another completely different me doing all kinds of stuff out in the world.

This feeling grows stronger when I hear comments like, "Remember when you did that thing back then?" and I draw a complete blank on whatever "that thing" may have been.

Like someone may say, "Remember when you ripped off that person's socks just because they took your fancy?" Nope, no memory of that at all. True, those socks are in my drawer, but as I recall, the person in question bought an identical pair and gave them to me as a present. Or, "Remember when a passing stranger said something insulting to you and you clobbered them with your tennis racket?" How could a scaredy cat like me, timid as a tadpole, do something like that? For whatever reason, the me that people seem to remember is violent and evil. Which leads me to think that, surely, there must be another me out there.

Every few years, when this feeling overwhelms me, I run out and buy a notebook, and I start a diary. I figure that way, if I'm accused of "that thing," whatever it may be, I will have proof that the charges are false. The problem is, I can't get into the habit of writing every day, so the diary soon goes missing in action, swallowed by the chaos that is my room. Then out of the blue it pops up, years later.

I came across one of these old diaries just the other day. It contains my entries from August and September six or eight years ago. Amazingly, I had no recollection whatsoever of the events it described. None. The entries seem to have been written by a complete stranger.

An American writer, now deceased, described his entire life by means of an itemized list, where every entry begins with "I remember." If he could do that, I suppose I should be able to convey my own life, or at least those two months, under the heading "I don't remember."

I don't remember spending a whole day wearing a mushroom-patterned T-shirt someone gave me with a mushroom-patterned hand towel wrapped around my neck.

I don't remember mistaking a "drink voucher" for a "shrink voucher," and how my heart skipped a beat before I realized my error.

I don't remember an exchange with someone who asked me what a "bear cicada" sounds like, and I growled in reply.

I don't remember a dream in which someone with the unlikely name Kazue Bokukinoko made an appearance.

I don't remember falling madly in love one evening with a dish of squid cooked in its own ink.

I don't remember the time I found a little person in my head who whispered "expectorate" every time someone said "at any rate."

I don't remember seeing a girl on a train with a yellow handkerchief that, on closer inspection, proved to be a banana skin.

I don't remember a whole day wasted fretting over a mosquito bite on the side of my right foot, just where the arch meets the heel.

I don't remember how much I missed watching a full bowl of miso soup slide across a wet table in a cheap diner.

I don't remember learning that an inchworm is also called a mulberry looper.

I don't remember that, in return for a gift of *yuzu*-infused aromatic cooking oil, I gave someone a packet of insecticide to get rid of spider mites.

I don't remember walking through Shinjuku station wondering where all the fun in life had gone and passing someone whose T-shirt read "Denizen from the Bowels of the Earth."

I don't remember roaring with laughter one solitary night when the wind got too strong. 🐵

Note from the translator: This story takes as its model the acclaimed *I Remember* by American artist and writer Joe Brainard (1942–1994).

Matthew Sharpe

———

2020 Triptych

1.

ANYTHING WORTH DOING is worth doing badly. Like surgery. It's the thought that counts, I told myself as I trepanned myself. There's always a sturdy bearded Midwestern man on YouTube who's willing to talk you through household tasks to a soundtrack of disco music, and I'm relying on Bill from Elyria, Ohio, for help in the creation of a hole in my parietal bone because I've tried everything else to relieve the irritability. Oh, you want a list of what I've tried? Sure, I have infinite time to provide that for you, I'm not going anywhere, just sitting here doing what Bill refers to as "letting your brain air out after you've removed the small circular piece of skull bone." Neurofeedback. Those pills. Cutting down on carbohydrates. Fewer eggs. Fewer salmon. Less weed. Less crank. Reducing angering stimuli. Meditating. Tantric breathing. Tantric sex. Regular Western-style sex. Pink Floyd. All the other shades of Floyd. Chanting. Chanting "You can do it!" Listening to cartoons with the sound off. Running. Running away. Running away in terror. Running away in ecstasy. Calling a friend. Calling someone I don't know at all and asking them for money for my preferred Senate candidate. Venmo'ing. The miracle of Venmo. Listing all the miracles I know of, ordinary things, breathing, the extreme unlikelihood of existing and knowing you exist.

2.

MY WIFE IS FELLATING ME while I order a pack of ten
surgical masks online. I hope finally to find a mask that
will not fog up my glasses. I also hope not to live in a
national death cult that I did not volunteer for. I hope
all the unnecessary dying will stop and we will return
to the good old days of necessary dying. To keep
things lively here in the apartment all day every
day she and I are improvising new routines. I lick her
while she's ironing or changing the cat litter. She
strokes me while I'm on a ladder changing a lightbulb.
She penetrates me with ordinary household objects
while I fold clothes from the dryer and utter the
scripted lines, "Honey, what is this new fabric softener
you bought, it smells like a mountain forest!" The
drudgery of marriage is optional, you just have to get
creative. Sex is the least of it. There are uses for
costuming, it turns out, other than sex. Like general
merriment. I dressed up as General Merriment
for a week straight instead of putting on work clothes.
Storming the fortress at Poland Springs. "The only
thing we have to fear is that guy at the top of the
hill with a shoulder-mounted rocket launcher." She
dressed as Major Aberration for the entire month
of April. We sang all three of his albums back to back
a capella. All while suffering. All while watching the
cooking scene in *Schitt's Creek* on repeat ad nauseam.
We slept on a bed of both nails and roses.

3.

IN THE TEMPLE OF THE SUPERMARKET I am lying down on the linoleum floor of the cereal aisle like a lozenge dropped from the wet mouth of an asthmatic child. I am seven years old and the floor has just been mopped. The mopper is a high school boy who treats the mop like his own hair—he never cleans it. The floor is wet and smells of rancid mint. I am lying on my belly with my face tilted to the side. The wet floor on my cheek. The cereal aisle. The cereal aisle is the brain center of the supermarket. The cartoon animals on the cereal boxes—the bear, the tiger, the pink rabbit, the meat-eating dinosaur, the mad-eyed dog— all are eyeing me like the Mona Lisa my mother showed me in a picture book of the Louvre. I am meant to be a lozenge, I know this at age seven, my purpose is to soothe. Everyone around me is sore. The air hurts their skin. They have been infected and they will never get well. I cannot heal them but I can soothe them. But not today. Today I will confuse and frighten them. I am delicious.

Crossings
A Monkey's Dozen

Unlike a baker's dozen (one extra!), a monkey's dozen is one short.
In this section you will find eleven delicious treats:
stories, poems, a graphic narrative, and a nonfiction book excerpt that
feature all sorts of crossings—the special focus of this volume.

When there's someone you can't forget
Making your heart lonely
Go out walking on your own
And leave your feelings in the fields

When there's someone you can't forget
Making your heart feel tender
Go out walking with the wind
And let it carry your memories away
(unknown poet)

Midori Osaki

Walking

translated by Asa Yoneda
and David Boyd

IT WAS PURELY IN ORDER TO FORGET Mr. Tōhachi Kōda that I left my attic room that evening and went out for a walk. Clouds in the sky, an evening wind blowing through the fields. Yet as I walked, instead of taking Mr. Kōda's face away from me, the wind seemed only to carry him back into my mind. So at some point, after walking a good distance, I stopped and decided that I should turn around. I might as well return to my attic and let my mind linger on Mr. Kōda there—no need to continue this pointless walk, which was failing to bring me any consolation. The face of a person one hopes to forget is all the more unforgettable in the midst of things like clouds and wind. —So I started on my way home, down the slope of the meadow, putting the wind that had been in my face until then behind me. Does having the wind at your back only drive you deeper into melancholy? By the time I arrived home, Mr. Kōda's image seemed even clearer in my heart.

The sliding doors and shutters were still open, and inside, my grandmother was talking to herself as she folded my clothes: a few simple dresses, summer kimono, and obi—which out of laziness I'd left hanging on the nails on the walls of my room.

My grandmother brushed the dust from the shoulders of my dresses into the hearth (all my clothes were covered in soot) and smoothed the wrinkles out of my threadbare everyday obi, oblivious to the fact that I was standing just outside, looking in. She was talking to herself, but everything she said was about me: I wonder if that granddaughter of mine's delivered those ohagi to Mrs. Matsuki yet. I hope she's there right now, eating with the Matsukis. That's all I ask . . . Perhaps they've already finished eating and she and

Mrs. Matsuki are out walking around town—that'd be nice. By the time they've had some sweet dumplings together, Mrs. Matsuki will have seen for herself how that poor child needs some physical activity and taken her out. That girl's been in dire need of exercise. She's been bitten by the melancholy bug and just stays cooped up in the attic all day. They say the melancholy bug is a kind of nervous exhaustion, and sweets are the best tonic for the nerves. Oh, I hope she eats her fill of dumplings and walks a good ten leagues before she comes home tonight...

My grandmother carried on, inspecting my flannel kimono and breathing on the collars of my silk kimono to get rid of the impressions left by the nails. Outside the window, I shook my sorry head and turned to leave again. Since I first left the house, I'd been carrying a lacquer box wrapped in a cloth: this should have reached Mrs. Matsuki quite a while ago but had not yet arrived, as my heart had led me astray.

Earlier this evening, my grandmother had suddenly decided to make a batch of ohagi. She made them in a great hurry, packed a dozen or so in a lacquer box, and told me to deliver them to Mrs. Matsuki. This mission was my grandmother's way of getting me out of the house (she believed my listlessness was entirely due to lack of exercise, from staying in the attic all the time), but not long after leaving, I'd forgotten about the box. Arriving at the meadow thinking only of Mr. Kōda, I found myself in an unhappier state out there with the clouds and wind, and came home again. At no point did I remember the box I was carrying.

Having left a second time, I had to get to Mrs. Matsuki's with no further digressions. I tried to remember not to forget the weight of the bundle I was supposed to deliver. It was nearly dinnertime, and I hadn't eaten. My grandmother had handed me the lacquer box and sent me out of the house on an empty stomach. According to her merry imaginings, I was to nourish my nerves by filling up on ohagi courtesy of Mrs. Matsuki, and then set off with her on a "ten-league stroll." Such, more or less, was the idea behind the box of dumplings.

I continued toward Mrs. Matsuki's house trying as best I could to avoid the meadows. But I was still thinking of Mr. Kōda, and I was in constant danger of forgetting about the ohagi. I swapped the box over from my left hand to my right and tried to focus on its weight; however, not even half a minute after taking the bundle in my other hand, my thoughts returned to him again.

Perhaps I should now tell you a little about Tōhachi Kōda, who held my feelings captive in this way. One day, before I had moved into the attic room, my elder brother Ichisuke Ono sent our grandmother a postcard. The message began, "Please allow me to introduce Mr. Tōhachi Kōda, a member of the medical staff at the hospital for hearts and minds where I am employed. He is an ardent scholar of the schizoid psyche." My brother continued: Tōhachi has recently decided to conduct a tour in order to collect materials for his latest research project. We have great hopes that he will return with data invaluable to the establishment of a new area in our field of schizo-psychology. Several of us threw a party last night to see him off, and I may have gotten a little carried away by the spirit of the occasion. Tōhachi left today and should reach you in due course. He will stay for a few days, and during his stay will require various modells. He is to be provided with every assistance.

I had considerable trouble getting my grandmother to appreciate the import of Ichisuke's postcard. She finally seemed to comprehend that we would be receiving a visitor, but what did my brother mean by *modells*? That was unclear even to me. As I wondered out loud to myself, my grandmother said:

"Won't it be in your dictionary? Young people like your brothers are always using these newfangled words. I really haven't a clue. I'm sure you'll find it in there if you take a good look."

"A model is the person a painter uses as the subject for their work, but I've never seen *modell* in the dictionary," I said.

"What a pickle. Well, if a model is a subject, then..." My grandmother was deep in thought for a while. "Why, a doctor's model must be a person who's unwell!"

My grandmother turned toward the ashes in the hearth with a heavy sigh: If a doctor's model is someone who's unwell, then there's no shortage of potential models. Isn't the world full of such people? Mrs. Matsuki's younger brother spends his days taking drugs and writing incomprehensible poetry. He must be suffering from some mental illness. From what I hear, he wrote just the other day that crows are white. Ichisuke says that at the hospital where he and our guest-to-be work, they treat afflictions of the mind. If Mr. Tōhachi Kōda arrives and requires a model, Mrs. Matsuki's brother can be the first.

Then, in the midst of this talk, my grandmother suddenly started to worry about rooms. "When our guest arrives," she fretted, "where is he going to stay? I don't think Mr. Kōda would get any sleep in the reception room. There are such lonely sounds there at night. The autumn wind, you know."

Taking me to the reception room, she had me stand right in the middle of it and said: "See what you make of this." Immediately, my ears filled with the loneliest autumn sound—the sound of the neighbor's banana tree swaying in the wind.

I moved into the attic that very day. After some consideration, my grandmother and I had decided to give the visitor my room. It was almost ten-foot square, and at some remove from the banana tree.

Compared to my old room, my new one was nearer the sky by one story, but it was terribly dark. There was just one window toward the top of the wall, with a wooden lattice. It was a simple attic that my grandmother used as a storeroom—no more than a small space between the triangular roof, which had no ceiling boards, and the bare floor. That said, a persimmon tree grew right up to the window, so my new quarters offered me an abundance of autumn fruit.

I picked a few persimmons through the lattice, and while eating one and then another, I set about appointing my room. This I was able to do almost entirely using items that were already in the attic. The long wooden chest lying along one wall was just right for sleeping on, so I hung a lantern next to it as a bedside light. This lantern had seen better days, and the paper was more or less torn to shreds, but even this could be turned to my advantage: if I were lazing about and wanted to extinguish the flame without getting out of bed, I could simply blow through one of the holes in the paper. Where I'd hung the lantern was perfect for this maneuver.

Next I made a desk out of four tangerine crates and the wooden mochi board that we used only at New Year, laid a reed mat in front of it, and placed an old oil lamp at one corner of the desk, which was still covered in starch. To complete the effect, I hung up every last piece of clothing that had been on the walls of my old room. I wanted to give the gloomy attic as much of the ambience of my old room as I could. My grandmother objected to me moving my summer dresses to my new room, saying, "It's already fall—wash your summer clothes and put them away." But I felt quite differently. While I sat on an old wicker basket, gazing at the clothes lined up in the same order that they had hung in my previous room and eating persimmons, my grandmother was downstairs running a duster over Mr. Kōda's room.

Mr. Tōhachi Kōda finally arrived around seven days after my move upstairs. By then, my grandmother was on the verge of giving up on him, saying: Our visitor must have had a change of heart. It looks like he won't be coming after all. No need for you to keep sleeping on that chest—come back to your old room. I too was thinking of moving back downstairs, because every time my grandmother made a fire in the hearth, the smoke rose into the attic and then took its time leaving through the lattice at the window. Mr. Kōda arrived precisely at this point. He had brought one large trunk, and no other luggage. With it, he took up residence in the room set aside for him, and after sleeping soundly for two hours, immediately started working on something at my former desk.

After dinner, as we sat around the hearth, my grandmother questioned Mr. Kōda about models and raised the subject of Mrs. Matsuki's brother. Mr. Kōda replied that he did not require models for his research (despite the undeniable fact that he went on to use me as one), and stood up to fetch a book from his trunk, which he brought back to the hearthside. It appeared to be a volume from an anthology of plays.

Mr. Kōda leafed through the book's pages for a while before handing the open book to my grandmother and asking her to read some lines out loud.

My grandmother was terribly flustered. She quickly shook her head a couple of times, and seemed at a loss for words. She tried to adjust her reading glasses, only to realize she wasn't wearing them. I got the glasses down from the lintel and put them on her face for her.

"Oh—"

My grandmother managed to utter only the first word of the line indicated, and could not continue. Mr. Kōda waited attentively, his gaze directed at the ashes in the hearth, but my grandmother had already placed the book in my lap, and said as she wiped the sweat from her glasses:

"Dear me, what difficult words. I'm afraid I can't help you."

At this point it became clear to me that my grandmother had been made to serve as Mr. Kōda's first model. Most likely, he was analyzing a person's voice and articulation as a way to explore the deepest recesses of their psychology. But with my grandmother as his model, Mr. Kōda had no success whatsoever; he stood up with a shake of his head, retrieved another volume from his collection, and handed it to me. Then—oh, what passionate words I was being asked to read! I could only look in silence at the book open in my lap, unable to say anything at all. "How skittish girls are," Mr. Kōda said. "My research will get nowhere at this rate. Let's try moving away from your grandmother." Then he took me to his room. My grandmother was falling asleep by the hearth, still wearing her reading glasses.

But even in Mr. Kōda's room, I couldn't read the words aloud.

"Your grandmother's still making you shy. I suppose we'll have to go upstairs. She shouldn't be able to hear you up there."

I lit both the paper lantern and the oil lamp in my room, then led him inside. Mr. Kōda waited for me to start reading with one elbow resting on the mochi board, but he soon noticed a dusting of starch on the sleeve of his jacket and went to the window to brush it off. He picked a few persimmons and lined them up on my desk.

At some point, Mr. Kōda and I both started eating persimmons. Abandoning the reed mat, Mr. Kōda pulled up a chair and proceeded to eat no small amount of fruit. Mr. Kōda's chair was the old wicker laundry basket that my grandmother had left in a corner of the attic.

Once I'd eaten a persimmon, I strangely found myself capable of reading the lines printed on the page. It was probably Mr. Kōda's demeanor as he sat on the upended basket eating persimmons that had put me at ease.

"Oh—Herr Humor, must you depart so soon? O'er fields and o'er dales, and oh, so many peaks and streams . . ."

This seemed to be a parting scene. As I read out lines like these, Mr. Kōda, in between mouthfuls of fruit, would read the man's part. His articulation was a little languid, on account of the persimmons, which gave our reading an even greater poignancy.

Although Mr. Kōda's stay lasted only a few days, we spent the entire time together, exchanging romantic declarations. When I was a townswoman, he became a persimmon-eating scoundrel, and to my Margarete, he was a persimmon-eating Faust. It was a measure of his solicitude that, to spare my embarrassment, Mr. Kōda always sat on the wicker basket, eating persimmons, no matter what we read. The anthology filled Mr. Kōda's luggage, and yet there was not a single love scene in it that we left unread. Then, oh—the day finally came when Mr. Kōda left for the next stop on his tour, along with that giant trunk of his.

I do not know what psychological observations Mr. Kōda made about me in his notebook. All I know is the emptiness that I experienced after he left. My mouth, which had grown accustomed to reading dialogue, felt bereft, and to fill that emptiness I ate one persimmon after another. Sitting on the basket seat that he'd vacated, I lined up persimmons on the mochi-board desk, and ate and ate. On the starchy surface, I wrote: "Oh—Herr Humor, you have departed too soon."

My grandmother kept ordering me to move back into my old room, but I remained upstairs in the attic. I closed the window lattice and coughed in the smoke from my grandmother's fires.

Meanwhile, knowing nothing of my feelings for Mr. Tōhachi Kōda, she believed my state to be purely due to a lack of physical activity, and aspired to make me do as much walking as possible. —And that was how she came to make those dumplings and send me off to Mrs. Matsuki.

MY DUMPLINGS DID NOT MAKE MUCH of a contribution to dinner at the Matsuki household. While I was out meandering, dinner at the Matsukis' had long since finished. The table had been cleared, save two items unrelated to the meal: a slim magazine and a jar of tadpoles. Mr. Matsuki was looking from one to the other with a decidedly ill-humored expression, while Mrs. Matsuki had a pair of not terribly clean-looking trousers on her lap, which she was in the middle of mending.

Mr. Matsuki swallowed half a dumpling with a disgusted look on his face, and said:

"At any rate, no poet gets things as backwards as Kyūsaku Tsuchida. Every single thing he says is turned on its head. What in the world does he mean by white crows? Sheer blasphemy. I can personally guarantee—I'll wager on all zoology—that crows are as black as can be. Young lady, go ahead and tell me what you make of this."

Mr. Matsuki passed the magazine to me. It was opened to the poem in question, which went, "The crow beats its white wings and laughs *ah-ah,* when the crow laughs my heart is full of joy." The poet was Mrs. Matsuki's younger brother, Mr. Kyūsaku Tsuchida, who was always writing poems that got things the wrong way round, driving the zoologist Mr. Matsuki to despair.

"At any rate, we must make him stop taking those drugs that unsettle his brain," Mrs. Matsuki said, still working on the pants. These had to be the poet's trousers.

"We should get him off drugs altogether. What kind of poet needs as many medications as Kyūsaku? He takes a digestive powder after a meal instead of a con-stitutional, and never goes to bed without a sleeping pill. Little wonder he thinks crows are white."

"Little wonder he only has to step out of the house to get his pants ripped in an encounter with a passing car!"

"That reminds me, he says his new poem is supposed to be about tadpoles. The horror! If someone doesn't intervene, he's sure to write about tadpoles shaking their tails of pure white. It's a desecration of science. So I went out and found some late-laid frogspawn and incubated them in my lab. Even Kyūsaku should be able to write something sensible with the real thing there to guide him. Speaking of which," he turned to me, "am I correct to assume that you've been suffering from a severe lack of physical activity? Then how about," he said to his wife, "you take the tadpoles to your brother and take the young lady along with you as far as the crematorium? That'll be just the exercise she needs."

But Mrs. Matsuki had more mending to do on the trousers, and so it fell to me to deliver the tadpoles.

I wrapped the jar in a cloth and, on Mrs. Matsuki's prompting, took the lacquer box with me as well. She said that I should make sure Mr. Kyūsaku Tsuchida ate all the dumplings he wanted if he seemed tired from working at his desk all day. He lived to the north of the crematorium chimney, Mrs. Matsuki explained, on the second story of the third building after the house with the bulldog and the tea olive bush; the rooms downstairs were probably still untenanted. I would know Kyūsaku's room by the brownish cloth hanging in the window.

I walked far on my journey, just as my grandmother had hoped. Yet I was unable to forget Mr. Tōhachi Kōda. I thought of him at the blooming tea olive, and I thought of him at the chirping of crickets. I spotted the autumn-brown window to the north of the crema-torium chimney, passed the empty rooms downstairs, and reached Mr. Kyūsaku Tsuchida's home.

I found Mr. Tsuchida deep in thought, trying to write his tadpole poem. When I set the jar of tadpoles in front of him, he looked extremely put upon, and immediately hid them in the darkness underneath his desk. He was of the belief that being confronted with real tadpoles when writing a poem about tadpoles made it impossible to write anything at all.

Then, with a most apologetic air, he asked:

"Would you go and get me an ounce of Migrenin? I ran out a couple of hours ago, and my head is killing me."

I took the amber one-ounce bottle he handed me and went to the pharmacy.

When I returned with the medicine for his head, Mr. Tsuchida had opened the lacquer box and was eating ohagi.

After a while he put down his chopsticks and, shaking his head, said to himself:

"I think I've had too many dumplings."

Mr. Tsuchida dug into his desk drawer and got out some digestive powder, then took half a spoonful. That was all that was left in the tin. He waited some time for the remedy to start working, shaking his head or turning to his notebook, but eventually, with what appeared to be great reluctance, he asked:

"Would you go and get me a tin of Ohta's?"

He then shared his thoughts on the relationship between dumplings, the stomach, and the workings of the mental faculties: people seem to believe that sweet things help alleviate mental fatigue, but overindulgence leaves the stomach heavy. When the stomach gets heavy, the pressure rises to the head, weighing the brain down. Doesn't it follow that ohagi, being so very sweet, are in fact ruinous to the work of the human intellect?

Mr. Kyūsaku Tsuchida was preoccupied with the state of his head—so much so he forgot to close the drawer of his desk. I could see that it contained nothing but a large assortment of medications.

So I had to set off for the pharmacy once again. What a busy night this was turning out to be for me, walking here, there, and everywhere! And what a homebody this poet Kyūsaku was! He must always be holed up in his room, taking his postprandial exercise from a tin and improving his mental acuity with brain-stimulating medications, all the while composing poems that left the Matsukis up in arms. —Busy with thoughts like these, I finally forgot about Mr. Kōda for a while.

When I returned with the tin, Kyūsaku had the jar of tadpoles on his desk and was muttering to himself while contemplating their movements. He seemed not to notice that I'd come back. "No more tadpole poetry for me! The moment I laid eyes on these tadpoles, it became utterly impossible to write about them. What troublesome creatures that Matsuki has sent over!"

Kyūsaku opened the seal on the tin and swallowed a large amount of powder, then turned to his notebook, but there were no signs of his having written even a single word of poetry. Meanwhile I watched the tadpoles in their jar. The unseasonable creatures were floating and sinking in the water, and didn't look too active. Maybe something was weighing on them, too . . . —Then the memory of Mr. Tōhachi Kōda

returned to me, and I let out a sigh. Kyūsaku took a deep breath as well, and said:

"So you're sad about something. When you're unhappy, it poisons the mind to look at creatures like these, so you'd better not. Look too closely at ants or tadpoles when you're unhappy, and your mind will start thinking the thoughts of an ant, and your heart will take on the feelings of a tadpole, and you lose track of your human self." He wrapped the jar of tadpoles in several layers of cloth and carried it to the bottom of the stairs. "At times like these, what helps is to look up to the sky and sing. Try it—sing something."

But I couldn't bring myself to sing anything at all. In the end, Mr. Tsuchida tore a page out of his notebook and wrote down the following poem for me. He said it wasn't one of his own, but something he'd heard somewhere once. On the piece of paper, he had written:

When there's someone you can't forget
Making your heart lonely
Go out walking on your own
And leave your feelings in the fields

When there's someone you can't forget
Making your heart feel tender
Go out walking with the wind
And let it carry your memories away 🐵

Hideo Furukawa

The Little Woods
in Fukushima

translated by Kendall Heitzman

Note from the editor: In the summer of 2020, the novelist Hideo Furukawa walked through his home prefecture of Fukushima, traveling more than 360 kilometers on foot, meeting people along the way and listening to them talk about how the 2011 triple disaster affected their lives. In 2021 Kodansha published *Zero F,* a book-length report of the experience. The first chapter of *Zero F* appears here in translation.

ON DECEMBER 15, 2019, we took my mother's remains to the gravesite as part of the forty-ninth-day services. I was the one to carry the urn that held her bones from the family house, where the Buddhist services had been held, to the cemetery where the Furukawa family plot is located. It was only 500 meters. The cemetery is just to the rear of the village. Most of the people in attendance went by car, but my wife, my sister-in-law, one of my nephews, and I went on foot. My sister-in-law led the way. There were rules, so we learned, about how to proceed through the village. "Hideo," my sister-in-law said, "the dead have their own route." Meaning that the four of us—or the five of us, I should say, counting my mother's bones— took a course through town that followed the rules of the world beyond and was completely at odds with what we did in our everyday lives.

A number of rituals had to be performed at the gravesite as well as on our way there, but I was still in an emotional state, so I don't quite remember what I did with whom or where. What was the sequence of events when we offered the ceremonial sake at the entrance to the site? The image that *is* burned in my mind is of the moment the gravestone was moved off the pedestal, revealing the cavity beneath, where the bones were placed. My grandmother's bones were there. They had been interred at the end of 1999, and that time, too, it had fallen to me to carry them to the grave. Before my grandmother's death, the family tradition had been simply to bury the bodies—meaning, in my bloodline, no one had been cremated before then—so in truth, there was no one but my grandmother in the family ossuary. Her bones were entirely a product of the twentieth century.

Such old bones, I thought, studying them. *It's been a long time, hasn't it, Gram?* And then the new bones were added to hers. My mother's twenty-first-century bones were poured—and "poured" really is the best verb to describe their kinetic energy—into the ossuary. It was over in a moment, but the afterimage is seared into my own visual repository.

When this was done, I headed back to the house with my sister-in-law and the others. This time we took the street that ran through the village in a straight line, cutting across the cemetery to get there. "Look," said my sister-in-law. I looked. "The graves in this section are all new," she said. "Every single family's." Even as she was saying this, I realized that they were all in mint condition, so to speak. The surfaces as smooth as a mirror (on the headstones), the carefully tended plots (one for each family), the sense that everything here was pristine...it all clicked into place for me. I understood exactly what I was looking at.

As anyone doing the math will have deduced, eight years and nine months earlier there had been a monstrous earthquake, which had toppled many of the gravestones in this cemetery. What might surprise you is how they were first put back together, using things such as instant adhesives, available in any store, for emergency quick fixes. Later they were properly replaced, but perhaps this is something that only happened at my family's cemetery. Suffice it to say that from then on I thought a lot about the plight of people who felt they had to do something about the family grave as quickly as possible, and were willing to go to such lengths to do it.

I could see my family house up ahead, at the end of the road. The first thing that came into view was the no-longer-used workshop (there is another workshop in a different location that is still called the "new workshop" despite having been there for forty years), and next to it a little clutch of greenhouses with plastic-sheet siding. Behind the workshop were more of the same kind of semicylindrical greenhouses, all in a row. My family grows shiitake mushrooms. They work at it 365 days a year. This is their entire livelihood, and between my father and my older brother, the business has continued for two generations now. The moment I saw the "old" workshop, all kinds of memories from my youth came flooding back. Long ago, it had housed a number of dryers, used to produce dried mushrooms, that whirred continuously, even through the night. Under the eaves of the workshop was a recently acquired—and by this I mean "something we shelled out a lot of money for"—automatic packaging machine. We would be out there packaging mushrooms (on trays for shipment) until eight, nine, ten at night. I was in third grade when it happened: I was helping with the work, feeding trays into the packager on a conveyor belt in my clumsy way, when one of my little thumbs got caught in the belt. If you visualize the end of an escalator when it reaches the next floor, and what would happen to a finger that was swallowed up by ("sucked up in"? "caught up by"? or perhaps I could just say "mangled by") the gap, you'll get a sense of what I faced. But my older brother managed to shut off the machine at the last second, and then put the belt into reverse. Thanks to him, to this day my left thumb continues to be happily attached to my hand.

Even as I describe these things, though, I doubt my own memory. Was I really only in third grade? It didn't happen when I was in fourth grade, or even fifth? Maybe when I was in third grade the work that happened under the eaves of the old workshop was

the prep for mushroom drying (in which we spread them over wire netting), and the automatic packager didn't arrive until later. Why I doubt myself is that, although my father would always say, "I started producing mushrooms when I was thirty," which led me to place it in 1966 or 1967, right before I was born or while I was a baby, my brother now swears, "No, I think it was before that, maybe two or three years earlier." Now that I think about it, it takes two years from the time a fungal strand is inoculated for the first flush of shiitake to appear. Considering that this was how shiitake were cultivated at the time—by growing them on decaying logs—perhaps by the time the initial crop was developed, harvested, and brought to market, my father really was thirty years old. Memory is more than mere data. Even if we don't intentionally lie, our memories can be unreliable.

The important thing is that I was born into a family of shiitake cultivators.

And also that when I was born, I was surrounded by cut timber, fungal filaments, and the forest.

IN THE TERMS OF THE TRADE, shiitake are classified as "forest products for special use." They aren't considered agricultural products. Because they are

a separate classification, I was conscious of the fact that I was born into a forestry family. Chestnuts, walnuts, wild vegetables such as *takenoko, koshiabura, fukinotō,* and *warabi*—all are forest products, as are shiitake mushrooms. And so, I defined myself as a child who was raised by forest products, things that come from the trees, the groves, the woods.

I still do. Even after leaving Fukushima when I was eighteen, and even after the events of March 11, 2011, when Fukushima became famous as a disaster site, I still do.

MY HOMETOWN, the city of Kōriyama in Fukushima prefecture, was a weak 6 on the Japan Meteorological Agency's seismic intensity scale. Eleven municipalities in Fukushima registered as a strong 6, but none of them approached the devastation in Kōriyama in terms of the number of houses that were deemed "completely" or "half" destroyed: 2,732. That number appeared in the *Mainichi Shinbun* on May 6, 2011; I was so interested that I saved the clipping. It reads: "In this year's earthquake, damage such as the collapse of houses and other buildings was particularly devastating in areas that were once part of Lake Kōriyama, an ancient body of water that is thought to have occupied inland areas of central Fukushima prefecture 100,000 years ago, according to research conducted by Tatsuya Kobayashi, 23, a native of the village of Tamagawa in central Fukushima and a graduate student in geography at the University of Tokyo." This "Lake Kōriyama" is "thought to have been largely filled in with mud 23,000 years ago, and sometime after that, what remained became swampland." The largest number of building collapses in Fukushima prefecture was on tableland where the foundation was thought to be generally solid.

After the earthquake—or rather, after the nuclear meltdown—all kinds of figures were thrown at us, trading in orders of magnitude, such as, for example, plutonium-239 having a half-life of 24,000 years, while uranium-238 has a half-life of 4.5 billion years. I was made to look at the same kind of numbers —the reckoning of *tempus fugit*—in regard to my childhood home. When I went to the house for the first time after the disaster, a geological formation from 100,000 years ago had me saying, "This is awful. This . . . this is awful." The city authorities had determined that the main house was "half destroyed." The entryway was intact, but taking just a single step inside, you could see that of the four walls of the main room, two were no longer there. What remained were a number of exposed posts and beams, and the floorboards—which had caved in. My mother and sister-in-law came out to greet me. (As I mentioned above, my mother is no longer with us.) Something my sister-in-law said at the time left a deep impression on me: "If this entryway had collapsed, the house would have been considered 'completely destroyed,' and we would have received a fairly large compensation."

In a later development, even the "half destroyed" determination was revoked (as I understand it, the area of the destroyed portion of the house as a percentage of its total footprint was recalculated), and we received nothing by way of compensation. But now the interior of the house from the entryway on back has been beautifully remodeled. Already, I have to really focus my mind to conjure up how it looked in ruins; that horrible image exists nowhere else.

OVER THE PAST SEVERAL YEARS, people have asked me the same question again and again: "After such a terrible disaster, I really thought Japan would change. For sure, I thought, Tokyo (as the capital, as the place that consumed all of that electricity produced by the Tokyo Electric Power Company's Fukushima Daiichi Nuclear Power Plant before the meltdown) would change. But nothing changed. Japanese society, the Japanese people, changed absolutely nothing about their lifestyles. Mr. Furukawa, how can this possibly be?"

I wish I knew.

Or else I reply along the lines of, *It is human nature to forget . . . whenever possible.*

But now that I am writing this out, the writer in me wants to do everything I can to get it right. So I'll try to answer properly. I have two ways of getting at this clearly and concisely. The first is to say that Japan (meaning, the Japanese people) has no sense of tenacity—at least not when it comes to the tenacity required for deliberative thinking. The second is that the media bear responsibility. The so-called mass media were too quick to cater to the desires of their masses, who are inclined to feel that Heaven is boring and Hell is thrilling. I harbor the same inclinations myself. If you assume Heaven to be "stories about recovery" and Hell to be "stories about disaster areas and entire prefectures that are struggling to recover," you'll get a pretty good sense of the situation. To be fair, there were quite a few stories about recovery, but they were formulaic and trite, because, after all, boredom is the province of the divine. If, on the contrary, there are forebodings of even greater tragedies on the horizon for the affected areas, now *that's* news worth watching. The moment the masses hear that things might get even worse for these people, they will feel the frisson of morbid curiosity. Two problems emerge from this. One is that, while it is true that a certain amount of thrill can bring interest to a story, when that thrill crosses the line into actual fear, people's minds snap shut.

Deliberative thinking, for the most part, is rooted in the everyday. The everyday is another way of saying "that which is continuous." But newsworthy events are the manifestation of the *non*-everyday—the continuous everyday's polar opposite. "Continuous," on the other hand, is intimately connected to "tenacity"—they are practically synonyms. So why did people stop thinking about March 11 and its aftermath? The reason is written into the logic of how news is generated.

But this leads us to a second problem.

We have established that utter fear was the driving force behind forgetfulness. Now, I could follow this up with, well, if that's the case, then what we need is news programming that will strike only a *little* fear into people, but if it is true that most people don't want this (and I'll go ahead and say they do not), then it is even more the case that the mass media are fundamentally incapable of providing it. That said, someone will try. There are surely people of that mindset in the news profession. Some of the really hard-charging journalists. I have no doubt. But I don't believe that this is my role (not to any significant extent, anyway). I have no illusions about that. Even if I were to try to get involved in that way, I am, in the end, a novelist.

To write novels is my main order of business. And so, as one of that breed known as writers, I will say this instead. In spite of myself—look, I didn't see this coming either—here is what I will proclaim: If something's tragic nature is emphasized, and it is widely recognized that there is value in depicting it as a tragedy, and it is then abandoned *for the very reason* that the tragic narrative was so desired, then maybe I want to write a tragedy, too.

In the end, I fight the battles that I am destined to lose.

It's in my nature.

In April 1955, Albert Camus gave a lecture in Athens entitled "On the Future of Tragedy." As Camus defines it in this talk, tragedy requires two opposing forces. Each has a claim to legitimacy, each has its own rational justification. This is so interesting. It's like a description of the face-off between advocates for nuclear energy and the anti-nuclear movement. Camus sums up the situation by saying that "the perfect tragic formula would be: 'All can be justified, no one is just.'" Interesting, interesting. I have nothing but respect for Camus (as a novelist, as a dramatist, *as a person*), but these words that he left to posterity certainly feel overwhelming.

Actually, I'm feeling a little too overwhelmed by these words. Let me start the story of my own family's tragedy with a selection from something a little more approachable than Camus.

YŌKO HANO IS A MANGA ARTIST living in the city of Shirakawa in Fukushima prefecture. I don't know her, so I was surprised to learn that, like me, she had grown up in Nakadōri (the central region of the prefecture), in the village of Nishigō, and that her family cultivated shiitake. I was even more surprised to learn that she has published a manga in which the main character is the son of a shiitake producer: *Chainsaw Rhapsody,* the second volume in her series *The Spring It Started*. I will here reproduce for you in its entirety the dialogue that is to be found on pages six and seven (together with some "stage directions"). A high-schooler is riding his bicycle and talking with his close friend on his cell phone. The friend will someday take over his family's dairy farm.

Meaning, he'll be a dairyman. Which would make the main character a mushroomman, I suppose.

April 4, 2011

Ken'ichi [the main character]: Yeah, for a long time now we haven't been able to ship anything. Supposedly it's going to open up again on April 10.

Genta [the friend]: Whaa—? Are you going to be OK, Ken'ichi?

Ken'ichi: Sure . . . You're the one I'm worried about, Genta. You're throwing out milk every day, right? Even though we're 80 kilometers away, that radioactive stuff came floating toward us.

Genta: Things have to be tough for shiitake, too, I imagine?

Ken'ichi: Yeah. We lost the *roji** crop for the spring. [*outdoor cultivation of shiitake]

Genta: Man, those are the most delicious.

Ken'ichi: It's outside. Absolutely everything is radioactive outside. We know from that nuclear accident in the Soviet Union, for a short time the milk is polluted, but the mushrooms are a problem for a long time. Well, in one sense, it's making stars out of us.

The two are seventeen or eighteen years old. When I came across this manga, I admit I got goosebumps all over.

I CAN'T REMEMBER exactly when I decided that I needed to interview my brother. But according to my date-book, I resolved that I was going to write something about him about a month and a half before my mother died. At that point, I didn't realize what was going to happen just a few weeks later: my mother's death. I wouldn't learn that it was on the horizon until nine days later (this I am also pulling from my datebook). I should say that my mother had been

in a nursing home for a number of years at this point. Her body had grown weaker over time, and now she was bedridden, as they call it. It was the onset of depression that had led to this decline. It got to the point where she couldn't eat anything. They inserted a feeding tube that goes through the abdominal wall directly into the stomach. But nine days later, I heard from my brother that she was vomiting the nutrient mixture she was getting through the tube. So clearly the feeding tube had to go. The facility would not take any measures to extend her life—the directive we all agreed to when she was first admitted. I got a phone call to the effect of, *What do you think, Hideo, we need to make a decision.*

I made the decision, and my other siblings made the decision. There are three of us: my older brother and me and a sister in between us. My sister and her husband produce rice and strawberries for a living. They are a full-time agricultural household.

We were told that once nutrition was no longer provided through the feeding tube, we should expect my mother to pass in the next week to ten days; the next few days were horribly stressful. That probably goes without saying. I went up to see her briefly during that window. It was on that trip that I said to my brother, "I want to interview you. Once things quiet down, obviously." I remember being in a very frazzled state of mind. Or perhaps I was utterly calm. Memories are not to be trusted.

In the event, my mother hung on for another twenty-five days before passing away.

They were strange days for me (and my wife), as we stood by in Tokyo. To make matters worse, the day after my mother died, my wife's father had a stroke. It felt as though the world was falling apart. It seemed to us that during those twenty-five days my mother's *death* was being drawn out. But she showed no cognizance of this. She had no way to show any cognizance of this. She was simply doing what she could to *live on*. I would be lying if I said that what I had taken to be an extended death didn't start to instead seem like an extension of life. I can't yet say what it might mean for a pregnancy to be extended, or for a baby to be given a reprieve. I don't have the words to explain it.

For a long time, I had steered clear of interviewing my brother (or any immediate blood relative) for the simple reason that it might cause alarm. Cause alarm to me, that is. It struck fear somewhere deep inside me, in my inner recesses. Mainly because, *as soon as I start thinking about him, I'll end up having to take a long, hard look at myself,* I thought. I knew that *once I do that, I will have no choice but to write about it.* I'll say it again: a writer is a writer by nature. And that's why I was dodging this one. Of course, I understood full well the terrible predicament that the 2011 earthquake and tsunami had left shiitake producers in, and I knew what other difficulties others with crops were facing. I felt it in the hollows of my hands. And yet, I couldn't speak on their behalf.

No way. Absolutely not.

Let me say something very simple here. I'll start with something clear and concise: I knew that if I were to shout out, in the wake of the Tōhoku disaster, "I stand here in support of my homeland, Fukushima prefecture," I would have to say as a precedent to that, "I loved my life in Fukushima." In the event, I did declare my support for the homeland. And the moment I did so, I shoved my own feelings into the classified files of my soul.

I am being completely logical about this, man . . . is what I think.

Ah, I used to be so logical about this, man . . . is how I shift this sentiment into the past tense.

Here I am now, moving forward with this sentence by sentence, and all that I can reasonably predict is that my discretion will go directly out the window. If I move ahead with writing about my older brother, this will certainly be the case. If I wish to tell the story of my brother, the purveyor of shiitake mushrooms from Fukushima, I will undoubtedly be ambushed by an urge that compels me to write about myself. I accept this truth with a hearty Fukushima, "Sounds about right. Whatcha gonna do?"

But before we go there, what if I reveal memories such as this one—and not just the memory but the entire scene it evokes. My mother had a license to operate a forklift. Behind our house was a submersion tank, a pool of water into which are submerged hundreds or even more than a thousand bolts (the cut logs of unprocessed timber on which shiitake fungal filaments are grown). This process, called "shocking" the log, requires a forklift. My mother was really good at operating it. In my early childhood, she would get up before five in the morning and work until after eleven at night. She was that kind of person, and it was that kind of family operation. And most of what she did was manual labor. I think of my mother as having been an extraordinary woman. Therein lies my respect, my love.

I have absolutely no doubts about the veracity of these feelings.

WHEN I WAS BORN, my older brother was eight, and three months later he turned nine, which would put him in third grade at the time. When I was born, the smell of the fungal filaments permeated everything in the vicinity and there was rich, organic soil in the forest. But this hadn't been the case for my brother. When my brother, Kunikazu Furukawa, was in first grade, our family decided to pursue shiitake production as the family business. At that moment it was still more a venture than a family business—they started with the idea that it *could* become the family business. They acquired 1,200 bolts and inoculated them with shiitake fungal strands. These bore mushrooms two years later. By the way, the fungal strands are inoculated into the bolts in spring (March or April), so as the shiitake operation grows, spring becomes "inoculation season," which can take an entire month. There are a huge number of bolts to be treated, and a correspondingly huge number of people—including temporary hires—doing exactly that.

The bolt starts out as a round log not quite a meter in length, maybe 90 centimeters. We use a power drill to bore holes into it, and then a hammer to pound small dowels called "plug spawn" into the holes. Over time, the fungal strands will colonize the inside of the log, turning it into the aforementioned bolt— a magnificent mushroom-growing log.

I have already said that my family cultivated shiitake year-round, 365 days a year. The spring that my brother was in first grade (meaning, right before he became a second-grader by the Japanese academic calendar), they first experimented with inoculating logs with shiitake spawn. Two years later, the first flush of shiitake appeared. Meaning, it was only after this that year-round cultivation became possible. Meaning, the same time I was born.

People generally understand that farming households have busy seasons and slack seasons during which farmers can do other kinds of work, and that this pattern produces a need for migrant workers, or seasonal labor. But not so with us. Our circumstances were horrid. Three hundred and sixty-five days a year, without a break. To be exact, every four years it was three hundred and sixty-six days a year without a break.

My older brother, Kunikazu, took over the business in the spring of 1976, after he graduated from high school. He was eighteen, and I was nine. And my sister was fifteen—the gap between her and my brother was three years, and between her and me was six years.

To me, my brother was always a giant. He was tall, so much taller than I was. Obviously. My father was stricken with polio when he was two years old, which left him with a bad leg. He was registered as having a disability. Never once did he carry me on his back. It was my brother who did that. He gave me piggyback rides (in standard Japanese, *onbu*), spun me around, played with me. That's what made me think of him as a giant. In March of my last year of junior high, when I was fifteen, my brother's first child was born. It was a baby girl, meaning I had a niece. But although technically my niece, she really felt like a much younger little sister to me. I gave her piggyback rides (which we called *oburu*—perhaps our dialect, I am realizing now), gave her milk (from a bottle, of course—I would heat up water and prepare the formula), change her diapers. I thought of my niece as a younger sister, in the same way that I thought of my older brother as a father.

Well, let's put a lid on all of this talk about me, and get back to Kunikazu.

This is the interview I conducted with him in January 2020. Since the forty-ninth-day services, another forty-two had passed.

"WE HAD CONVERTED over to 100 percent mushroom beds. You thought it was the year before the earthquake? No, no—it was earlier than that. We started experimenting with shiitake mushroom beds in 2000. We were still doing the log inoculations. At first, we were doing a ratio of half the shiitake from the bolts and half from the mushroom beds. You're probably wondering why we started doing the mushroom beds in the first place, so I'll try to give it to you in a proper order. At any rate, if we hadn't switched to 100 percent mushroom-bed cultivation, it would have been completely hopeless. I mean, we *did* switch to 100 percent mushroom-bed cultivation, and it was *still* completely hopeless."

My brother Kunikazu was explaining to me how he had narrowly escaped having to shut down the business.

I mistakenly believed that the family mushroom business had entirely switched over to mushroom beds in 2010. That was not the case. Through a series of twists and turns—well, through a process of trial and error to which they felt driven by external forces—they converted at an earlier point to using exclusively mushroom beds. I left home in March 1985, during the inoculation, in the time when humble logs become bolts, so I don't know a thing about cultivation using mushroom beds. I couldn't even tell you the basics. But I know that it doesn't require setting up bolts in the woods (in specialist terms, "creating a laying yard"), nor is a crop exposed to the elements—meaning, it's not something that is done outdoors. Mushroom-bed shiitake are raised in greenhouses.

This became the difference between survival and ruin.

The situation was grave, I will note for the record once again. After the hydrogen explosions in the building housing the nuclear reactor at the Fukushima Daiichi Nuclear Power Plant (on March 12, 2011, and again on the 14th and 15th), mushrooms were considered "dangerous for consumption." Perhaps the situation would be better described by saying *Fukushima* mushrooms were considered to be dangerous for consumption. Information on which agricultural, forestry, and marine products easily absorb radioactive material such as cesium was instantaneously made available to everyone at that time. Among forest products, there were a variety of mushrooms and edible wild plants being tracked. I had a real sense that shiitake were, in a word, feared, so they couldn't be sold, and prices plummeted. I could feel that reality even from Tokyo. In any case, there was an active effort to avoid stocking the region's goods, so there wasn't anything from Fukushima on the supermarket shelves even if people were willing to buy them.

And, for shiitake cultivated outdoors, there was also a restriction on shipping them.

This began on April 10, 2011, when the Ministry of Health, Labor and Welfare announced that they had "detected radioactive cesium at levels that exceeded provisional regulation levels in shiitake grown in Iitate village, Fukushima prefecture." Three days later, the shipment of shiitake that had been cultivated outside in any of five cities, eight towns, and three villages in Fukushima prefecture was prohibited. A limitation on intake was assigned to shiitake cultivated outside in Iitate village. On April 25, another city was added to the list that prohibited the shipment of shiitake that had been cultivated outside, while another had its shipping restrictions lifted. But however you looked at it . . . however you looked at it, things were headed in a bad direction.

Shiitake cultivated in mushroom beds were allowed to go to market, but there was a problem.

I knew nothing, truly nothing, about mushroom beds, but I boned up for this very interview with my brother. They use something called a mushroom block as a sort of artificial log-*cum*-bolt. The medium is a nutrient source mixed with sawdust from broadleaf trees and allowed to harden into a block. You will note that sawdust is a crucial component. Where was Kunikazu procuring his sawdust? In Haramachi. It is currently a ward in the city of Minamisōma, but until 2005 it was an independent city.

I imagine the factory was in the eastern foothills of the Abukuma Highlands.

If so, that would put it right next to Iitate village.

"If we had gone on like that, we would probably have been using polluted sawdust, stuff from a place with a high level of radioactivity. But we changed suppliers with unbelievable timing. In March—meaning, in March 2011—we had switched to a vendor in Marumori, in Miyagi prefecture. I thought it was a great stroke of luck. It was sawdust from outside the prefecture, so I thought we would be OK, we could continue on with our mushroom-bed cultivation, keep on trucking. And then the report hit."

"The report?" I asked.

"It was radioactive."

Oh, man. That was all I could say. The town of Marumori is the southernmost place in Miyagi prefecture, located along the lower reaches of the Abukuma River. Three months before this interview took place, it had been devastated by Typhoon Hagibis, so I recognized the name when he said it. *Oh, that place,* I thought. "That place" borders Fukushima prefecture. Right after the nuclear meltdown, the cloud of radioactivity moved in a northwesterly direction from the Fukushima Daiichi Nuclear Power Plant. And Marumori was *right along that path.*

"With that, I couldn't procure any more sawdust. I had some blocks that I had finished preparing before all of this, and they fruited. So I was able to produce a crop of shiitake. And I was able to ship the shiitake. What I couldn't do is sell them. Even though, of course, there was no trace of cesium on them, there wasn't a thing I could do to sell them. And I couldn't prep any more mushroom blocks. Finally, in the fall—"

He's talking about the fall of 2011.

"—I managed to buy some sawdust from a place in Yamagata. But it was sawdust made for harvesting nameko mushrooms. It's different. It's just a little different. OK, it's completely different. Here was another problem. So we got hit with this double whammy—no one to buy them, no way to prep the beds, so *it was all completely hopeless* that year."

I figured it wouldn't do to try to drag anything more out of Kunikazu, so I used my standard, "Oh, man," with a groan. Then I straightened my back and repeated it a few times, dragging out the last vowel each time: "Oh, maaaan."

"At the end of the year, we received a settlement from the power company. With that, somehow, some way . . ." he said, bringing the narrative of the hardships of 2011 to a close for the time being.

From there, we went back to the time when my brother Kunikazu was a young man and I was a child, nine years younger than him.

NO ONE REALLY KNOWS THIS, but 71 percent of the total surface area of Fukushima prefecture is forest. It boasts the fourth-largest total forested area in all of Japan.

No one really knows this, either, but in 2010 Fukushima prefecture ranked seventh in timber production, and first in the number of logs supplied to other prefectures for mushroom cultivation.

And no one really knows this, but in that same year, the amount of fresh shiitake produced there was seventh in the country.

No one really knows this except for my brother and me, but when we entered the little wooded area where we had the laying yard for the bolts (we had created a number of these "wood in the woods" areas), there were squirrels, there were bamboo partridges, there were pheasants.

Perhaps this is something that only I would remember, but I loved everything about the plug spawns that we used to hammer into the logs to inoculate them: their texture, their elasticity, their smell. I felt that I had a lot in common with these fungal strands. And then, the cut ends of the logs, their rings visible. In the spring, during the aforementioned "inoculation season," a pile of the logs, well over 10,000 of them, would be stacked up in front of the work area at our house. This too was a forest. My own private forest. I would even go into this cultivated forest from time to time and hide out for a while. Sorry, I can't go into details.

And yet, the family operation (and my role in it) was just *brutal*.

My older brother, Kunikazu Furukawa, took over the business in 1976. He was eighteen. Did he do it because he was so attracted to the cultivation of mushrooms? "Nope," Kunikazu answered straight out. To begin with, he said, the family business was *brutal*. Where have I heard that before? In our house, children were laborers. That is a brutal life. "Sundays were depressing," Kunikazu says. At the time, there was still school on Saturdays; it hadn't yet been cut down to five days a week. Sundays were depressing because physical labor was waiting for him on his one day off.

Best not to get him started on long holidays, or the lack thereof.

But, he took over the family business. The shiitake operation had been scaled up in size, and my father had come to the determination that "if things carry on like this, you should be able to live a pretty secure life well into the future." He had ordered Kunikazu to take it over. At the time, Kunikazu had nowhere to escape. His little brother Hideo, on the other hand, *would* have a place to escape. But at the time I was nine years old and figuring out life.

To be sure, life was on the upward swing. In 1979, we built a new house (the one where the main room next to the entryway was "half destroyed" on March 11, 2011).

In the mid-1980s, the winds of change reached our house.

Dried shiitake produced in China began to flow into the Japanese market.

My brother stopped producing dried shiitake. It wasn't worth it anymore, he said. They focused exclusively on fresh shiitake, but from a financial perspective, they were feeling the pinch.

In 1992, my father was still alive and well, but he handed over financial control of the business to my brother.

In the following year, fresh shiitake from China entered the Japanese market.

My brother had a bad feeling about this.

In 1997, the supply of fresh shiitake from China suddenly increased. Kunikazu described this as landing with a *whomp*. At this point, domestic fresh shiitake went into free fall.

In 1999 and 2000, imports of Chinese shiitake continued to rise. The family's losses increased, and their debts mounted.

"That's why we turned to mushroom beds," he said. Kunikazu, my brother.

The operation shifted away from inoculating logs. At first, they did half bolts and half beds. They started out by buying prefabricated mushroom blocks that had already been inoculated, also to minimize the initial risk. "The cost of production went down, and the yield went up, so we switched over completely to bed-mushroom cultivation. At first we were buying the mushroom blocks, but we did some research, and starting in the spring five years later, we began producing our own mushroom blocks."

This was in 2005.

Earlier than that, in 2001, government safeguards were implemented, in the form of emergency restraints on imports, measures to protect domestic producers from sudden increases in imports of designated products. Fresh shiitake, spring onions, and tatami rushes were all three protected.

Between 2001 and 2005, deflation steadily chipped away at the business. And yet, it somehow picked up. "Have we finally achieved altitude now?" Kunikazu dared to wonder.

In September 2008, a financial crisis on a global scale peaked with the collapse of Lehman Brothers. Another serious blow.

They rode out that storm.

And then came March 2011.

WHEN I DID THE MATH to figure out how old my brother was when it happened, I realized that he was the same age as I was now, interviewing him: fifty-three.

I'LL TELL YOU ABOUT my mother's wake. What happened at the wake for the mother of my brother, Kunikazu, and me, Hideo, and my sister . . . well, this piece isn't about my sister, so I won't give her name.

I went around and poured sake for the people who came, table by table. I came to the table for my mother's relations. My father's side of the family was much more active in our lives. So, truthfully, I am not all that close to my mother's relatives.

"Hey, Hideo, have you heard this one?" a cousin asks me.

Maybe I know it.

"It's about when your mother learned that she was pregnant with you."

Maybe I know it.

"She came to consult with my dad. 'You're my big brother, what do you think—should I have this baby? We're so busy with the shiitake. I don't have any time to look after a child. But I'm pregnant. Should I keep it?' she asked him. And my dad said, 'Yeah, you should.' Did you know that?"

I know it.

I didn't know that I had been saved by my uncle like that.

I was hearing that part for the first time. But I knew it.

When I was maybe thirty-two or thirty-three—my memory is a little fuzzy on this—I was riding with my wife in the car my mother was driving, and she confessed this for the first time. I was going to abort you, she told me. She said that she thought it would be impossible to raise me, so that's what she was thinking of doing. The version that I heard from her was, "Grandma said to me, 'I'll take care of it,' so I had you." In the end, I have to think that I was born after receiving a reprieve from my grandmother and uncle.

My sister (who was at the same table, paying the same courtesy-in-a-bottle to the relatives as me) didn't know the story. My brother still doesn't know, I imagine. It's possible he will learn about it for the first time when he reads these words.

I WAS CLUMSY, not fit for manual labor—in other words, completely unsuited for the job. I made mistake after mistake. I injured myself time and time again.

Over spring break at the end of my first year of junior high (at the end of which I would begin my second year of junior high), when I was in the middle of inoculating a log, I bashed my own finger with the hammer. The index finger on my left hand. I was forced to leave the front lines of the war known as "inoculation season."

There was another time in the summer of the same year. I was transporting bolts into the forest, driving a three-wheeled truck (designed for forest work, the brand name was Derupisu). At the laying place in the mountain forest, in a little wooded clearing, I gunned the Derupisu by accident, and drove it straight into a tree. I didn't have the presence of mind to hit the brake, I panicked so much. I took a blow to my ribs on my left side. Naturally, I was reprimanded. My father gave me a good dressing-down. My father's scoldings were of a category all their own. He had the pride of a person with a physical disability, so when someone without his disability couldn't do something that he could (pull his own weight), he chalked it up to laziness. I have no good counterargument here.

I didn't add a lot of value to our family business.

Every time I was told I was inept, the words had the power of a curse.

I can give you some other good examples. As a child I was afflicted with chronic sinusitis. I was always sitting in some corner of the house, my nose dribbling. My aunt admitted later that until I went to school, quote, "I thought you were a moron." I was hyperactive, I had my own mixed-up sense of how the world worked... let's see, what else? I'll add that I was frail, and I had asthma. There was a certain couple who hadn't been able to conceive a child who said they were interested in adopting me. But it didn't happen. I don't know the particulars of why it fell through. I had the feeling that there was something about me (innate to me) that was off-kilter. As I said, I was figuring out life.

I'm sure I was in second grade the time I left our house, walked away from the village, crossed some rice paddies, and just kept right on walking. A missing persons report was filed on me.

When I was in sixth grade, I contacted relatives who were living in Yokohama, in Kanagawa prefecture, to consult with them about possibly going to junior high in one of the Yokohama public schools. But my dreams of getting out that way didn't come true.

About this phrase, "getting out." I wanted to get out of my house. "I wanted to get out of my house" meant "I wanted to get out of Fukushima." I wanted to leave Fukushima behind me. Looking back, I can see that I already felt that way as a second grader.

MY BROTHER, Kunikazu Furukawa, even today cultivates shiitake. He also has a *kikurage* mushroom crop. Demand for *kikurage* is on the rise.

Back to 2011. To the days just after 3.11. Kunikazu wasn't able to sell any shiitake outside of the prefecture, so he sold where he could in the area. He sold them at direct distribution outlets run by Japan Agricultural (JA) Cooperatives and at various stores in a supermarket chain based out of Kōriyama. Both of those routes suffered from a dearth of mushroom buyers. The people of Fukushima prefecture were not interested in buying any scary shiitake, which along with other mushrooms had become synonymous with "radioactive contamination." The economic damage was increasingly dramatic.

"When there was news of a suicide in the village of T—," Kunikazu began, naming the place in question. A full-time farmer in Fukushima prefecture saw no hope for the future and had killed himself. "I was pretty...pretty shocked. I just thought, when things come to that, what happens?"

He was delicately glossing over something. He was saying in a roundabout way, if he were to make the same choice, what would happen? And, of course, what I take from that is about humans in general: When an option you hadn't particularly thought a lot about is shoved in your face, you suddenly realize that it exists as an option. Information expands your options. When said information is the fact that someone out there chose death, you can choose it, too.

But I don't know anything about the person who committed suicide in the village of T—. There were bigger stories (in terms of their shock value), such as when an organic farmer in Sukagawa City committed suicide late in March 2011, or when a dairy farmer in Sōma City did the same in June of the same year. The former was a good friend of my sister and her husband.

ABOUT MY SISTER.

I'm not researching her story, so in principle, I feel I shouldn't write anything about her. I'll just say one thing, which is related to my own story. There were no books in our house. There was nothing "literary" to speak of, nothing enriching, nothing like a set of great works of literature. My brother has also said this, but we never had any picture books in our lives when we were children. I first encountered an actual book during the winter I was in second grade. I took a book that belonged to my sister, then in her second year of junior high, and read it. It was a work of children's "literature" by Satoru Satō, called *A Little Country No One Knows.* In it, there is a little hill, meaning, a little woods, and an imaginary, happy country. To put it simply, I was on fire for this book. To the point that I danced through the flames. There was another forest in there, and it offered hope.

After that, reading became part of my life. I have since fostered the belief that, for me, books were a tool directly related to my survival.

I have never told my sister this. Anybody else probably would have.

THE LAST THING MY older brother Kunikazu talked about, starting with "And yet…," was how he decided in 2011 to continue on with the family business (in shiitake production).

"Mushrooms are a symbol of nuclear disasters, so there was no way that we could stop."

That was his declaration.

I was about to cry.

WE HAVE THE FOREST. We Furukawa siblings have the forest. We three siblings. And so do other sets of siblings out there. I left Fukushima of my own free will, so I think there is nothing that someone like me can say about life after the nuclear accident. Yet somehow I am in the position of cheering on Fukushima, to the point where I have spoken about it publicly, both in Japan and abroad. I have kept on speaking my truth—or, at least, *a* truth. Now, as to where this work goes next. People might want me to tell my entire story in detail, but I would just point out that that isn't so easy. I understand this in the marrow of my bones. Since I know this is the case, isn't it best for me to switch modes at this point, to listen to other people tell their stories, and to listen attentively? It's possible I will get everything wrong, but even so…

Even so…

Even so, I am convinced that if all we do is adopt the stance that reconstruction should just be about getting things back to the "good old Fukushima" (of pre-March 11, 2011), there are things that will never be restored and there are people who will never be made whole again, so maybe (just maybe) something good can come from this modest contribution.

…just maybe, I think to myself.

I will leave it to my own clumsiness to take care of the rest.

February 2020 🐒

Note from the translator: The quote from Albert Camus is from his essay "On the Future of Tragedy," published in *Lyrical and Critical Essays,* translated by Ellen Conroy Kennedy (New York: Knopf, 1968), p. 301.

Kyōhei Sakaguchi

The Tale of Malig
the Navigator

translated by Sam Malissa

I'LL TRY TO TELL YOU ABOUT the path I've traveled. I don't know how long I've followed it, but it's been a strange voyage—though maybe voyage isn't quite the right word. What else could describe what I've been through? Perhaps a festival. A festival from long ago. The story begins when I was still very young. Maybe only just starting to walk. I had no father or mother. At least I don't believe I did. I can't be certain. I didn't feel at all lonely, so I guess I never thought about it. Having no parents didn't worry me, and no one else ever mentioned it. Everyone was always laughing and bustling around. I was good at finding water, which I always did while dreaming. When I dreamt, I was fast asleep. I'd tuck myself under a blanket of broad leaves and fall into a deep slumber. There, even if it was the middle of the day, it would suddenly become my night. My head could always find the night. I would drag out the moon and stare at it. The moon was purely in my head, so its light was odd and its shape wasn't quite round. But no one cared that it wasn't a perfect circle, least of all me. It was the moon. I didn't even know the moon's real shape until I went to sea. No one had ever told me. I thought of the people I was with as family, though we weren't related by blood. Our faces were different, as was the color of our skin, so we must have come from all over. I didn't know about such things, perhaps because where I lived there was no such thing as history—in the sense that history is a story of something that has ended—but I was still living, and where I lived was strange, as deep as you can go into the mountains and then deeper still. A place no one could reach. Only someone raised there could find it. It was shaped like a basin. We knew absolutely nothing about the sea. Only later did I learn that if you cross the mountains, and then cross yet more mountains, all roads lead to the sea.

But I grew up in the mountains. I was there from my earliest memory. The smell of damp black earth was everywhere, and once a day rain poured down, changing the landscape completely. It could be the sunniest day when clouds would suddenly appear and then weigh down on me, as if to cover me in layers. The clouds would swallow me up. I could hear the voices of the adults around me, but I couldn't see

anyone through the thick fog. It's not that I couldn't see them—they were gone. Everyone was gone. Once a day, every day, I'd be left on my own. I was used to being by myself, even when it wasn't raining, because I had no mother or father. I was on my own for bedtime, but I could sometimes find children who let me snuggle in like a brother. When the clouds swallowed me, though, I was entirely on my own. The adults used to shout at us to shelter under the broad *takusa* leaves when it rained, but I ran all over looking for them and couldn't find any. I'd thought that I couldn't see anything because of how hard it was raining, but never once did I crash into a tree, so I realized that it wasn't just the people who disappeared, but all the rocks and plants—everything. If I told anyone about this they'd never have believed me, so I kept it to myself. No matter how I ran, the rain would find me. There was nowhere to hide. Soon enough I no longer bothered to run.

When the clouds swallowed me, I would just sit there quietly. The rain would fall and enter my body. When I held out my arm, there would be droplets clinging to it. I'd stare at the scenery reflected in the droplets. Everything around me had disappeared, but somehow I could see the whole world in those droplets. Sometimes I could even see sunshine. It would light up places that were normally dark and hidden, revealing them. This felt special, and I came to look forward to the rain. I was alone, but I wasn't lonesome.

The rain would seep into my body, and I would gradually fall asleep. My body was jet black and damp, and smelled of soil. Water flowed in from different places, recalling various landscapes reflected in its droplets. There was sunlight in that scenery, and air to breathe, and all kinds of creatures breathing it. I could see them moving. For the full hour of the downpour I would sit, exploring. When the water fell asleep, the scene inside it would shift to night. There was nothing to reflect the light and it fell into total darkness—the same dark hue as my body, so I couldn't tell one thing from another. When I slept, the water weighed down on me like metal. Such tiny droplets, but they were so heavy they left indentations in my skin.

Sometimes the adults would vanish. We never knew when this would happen, and just as we forgot that it would, it did. Right in the middle of the day, and they were nowhere to be found. I was fine being on my own, but the babies and younger children would start to cry. Crying didn't bring the adults back, though, and before long the children would fall silent. We could only tell the passing of time by how hungry we got. We had to eat something, so the older children came up with the idea of catching birds. We knew the birds were living things, like us, so we named them, just as we named babies. Birds with names didn't return to the woods—instead, they built nests in the eaves of houses. Why didn't they fly away? I didn't have a bird. Because no one had ever given me a name, I had to name myself. Everyone called me Malig, which means bird. I had no parents, so they called me bird. I didn't like that, so I gave myself a name. But I didn't tell anyone what it was. I've never once said it out loud. So even now, people still call me Malig.

Whenever the adults disappeared, I would catch the scent of my favorite seeds. They're from a plant that grows underground, that spends its whole life buried and never comes out. Only when it dies does it become a thin strand of smoke that rises from the ground, just for a moment, and then it's gone. That's its flower, and it's said that if you find it you'll have good luck. It's called the *taa* seed, and I was always good at finding its flowers. It has a faint perfume, so it was easy for me to sniff out, even though none of the other children had ever found one. Maybe I just have a good sense of smell. It was strange, though—the other children seemed to forget everything, so when the adults vanished again that day, they were all beside themselves with fear. I remembered that something similar had happened before, when I had first learned to walk, I think. Back then, too, I could smell *taa*. A sweet smell, like deep-red spice. I remember things from the way they smelled, maybe because no one ever played with me or cuddled me. Whenever I picked up a scent, I sensed that I could hear the adults moving around me. Soup made from *taa* is tasty, but on days when the adults disappeared the *taa* would be spread around

on the soil, and I slept alone, apart from everyone else. I went off to a dark place where I couldn't see the roofs anymore—it didn't scare me, rather I felt safe because I knew no one would come there, and I nuzzled into a soft woven-grass basket and slept. Occasionally I would mix in with another family, playing with the children and little ones, and I would grow tired and spend the night in their house, but usually I would just find a dark place and sleep alone.

THE PERSON WHO WOVE the basket for me was Mehsa, who may have been a man, but also could have been a woman. I never knew for certain. Sometimes Mehsa had a beard, sometimes they wore their hair down to their waist, smelling sweet and looking something like a mother. They could make just about anything. Sometimes Mehsa took weapons and went hunting with the men, not returning for several days. They were good at cooking, and they had no family. Mehsa gave me my first taste of liquor, and they killed a small animal and separated out all the bones and organs on the ground, patiently showing me how the body fit together. Mehsa was well muscled, with no breasts but an ample backside. It was like their body was half male and half female, both strong and soft, so to me they were both father and mother. There were times they came back from a battle covered in blood, and sometimes, near where I slept in the dark, a group of men would get on top of Mehsa, who would mewl and howl like a cat. Often Mehsa spread *taa* on their body and painted patterns on their face.

Mehsa is gone now. Whenever I catch a whiff of *taa* I remember Mehsa's breathing. Warm exhalations beside me, Mehsa sweating. Mehsa, rough like a father, soft like a mother. I don't know where they've gone. I don't know if they are dead or still alive. Whenever I see a *taa* flower, I think it looks like Mehsa. It was Mehsa who taught me how to make it through the heavy rains, though they never told me I should do this or that. Mehsa couldn't speak, so I never heard their voice. I don't think they ever uttered a single word. The only thing I ever heard was that feline mewling. It seemed like the men were tormenting Mehsa, which filled me with loathing, but it was also the only time I heard Mehsa make any sounds, so it gave me a peculiar feeling. *I'm not alone.* It was the only time I had that thought, and I held on to it. I felt sorry for Mehsa, but lying there with my eyes shut, pretending to sleep, for just one moment I felt like I was part of a family. I could see it right there in front of me.

Mehsa's house was the reverse of other houses. Instead of the roof protecting us from the rain, it was flipped over and placed in a bowl-shaped hole dug into the ground. Mehsa would sit on top of the inverted roof. There were no walls, and I wondered if that was okay, but Mehsa was good at weaving and could make just about anything out of *takusa*. When the rains came, they would quickly weave the leaves into hats. Mehsa treated the whole forest like their house and didn't distinguish between inside and outside. At least, that's what I thought they believed. Mehsa had no voice and lived their life in silence. I asked Mehsa, if the forest is your house, then where's the outside? Mehsa picked up a big acorn and shook it. It rattled. The outside is in here, Mehsa said. Wait, I just remembered, I *had* heard Mehsa speak. I don't forget things, so this must be true. I remember Mehsa's voice. Not just their cat-crying voice; I know their calm, quiet voice too. Mehsa was a good cook, often making deep-red soup from *taa*. They shared it with me for dinner. Even just a little bit would fill me up, and because most of the rest of the time I was hungry, this made me happy. Mehsa didn't teach me about all the different things you could eat. They were always saying that we only needed a little bit for each meal. No need to eat much, Mehsa said. They taught me many ways to fill up on just a little bit of food. Don't worry about eating, they said. Be eaten. When the time comes, become someone else's meal. Yes, now I can remember Mehsa's voice. We talked. Talked and talked, for hours on end. After having soup, after I woke to the morning, after the next night fell, we talked. It was bright out, so I assumed the morning had come, but maybe it was all just one long night.

I THINK IT ONLY HAPPENED ONCE, on that one night. It seems now like it was more, but it was just that one time. It felt like Mehsa had always been with me, but it may only have been for a few days. My memory is clear, but I always picture Mehsa like a ghost. They may not have been an actual living person. It's possible they had died long, long ago, or that they had never even been a human being. But I can recall Mehsa's smell quite vividly. Even now it lingers somewhere deep inside my nose. Sometimes the smell is strong, which makes me remember Mehsa's body. A bountiful body, the body of both father and mother. After that night, Mehsa disappeared. The last time I had their soup it was extraordinarily delicious. As usual I only ate the tiniest bit. There was a stone set in the earth, hollowed out by the rain into a bowl that Mehsa used to serve the soup. I got down like a dog and slurped it. The same flavor as always, but somehow different. Usually when Mehsa fed me they would go off somewhere and leave me on my own. They would disappear into the forest, but that time they sat with me quietly. Mehsa faced me and spoke. It was the first and last time I ever heard them speak. But having heard their voice, I started to think about other times with Mehsa, and it makes me feel like I had heard them speak before. Maybe that night was just the first time I had heard Mehsa talking. They called me by my name. Not Malig. The name I had given myself. Or maybe it was Mehsa who gave me that name. That moment feels like a turning point, when the flow of time shifted. I could then smoothly go back to times I had lived before. Time was now like a village, or like a forest ringed by mountains that I could walk around as I pleased. And I could hear Mehsa's voice. I was called by my name, and I had a family. No father, no mother, but I was the child of the trees. Deep in the forest is a single small stump, but aside from that, no one touched any of the trees. No one could cut them down. The forest was eternally lush, not a single blade of withered grass. I am the child of that lone felled tree. It's the world of the nameless. No tree is like another, but none of them have names. Mehsa is nowhere to be found. Only their voice, all around like birdsong. Each voice sounded like it belonged to someone different, but to me they all seemed like Mehsa. Young Mehsa, and Mehsa grown old. It was the first time I had seen that place, the first time ever, but I was aware of my self that had known it since long ago. This self was separate from me, and it knew many paths. It brought me along to many different places. It has no form, and I have never seen it. Who I do see before me is Mehsa. Voiceless Mehsa, standing silently in front of me, eyes closed, working their jaw. Chewing something. Like always, Mehsa wasn't eating but was forever chewing.

Mehsa, who cannot speak, whose voice rings out through the forest like birdsong. The forest where I was seated and the forest where I could hear Mehsa's voice were separate, and I could see both of them. I was *in* both of them when my eyes were open and when they were closed. When I closed my eyes I could hear Mehsa's voice more clearly—it was all happening at the same time—and the familiar scents of the forest flowed through my nostrils to a deep place inside me. I remembered all manner of different things, or at least my self that was sitting there did, while my self in the other forest walked around, searching for birds. The time long ago when a fish in the forest river bit off my finger was right there in the color of the thicket just last night. It had the shape of plant life, but when I sniffed it, when I touched the leaves, scenes from the past flickered into view. Without any light I shouldn't have been able to see anything, and there was no light at all. But the darker the night became, the more blinding the scenes appeared. This had never happened to me before, but in the moment it didn't feel like it was the first time. Inside me there's an old man living in the woods. He's a different person than I am, and he was not born of my body. This goes beyond being something that I simply know. The forest is full of things that I don't know, things that I'm seeing for the first time, which excites me, and I walk and walk without ever stopping, though it's always night, and the sun never comes up. Or maybe the forest is just too dark. I can't imagine that it's not morning if I'm hearing so much birdsong. That's how active the birds are. Mehsa's voice reverberating through the trees, calming me. There is nothing to be afraid of. Even though I had always been so frightened of the forest.

I can go there any time, it feels like I'm there right now, and I never forget any of it. Ever since then, I have been in the two forests. I no longer set my rhythm based on the movement of the sun nor the emptiness of my stomach. I can eat whatever's close by, which appears in the other forest as plentiful seeds and fruits, so all I have to do is reach out my hand and put something in my mouth. A single day is no longer marked off by the sun, and the days get longer and longer. I'm somewhere in the woods, walking away the days. When I'm tired, I rest. I can hear the voices of the forest creatures, but I never see any of them. I may very well still be living out that unending night. I feel sure that a long time has passed since then, but I also feel like nothing ever ended. When I'm thirsty, no matter where I am, spring water appears. If there's a rock face, water gushes out of it. Sometimes water bubbles up right from the ground. I feel like Mehsa may be watching me. Sometimes they raise a finger and signal me to go left or right. But I can't simply follow the directions. There's no bridge connecting the two forests, so while I may receive guidance here to go to the right, in the other forest there is no left or right. I can only come to a stop. Each time that happens, there's a direction my body wants to follow, there are things it wants to do. I've decided to simply watch. If I deviate even the slightest bit, my body goes all strange. I need to remember how to use my body. It should only last for a moment. That's what I think every time I see Mehsa. It doesn't make sense that the sound would go on and on for this long without ever stopping. But I decided to stop thinking about it. Even now I can hear the tumbling of small rocks, which I'm sure happened decades ago, but I'm still in the two forests. Mehsa never died here. Here, they've been living all along, calling out the whole time. Even today. I can hear their voice. I can't understand it, but I decided to stop thinking about that too. Since I started to realize that I understand the things I'm feeling, I've been able to keep walking onward. I've gone back to the place I was born and reunited with the people I promised to meet again. They remember me. It's the first time I've ever met them, but my self who knows the paths embraces these people with apparent fondness. In this way, little by little, I separated from myself, I untied the threads that bound me, and as I let myself go slack and slacker still, I gave birth to many children. Baby boys who looked like old men, and baby girls too. As soon as they were born, they toddled off every which way, and this worried me, but I didn't reach out to stop them. At a certain point I got down on my hands and knees and began to crawl through the forest, just like they did. I brought my mouth down to sip the water that bubbled up from the earth. A little stream looks to me like a big river flowing lazily by. I'm tiny, like an ant, and I've been crawling for years. In the next moment I grow large. When I hurt myself I can use grasses to treat the wound. I now know which way to go. As I walk I see that the river has finally reached its end point, or so it seems, because the flow stops. I walk onward and find a pool of water. A pool so large that I can only barely make out the far shore. 🐵

Four Modern Poets on Encounters with Nature

selected and translated by Andrew Campana

Fude Iga (1913–1967)

渡り鳥とかりうど

夕暮れの寒空を　渡り鳥がただ一羽
おまえはどこへ行くの　どこへとまるの
羽も落ちそうな　かっこうをして
私のおうちへ　おいで
上等のご馳走はないけれど
あたたかいものをあげよう
私も淋しい一人ぼっち
旅のお話でもきかせておくれ
私は弓も矢も持っているが
おまえを撃たないよ

THE MIGRATORY BIRD AND THE HUNTER

One migrating bird, all alone in the freezing evening sky
Where are you going? Where can you stop?
It looks like your wings are about to fall off
Come to my house!
I don't have any fancy treats for you
But I'll give you something warm to eat
Just like you, I'm all alone
Come, tell me about your travels
I have a bow and arrow
But I won't shoot you!

一粒のベカンベ（ヒシの実）

道ばたで一粒の
干したベカンベ落ちていた
塘路古丹の道ばたで
きかん坊ぼうやが
手に持っていたのに
落ちたの知らず走り去る
そこへひらひら蝶がくる
白くきれいな蝶がくる
また見たことのないものがある
ベカンベの上を右左
なんですねと　もぐら持つ
私は草のなかにいるけれど
私の知らないものはない
お日さま 私の敵みたい
私のこの目昼知らぬ

Rukata shine bekanbe
Sattet bekanbe an
Tooro kotan rukata
Irara ponco
Tekeoro omawa
Hacir kai
Pirapira kani retar
Maraure et koranwa
Bekanbe samakeni as
Nenmaka etwa inkarayan
Neppadanaa eccur
Kuani munoro an
Kuani

A SINGLE BEKANBE

On the roadside, a single *bekanbe*—
A dried water caltrop—had fallen
A naughty boy had been holding it
On the road of Tōro Kotan
But he ran by not knowing he had dropped it
Then a butterfly flitted by
A beautiful white butterfly
This is like nothing I've ever seen
It said, fluttering around the *bekanbe*
Can I help you? asked a mole
I might live in the grass but
There's nothing I do not know
Though the sun—it seems to be my enemy
Daylight is unknown to these eyes of mine

Fude Iga (1913–1967)

紫雲台

春くれば青い空をみて
夏くれば広い海をみて
秋くれば美しい野山を
冬くれば白い世界を
この四季を忘れる人はいないけれど
世を終わりて この地
寂しき紫雲台の冷たい土と石の下
悲しく眠るしかばねや
楽しく眠るものもあらん
先祖代々眠る土地
この地は人の嫌う場所
されどこの地はほとけの国
地下には立派な都市ありて
われらの先祖が王であり
明治以前の時代から われらの知らぬ時代から
金と銀との城つくり
ダイヤモンドの電燈で煌めきさざめく城ありて
その名を第二のいこい城
次々訪れる人あれば
ダイヤを照らして迎え入れ
地上の文化の遅れを聞き
深くため息つくという
春には春の遊びあり
夏には深い水海へ
秋には月へでかけたり
冬にはシベリアへロケットで
地上の人には見えねども極楽浄土は地下にあり
誰にもさそいは出さねども
神のお召しがあればすぐに
第二のいこいの城めざし次から次へつづくでしょう
そこには富も貧もなく
煌めく明かりを中にして手をとりあって環になって
鶴の舞でもして遊び
蝶の舞でもして遊ぶ
ああそれとも知らず地上では泣きあって
花だ水だ線香だと年に一度の墓参り
物を供えてくれるより
きれいに清掃してほしい
紫雲台の地下には
黄金城があることを忘れずに

SHIUNDAI

When spring comes, we look out at the blue sky
Summer, the wide ocean
Autumn, the beautiful hills and fields
And in winter, the white world
No one would ever forget these four seasons
But in this place where you go once your life is done
Under the frigid stones and soil of the desolate Shiundai cemetery
The dead sleep in sorrow
Though some rest in happiness
The land where our ancestors have slept for generations
Has become a place that people hate
But this is the land of our dead
There is a grand city underground
Where our ancestors are kings
From before the Meiji era, from ages we do not know
They made a castle of gold and silver
A castle that glimmered with electric diamond lights
Called the Castle of Second Rest
When people visit, one after another
They are welcomed with diamond light
Those below hear about the backwardness of the cultures up above
And sigh deeply
In spring there are special games
Summer, trips to the deep ocean waters
Autumn, to the moon
And in winter, you travel by Siberian Rocket
Even though those on earth can't see it, the Pure Land lies beneath the ground
We do not invite anyone down here
But as soon as the gods call them
Those above will come to the Castle of Second Rest
There is no wealth here, nor poverty
We hold hands in a circle around the glittering lights
Dance the dance of the cranes
Dance the dance of the butterflies
Up above, they know nothing of this, and weep over us
Once a year they visit our graves with flowers, and water, and incense
But rather than these offerings
We want them to clean up our graves
And never forget that there is a golden castle
Under Shiundai

Matsusaburō Ōzcki (1926–1944)

雑草

おれは雑草になりたくないな
だれからもきらわれ
芽をだしても　すぐひっこぬかれてしまう
やっと　なっぱのかげにかくれて　大きくなったと思っても
ちょこっと　こっそり咲かせた花がみつかれば
すぐ「こいつめ」と　ひっこぬかれてしまうだれからもきらわれ
だれからもにくまれ
たいひの山につみこまれて　くさっていく
おれは　こんな雑草になりたくないな
しかし　どこから種がとんでくるんか
取っても　取ってもよくもまあ　たえないものだ
かわいがられている野菜なんかより
よっぽど丈夫な根っこをはって生えてくる雑草
強い雑草
強くて　にくまれもんの雑草

WEEDS

I don't want to be a weed
Hated by everyone
When you sprout, you're quickly yanked out
Even when you think you're finally grown,
    hiding in the shade of the vegetables
If anyone catches sight of your little secret flowers
They'll snatch you from the ground, shouting,
    "Another damn weed!"
Everyone despises you
They'll heap you up as compost and let you rot
I don't want to be a weed like that
But where do your seeds float in from?
How the heck can you be picked and picked, and
    never give up?
Weeds grow much stronger roots
Than any vegetable so tenderly cared for
Weeds are strong
Hated, but strong

夕日

夕日にむかってかえってくる
川からのてりかえしで
空のはてからはてまで　もえている
みちばたのくさも　ちりちりもえ
ぼくたちのきものにも　夕日がとびうつりそうだ
いっちんち　いねはこびで
こしまで　ぐなんぐなんつかれた
それでも　夕日にむかって歩いていると
からだの中まで夕日がしみこんできて
なんとなく　こそばっこい
どこまでも歩いていきたいようだ
遠い夕日の中に　うちがあるようだ
たのしいたのしいうちへ　かえっていくようだ
あの夕日の中へかえっていくようだ
いっちんち　よくはたらいたなあ

SUNSET

Coming back home towards the setting sun
Reflected on the river
A sky burning from end to end
The grass on the roadside is burning too
It's almost as if our clothes are about to catch fire
All day long we were carrying rice plants
Tired and achy, right down to our hips
But as we're walking towards the sunset
The setting sun soaks deep into our bodies
And it feels almost ticklish
It feels like I want to keep walking forever
It feels like my home is in the faraway sunset
It feels like I'm going back to the happiest home there is
It feels like I'm going back home into the setting sun
After a good day's work

Sōnosuke Satō (1890–1942)

仄かなる午前の風

村村へつづく庭の木の盛り上れる方より
わかき午前の日のかがやきと匂やかなる風は
いきながら空氣の娘のごとくにも近より來る
わが影をきよらかにめぐり半身に日を彩りつつ
そこらなる花花と蕾とをあたたかく一致せしめ
うすき喜びの電氣を燦めかして
椅子のほとりを黄金の日時計ともうたがはしめ
又はうつくしき地の光明臺の如くにも
はるかなる南風のほのほをひびかせ
うちあけたる朝の情熱をひたひたと滴らし
わが身の上を青空のさなかにすき透らせ。

A FAINT MORNING BREEZE

From the swell of garden trees that lead to the village
The glow of the new morning sun and the fragrant breeze
Draw near like the daughters of the air
Cleansing my shadow, coloring half my body with sun
Warmly matching the surrounding buds and flowers
Sparking my soft joy into electricity
Making the edge of my chair seem like a golden sundial
Or a gorgeous shining earthen pedestal
Let the blaze of the distant southern wind ring out
Dripping with the passion of the open dawn
Let my life story appear across the sky!

美しき冷感

障子をからからと開け放ち
さて水無月の灯を膝のほとりに引きよせて
宵の色こめたる野の面にふれよ
走る灯のはてはもうろうたる水となり
しつとりと藍いろの闇は獨座の裾をめぐる
あたらしき家の香を喜べ、私よ
傾けるオリオン星は肩のほとりに火花を與へ
ほのぼのもゆる庭のヂキタリスの影をはしる
おおこのひろびろとして、身にしみわたる
うつくしき我が宵の冷感!

A BEAUTIFUL CHILL

Open the rattling shoji screen
And draw the lights of June into your lap
Touch the face of the fields, full of evening colors
The running lights end in hazy water
Damp indigo darkness encircles the edge of my
    solitary seat
To myself I say, rejoice in the fragrance of your
    new home
The tilted stars of Orion honor you with sparks upon
    each shoulder
Running through the shadows of the gently
    blooming foxgloves
Oh, this vastness permeates my body
The beautiful evening chill!

Awajijo Takahashi (1890–1955)

21 HAIKU

跫音におどろく蝌蚪や水浅し
Tadpoles frightened
by the sound of footsteps—
shallow waters

傘さして馳け来る女春の雨
Opening her umbrella
a woman comes hurrying
spring rain

塀越えて蝶一つまたひとつ
Over the fence
one butterfly
and then another

部屋明し蛙鳴く夜の針仕事
Lighting a lantern
for a long night of needlework
listening to croaking frogs

夜桜に通りすがりの尼法師
Cherry blossoms at night
a group of nuns
pass by

おもむろに鶴歩み出づうらゝかな
Cranes stepping out
slowly
how peaceful

ゆるゆると鳴つて通りぬ春の雷
Taking its time
to rumble and move on
spring thunder

初蝶を見失うたる檜垣かな
Losing sight
of the first butterfly of the season
in the cypress fence

蛙の子押しかたまりて安堵かな
Tadpoles
huddling together
how reassuring

風に堪へ花を去らざる揚羽蝶
Buffeted by the wind
but still clinging to a flower
a swallowtail butterfly

降りそゝぐ雨にかぐろし蝌蚪の陣
Pitch black
in the steady rain
a squadron of tadpoles

女どちいとしあはせに青き踏む
A group of ladies
thrilled to tread
on the new grass

闇の金魚いとしみ見れば動きけり
Goldfish in the dark
I look at her tenderly
and she's already moved on

早こゝに鹿居て嬉し夏柳
I'm so happy
the deer are already here
summer willows

おのおのの心覚えや対浴衣
We each remember
different things
in our matching yukata

白扇や若きお僧の落ちつかず
White fan—
the restlessness
of a young monk

とぶ蛍草にとまりて消えにけり
A firefly
landed on a blade of grass
and vanished

光濃く蛍火水をはなれけり
Light growing stronger
the fireflies' glow
drifted from the water

空蟬を林のみちに拾ひけり
Picking up
an empty cicada shell
on my path through the woods

手につたふ露の雫や蛍籠
Carrying drops of dew
in my hand
like a cage of fireflies

ひらくより大蛾の来たる月見草
Just as it opens
an enormous moth enters
the moonflower

FUDE IGA (1913–1967) was born in Kushiro, Hokkaido. Her first language was Ainu, and she composed many Ainu songs and poems. Her daughter, Mieko Chikappu (1948–2010), was also a well-known poet and an expert in Ainu embroidery.

MATSUSABURŌ ŌZEKI (1926–1944) was born in Kurojō village, which became part of Nagaoka in Niigata prefecture. He wrote these poems as an elementary school student. His teacher and mentor, Michio Sugawa, participated in the Daily Life Writing Movement (*seikatsū tsuzurikata undō*), a pedagogical principle encouraging children to write about their experiences. Ōzeki joined the Imperial Japanese Navy and was killed in a torpedo strike in the South China Sea at age eighteen. After the war, his poems were posthumously compiled and published by Sugawa under the title *Yamaimo* (Yam).

SŌNOSUKE SATŌ (1890–1942) was a prolific poet and lyricist, born in Kawasaki. He founded the literary coterie Shi no Ie (House of Poems) in the 1920s and was influential in the development of free verse in Japan.

AWAJIJO TAKAHASHI (1890–1955) is the pen name of Sumi Takahashi, born on Cape Wada, in Hyogo prefecture. She was a member of the haiku coterie Unmo (Mica), and became well known for haiku evoking poetry from centuries earlier.

Kikuko Tsumura

The Kingdom

translated by Polly Barton

IT WAS NAPTIME AT KINDERGARTEN when Sonomi first noticed it. Unable to sleep, she was looking up at the light streaming through the gap in the curtains, and so she came to discover that if she stared at the light with her mouth open, Delilah the stentor would appear. Strictly speaking, she didn't actually need to have her mouth open for it to work, but Sonomi felt that opening it better conveyed her desire for Delilah's presence.

As Sonomi was gazing up at the light, particles of pink, yellow, and sometimes pale blue would form, strewn across the unexciting kindergarten scene before her like stars in a galaxy, and then, eventually, tiny Delilah would make her entrance. Mostly Delilah would come drifting from the top of Sonomi's field of vision to the bottom. Just when Sonomi was thinking that she'd disappeared, Delilah would descend from the top once again. Very occasionally she would move from left to right, but most of the time her movements were vertical.

When she first noticed the tiny figure, Sonomi had no idea what kind of thing Delilah was, and had mentioned to her mom and her kindergarten teacher that when she stared at the light she would see some kind of creature. That was until, at home one day, poring over the "Primitive Organisms" pages of her *Illustrated Book of Creatures, Volume I: Invertebrates,* she discovered that the thing she could see was very similar in shape to a frail-looking little organism called a "stentor." From that point on, Sonomi stopped mentioning the matter to people. After all, if the thing that would materialize unexpectedly amid her pink and yellow galaxy was a stentor, then it was no longer "some kind of creature."

According to the *Illustrated Book of Creatures,* stentors dwell in bogs, rivers, and similar environments, but as far as Sonomi was concerned, if something that looked identical to that would appear whenever she gazed at the light and focused her attention, then that was a stentor—its natural habitat was of little interest. At first she called it "Miss Stentor," but after a while she realized that was a bit like someone referring to her as "Miss Human" and decided to give the creature a proper name. She pondered for a week about what sort of name might be suitable, and came to the conclusion that, bearing in mind the exoticness of the galaxy in which the stentor appeared, a foreign name would be good. Most of the foreign names that Sonomi knew were the ones for the characters who appeared in the illustrated Bible stories she was given every month, and it came down to a choice between Isaiah, whose sound she liked so much, and Delilah, whom the illustrations showed as very beautiful. In the end, though, she considered that she did dearly want a female friend and settled on Delilah. Sonomi had "friends" from kindergarten and her neighborhood, but it would also have been true to say that she didn't have any real friends. There were several people her age who would do things like invite her to their birthday parties, go with her to swimming lessons, go crazy at her because her art smock was covered in glue, go crazy at her because she went jumping in puddles with her gumboots on, go crazy at her because her leg had accidently sneaked under the blanket of the person next to hers during nap time, and so on, but she didn't have any friends of the kind that she truly wanted. Sonomi herself thought of those people as sort of friends, but the fact that she came to rely so heavily on Delilah was perhaps a sign that somewhere deep down she knew that really they were no more than acquaintances.

ONE DAY, a classmate waved to her from the steps of the slide, and as she went running over, Sonomi tripped and fell. *I wasn't telling you to come running over,* her classmate said in an exasperated tone. She called the teacher over to where Sonomi was sitting on the ground, nursing her right knee. The knee was pretty sore, but Sonomi didn't cry. Sonomi fell over a lot, so she was used to injuring herself, and to seeing her own blood and cuts.

There must have been a sharp stone or something similar on the ground where she'd fallen, because that day the cut on her leg was slightly deeper than usual. The teacher escorted her to the classroom, saying they had to dress it, and there she rubbed some yellow liquid on the cut. Watching the cottonball soaked with antiseptic being applied to her knee, Sonomi forgot about the pain and instead felt a thrill surging through her. Usually when she hurt herself, the most

she would get was a bit of the clear liquid and a Band-Aid stuck on top. The clear liquid really stung, and it was boring. Sometimes, when Sonomi saw the naughtiest boys in class with yellow liquid and gauze dressings larger than any Band-Aids, she would feel a deep pang of envy and stare at their cuts. This time, her yearning had born fruit. Over and over, she peered down at the sight of the yellow liquid, such an unnatural color against her skin, soaking into the cotton gauze of the dressing and leaking beyond the wound. Returning to the slide where her classmate was, she waited patiently for her to ask, *why's your knee so yellow?* But the only question the girl posed was, *I never told you to come running over, okay, so you didn't go telling the teacher I did, did you?*

Sonomi was left with no option. Stepping away from her classmate and pretending to try and locate the bird who was chirping in a nearby tree, she lifted her eyes toward the sun and attempted to summon Delilah. After she'd been looking up at the light for a while, Delilah appeared, descending slowly from the top to the bottom of her vision, then retracing the same route.

Without using specific words, Sonomi reported to Delilah on the wound on her leg of which she was so proud. She let Delilah know that she'd finally been promoted from the rank of person given transparent liquid and measly Band-Aids to the rank of person given yellow liquid and gauze dressings. Over the course of Sonomi's report, Delilah traveled three times from top to bottom in expression of her admiration for this weighty transition.

Sonomi, you gotta stop doing that thing so only the whites of your eyes show—hearing a classmate approaching, Sonomi blinked and pretended to be examining the tree. *Yeah, it's freaky,* someone else said, standing in front of Sonomi and blocking her path. This classmate was tall—Sonomi's eyes were level with the girl's shoulders. The light streamed through the gap between her and Sonomi, so that Delilah began skating slowly across the surface of the girl's perfectly waved hair, the kind of girls' hair you see in picture books.

Sorry, Sonomi said. She hadn't done the slightest thing wrong, but it was too much of a hassle to have to justify herself. So she said it again: *Sorry.* What she didn't say, though, was: *I won't do it again.* She knew how dumb it seemed just to say "sorry" and not follow it up with anything, but there was no way she was going to say the other bit. Her classmates could have her robotic apology, but they weren't going to take her light, her Delilah, and her wound away from her.

ON THE WAY HOME from kindergarten, they stopped into the drugstore and Sonomi's mom bought some gauze. Feeling enraptured by this change that had taken place in her life, Sonomi asked her mom, *Will we change it every day? Every time you get in the bath,* came her mom's reply.

The way the wound looked after she'd been in the bath was also a matter of great excitement to Sonomi. She was already excited by how her fingers would go all wrinkly after being in the bath, but the sight of the bit surrounding her wound turning white like the inside of a Filet-O-Fish was even more wonderful. While her mom was in the bath, Sonomi whiled away the time by sitting on the plastic bath stool and looking up at the light on the ceiling to summon Delilah. Sonomi's mom was aware that Sonomi had a habit of opening her mouth, rolling her eyes back so far into her head that only their whites showed and looking in the direction of the light, but she didn't tell her not to, only hoped to herself that Sonomi didn't do it too much at kindergarten. Sonomi was her first child, which meant she didn't really know whether Sonomi's behavior was weird or not. It had been a concern to her when Sonomi had started talking about seeing strange creatures, but of late she'd not spoken of them at all, which was a relief.

When she was out of the bath, Sonomi's mom put some clear liquid on Sonomi's knee. Sonomi voiced her disapproval, saying, *why are you putting the see-through one on, doesn't it have to be yellow?* Her mom answered, *your teacher said that the clear one was fine.* Having once been granted the right to have the yellow liquid, to have that right taken away after just half a day felt to Sonomi like a demotion, and despite not having cried when she fell, or when the cut was disinfected and the liquid put on, she now felt herself close to tears. *Buy some of the yellow one,* she said to her mom, who said, *okay, we'll go back to the drugstore tomorrow.*

HER MOM HAD ASKED her kindergarten teacher to keep Sonomi from running around for the moment, as it wouldn't be a good idea for Sonomi to hurt herself again while her cut was still healing, so the next day at break time, Sonomi found herself sitting quietly in the classroom. Sonomi liked playing outside, but she also liked to stay inside reading books and making things with clay.

That particular day, Sonomi was drawing pictures in oil pastels with a girl from the class next to hers who had a cough. Sonomi didn't know the girl at all, but when Sonomi drew a picture of Delilah and told her it was a stentor, the girl didn't pull a face, and she didn't reproach Sonomi for staring up at the light either. When Sonomi asked the girl why she was coughing, the girl told her she had asthma. When she was actually wheezing she looked to be in pain, but probably because she was so used to her condition, two seconds after a bout of heavy coughing, she would look up again with a smile. This seemed to Sonomi unbelievably unnatural and very appealing.

Sonomi hadn't felt like speaking about the cut on her knee with the other kids in her class, but sitting with the girl with asthma, she felt like talking to her about it, so she did. *Do you know what, yesterday I fell over sooo hard, and I hurt this knee, and so then the teacher put this yellow liquid on it, and she put a gauze dressing on it too.*

The girl widened her eyes and then looked down and coughed. The sound she made wasn't of the cute *cough, cough* kind. It was a great big noise like a vacuum cleaner was attached to her throat, yet still she directed her eyes toward Sonomi's knee and pointed at it, saying, you've got a gauze dressing again today. Sonomi said, regretfully, *yes, but I don't like that the liquid isn't yellow.* At this, the girl said, pensively, *that's maybe like how when they changed my asthma medication from the big pills that were really hard to swallow to smaller ones I felt kind of let down because I didn't have to try so hard anymore.*

It was the girl from the other class who brought up the subject of smell, coming out and saying, *does your cut smell funny?* When Sonomi shook her head, the girl said, *it's not really a smell that cuts have, I guess it's the smell of the Band-Aids stuck on them, but they smell like nothing else I've ever smelt.*

Is it a bad smell? Sonomi asked, to which the girl replied, *it's not bad, but it's not nice either,* and then she started to cough. Sonomi was immediately taken by the urge to peel off the gauze from her knee and smell her cut.

The girl's coughing fit was showing no sign of easing up, so Sonomi started rubbing her back, and then the teacher came to lead the girl away, saying, *let's go and take your medicine, shall we,* and the two disappeared into the corridor, leaving Sonomi alone. Sonomi felt sad that the girl had left, as she'd wanted to talk to her more, but she also felt a sense of luck at being left alone after hearing such a great tip, and moved into the sunniest corner of the classroom.

Very carefully, pulling off the tape that held it in place, she peeled back the gauze on her knee. The neither-bad-nor-nice smell the girl had been talking about formed an interesting combination with the austere, medicinal smell of the liquid, but if anything it was the appearance of the cut, its blood now dried so she could see the contours of the entire wound, that held Sonomi transfixed.

Central to the circular patch where the skin had been scraped off and the red blood had coagulated was a slightly skewed triangular section of leftover skin. The longer Sonomi stared at it, the more this triangular section came to look like an island, floating on a red lake.

Sonomi had the urge to peel the triangle right off, but she clenched her right hand into a fist and resisted the impulse. She couldn't go doing something as wasteful as that. She stared fixedly down at her knee, and eventually settled for licking the red part, just a little bit. Mixed in with the bitterness of the liquid was the taste of blood. Blood tasted slightly like the sea. Sonomi had been to the sea just once. She raised her head a fraction and inspected the cut again. It seemed to her that she could see a castle, and fields, and flocks of birds on the island.

AS SHE WAS STARING DOWN at the cut, unblinking, Delilah made an unexpected appearance. Sometimes, when she was lucky, this would happen. Without Sonomi even

asking her to, Delilah would show up and begin falling from the top to the bottom of her field of vision.

When Sonomi quietly looked down, Delilah appeared superimposed upon the cut on Sonomi's knee, before sinking to the floor of the classroom. Then she appeared in the upper reaches of Sonomi's field of vision and started descending again.

It wasn't as if she'd never had intimations of the thought before, but this time, Sonomi felt without any doubt that Delilah was a holy being. Again and again Delilah descended, moving through the light as if in celebration of the kingdom of Sonomi's wound. There in the corner of the classroom, Sonomi felt that the world was utterly complete. It was a deeply exciting feeling.

A DAY LATER and Sonomi was permitted to go outside again, but she found that she was already excluded from the games that her classmates were playing. Trends moved fast in the world of the playground. While Sonomi had been taking it easy in the classroom for a day, her classmates had become obsessed by a game where you used red leaves as currency to buy falling camellia flowers, and when Sonomi, who didn't fully understand the rules, presented her classmates with yellow leaves that she'd picked up, they looked at one another and laughed, then told her that they couldn't give her any camellia flowers for *those.* Remembering that there were camellia flowers fallen on the road on the way back from kindergarten, Sonomi figured she could just pick up those ones, and went to sit in the sunny corner of the sandpit to peel back her dressing.

It was the third time she'd peeled it back that day. With every opening, the story of the cut on her leg would develop. The triangular island floating roughly at the center of the round red lake was currently ruled over by a queen. The queen was beautiful, although she wasn't young, and she was extremely dignified. On the island, apples and pears were harvested all year round and sold off to other nations. The apples and pears were incredibly delicious. The queen had recently sent her daughter, the princess, off to another country to be married for diplomatic reasons, and had just received a letter from her daughter saying that although it appeared from the outside that things between her and the prince were going well, the reality was that relations between them were rather icy. She hinted that she wouldn't be surprised if he divorced her, which had put the queen out of her mind with worry. The prince's country was the biggest importer of apples and pears, so the queen wanted to make sure that things remained peaceful.

Every day, the queen would sit on her throne, which was positioned in a sunny spot in the palace, roll her eyes upward, summon Delilah, and pray for her daughter's happiness. Delilah would tell the queen that she was watching over the princess. When she was out of sight of her husband, the princess would also roll her eyes upward and pray to Delilah.

So deep in thought was Sonomi about the kingdom on her knee that she didn't even notice the teacher approaching. *Don't you want to play with the others?* the teacher asked, so Sonomi thought a bit, and then said, *if the girl I met yesterday is there.* Sonomi wanted to talk to the girl about the kingdom on her knee.

The teacher shook her head and told Sonomi that the girl was off today. *Will she be here tomorrow?* Sonomi asked, to which the teacher said she'd ask the girl's homeroom teacher.

The number of peel-backs increased day by day, which meant more and more chances for the cut to be exposed to the air. It often happened that the tape holding the gauze in place would dry out and lose its stickiness, so that the dressing hung down below her knee, a state of affairs that her mom and the teachers would fix whenever they noticed it. Now, in addition to the combination of gauze dressing and the either yellow or clear liquid, there was a cold white spray that would sometimes be applied to the cut. It's snowing in the kingdom, Sonomi would think, when the spray came out. On occasion it would occur to her that sudden snowfall like that might prove detrimental to the apples and pears, and she'd feel a pang of worry. The teachers' and her mom's ministrations seemed to be having an effect, because Sonomi's cut gradually began to heal, the gauze dressing was removed, and most of the time she just wore a big square Band-Aid.

The kingdom itched. Sonomi would scratch her cut carefully, from on top of the Band-Aid, and would then grow wildly curious as to whether that scratching was having an effect on the kingdom, so she would peel back the Band-Aid to check. It seemed as though the triangular island was growing in size, but the real issue was that the red lake seemed to be getting smaller by the day. There was a band of yellow liquid around the rim of the cut that had now hardened, and Sonomi wondered if that was perhaps to blame for the lake's shrinkage. Sonomi knew from experience that the yellow liquid was really very salty, and so the apples and pears in the kingdom soon began to be affected and turn salty as a result.

Identifying the yellow tide as her nemesis—after all, it was making the red lake smaller and spoiling the apples and pears—Sonomi would constantly peel back the Band-Aid to check on the cut's condition, and if the yellow section had grown too much, would peel off little pieces of it with her fingernail and remove them. She mostly disposed of the chunks of tide she had removed by putting them in her mouth.

In the end it wasn't a teacher or her mom who saw her doing this and got mad, but a classmate. Sonomi didn't understand why it made the girl so upset. Maybe she thought it was gross, or maybe she was just feeling bad and was looking for an excuse to yell at someone. In any case, when Sonomi peeled back her Band-Aid during a break during song time and was pulling off chunks of yellow from the cut, the girl next to her suddenly shouted, *you shouldn't do that, it's bad!*

The girl explained what was happening to another classmate sitting on the opposite side of her, saying, *it's bad, right?* before going on to spread the news of Sonomi's act of folly to the person in front of and behind her, so that the surrounding area became a hailstorm of "you shouldn't do that"s. More than feeling sad or scared, Sonomi felt taken aback, and in her astonishment, moved the piece of yellow tide invading her kingdom's lake that was stuck to her finger into her mouth. It tasted salty.

Hearing the commotion, the teacher came over to see what was going on. Sonomi's classmates set to work seeking backup for their criticism of Sonomi's actions, but all the teacher said to Sonomi was, *Sonomi-chan, if you do that it'll be harder for the cut to heal, and it'll carry on hurting.* The sound of the teacher's voice somehow flicked a switch in Sonomi and, feeling the tears welling up in her at last, she began to cry. Clearly feeling a little sheepish, the classmates who had been accusing her slunk away, but Sonomi didn't stop crying. As she looked up at the ceiling and wailed, she walked over to the sunniest corner of the classroom.

Wiping her eyes with each of her arms in turn, she blinked hard and summoned Delilah. In those tear-veiled eyes Delilah moved faster than usual, racing from the top to the bottom of Sonomi's vision.

The teacher's hand fell on Sonomi's shoulder. *If you wipe your eyes like that the germs will get in,* she said, handing Sonomi a tissue. Sonomi used the tissue to wipe not her eyes but her nose, which was running, then stuck the tissue into the pocket of her smock and wiped her tears away with her arms, still sobbing. The teacher, who was now kneeling, looked down at the floor, her hand still on Sonomi's shoulder.

Delilah didn't pass any kind of message to Sonomi, instead she moved through her field of vision over and over, beckoning Sonomi's consciousness away from the corner of the kindergarten classroom and toward the kingdom on her knee. I bet the princess who was sent away from the triangular island didn't cry in such an undignified way as this, Sonomi told herself. She took the tissue out of her pocket, blew her nose, and wiped her tears with her arms.

TIME PASSED, and the kingdom continued to change shape. In spite of Sonomi's efforts, the red lake not only fell prey to the yellow tide's invasion but was also gradually encroached upon by the encircling territory and forced to join with it. The red lake developed a thin purple skin, swelled up, and rose to an even higher altitude than the triangular island.

Yet surprisingly enough, this development didn't leave Sonomi feeling too sad. This was because she had watched a short animated film about volcanoes on a DVD her dad had rented for her. The story was about a volcanic island that sang continually for its true love, and it was only when that island began to sink that its

true love (who was also an island) rose up from deep in the sea where it had been sunk all that time and revealed itself, which made Sonomi think that the same thing was happening on her knee. In other words, the triangular island was actually a volcano, and had kept on singing, and now the purple territory beneath the red lake had risen up and appeared.

By that point, Sonomi was going without a Band-Aid on her knee, and the only treatment her cut received was the spray that her mom would apply now and then, when the mood took her. It barely hurt anymore, either.

Occasionally Sonomi would consult Delilah about how things were going in the kingdom. While the kingdom was surrounded by a lake its peace had been assured, but how was the queen faring now that her kingdom had joined up with the surrounding territories? There was a lot of snowfall of late as well.

As ever, Delilah just drifted wordlessly through Sonomi's field of vision. She seemed to be saying that however good or bad the situation got, she would be there watching over things, in spring and in winter alike.

SONOMI'S CUT SEALED over completely, and the area of purple skin kept shrinking, until it became virtually indistinguishable from a regular knee. The kingdom had disappeared. As if in mourning, Sonomi now hardly spoke. Whenever she summoned Delilah, rather than talking to her as she had before, she tended to simply gaze at her. Delilah drifted slowly from left to right, as if lamenting the disappearance of the kingdom she had been protecting. This was something of a rarity, because she usually traveled vertically.

It was around then that the girl with asthma showed up again. One day when Sonomi was playing tag in the playground, she noticed the girl sitting in the corner of the classroom and went dashing over to her. And fell dramatically. She picked herself up immediately, though, approached the asthma girl who was sitting on the boards by the door where people took off their shoes, avidly reading a book about growing morning glories, and said, *good morning!* The girl replied, *good morning,* and breathed like a vacuum cleaner. Sonomi forgot that she was supposed to be running from the person who was it, sat down next to the girl, and told her about her knee. *Sounds like a really unusual cut you had,* the girl said, impressed.

Yes, it was a really rare kind of cut, especially the fact that the skin was scraped out so it looked like there was an island right in the middle of a lake. There was a queen living on the island, and lots of apple and pear trees. But the island was absorbed by the surrounding land and disappeared.

The girl listened quietly to what Sonomi said. *Was the princess who went off to be married okay?* she asked, and so Sonomi replied, *I don't know. I hope she's happy. She must have felt worried because she'd only just got married,* and the girl said, *and that's why she wrote a letter to her mom.*

Sonomi had run out of things to say, and she was squinting at the light in an attempt to summon Delilah when the girl said, *you've got a cut on that one too,* pointing at the knee Sonomi had scraped when she'd fallen over moments before. *If you look carefully, it looks like lots of little lakes,* the girl said. It was true: when Sonomi moved her face up close to the knee, it looked as though there were hundreds of little lakes dotting the skin.

When I was off school I read lots of books about the countries of the world, the girl said. *That's how I saw that there's a country with a thousand lakes in it. Where?* Sonomi asked, directly. The girl coughed badly, then said, *in a really cold part of the world.*

Looking down at her knee with the fresh cut, Sonomi imagined red lakes speckling the snow, going on and on for as far as the eye could see. The princess of the triangular island had gone off to that country of snow and lakes to be married, and her new environment must have made her worried, Sonomi thought.

Sonomi raised her head to tell Delilah all about it, and searched her out in the light. *I'm watching over her,* Delilah said, as she descended. *I'm watching over you. As long as you believe in me, I'll keep on appearing.* 🐵

The Cave

Satoshi Kitamura

The End

Stuart Dybek

———

Lessons

LESSON

Out of the glare, a strange boy
becomes recognizable as my most
scholarly student, Aubrey Aubert,
who just yesterday was dressed
in the uniform for school—horn
rims, gray trousers, yellow shirt.

Now he stands half-bare,
myopic, holding a trident-tipped
spear, the dripping stringer
of octopus cinched at his waist
still twitching, its tentacles
swaying like a hula skirt.

His trident jabs the way his hand
rises in class. Always first,
able to anticipate questions before
they're asked, he answers:
"To kill the sea-cat, me son,
you have to bite his eyes."

THE LESSON

*It seems to me you don't dare express yourself as
you feel.*

I had played his nocturne in C minor, left hand
tolling, the right braiding water, as if it were late
evening and I was performing at a salon.

A velvet drape was usually drawn, but today he
stepped out onto the balcony above the Boulevard
Poissonnière.

My friends envy the view but not the stairs.

One could see from Montmartre to the dome
of the Pantheon. The traffic of carriages clattered
from the cobblestones below. Bells from church
steeples across the city were striking the same hour,
each with its own cadence and decaying sonority,
all signaling that the lesson should be over. There
was a scent of thunder moving closer.

*I see timidity is a kind of armor you wear. Be
bolder, let yourself go more. Not just the hands, the
body must be supple to the tips of the toes.*

He sat down at the piano. I closed my eyes. Goethe
called music the language of the inexpressible.
I had a thought, the same was true of rain. By now
the boulevard must have become a torrent flowing
from umbrella to umbrella. Was some passerby,
hair plastered, face slick, gazing up stunned to
hear in a downpour the frightening beauty each of
us keeps shut within? My blouse was spotted. When
I touched my face, my fingers came away wet.

*Forget you are being listened to and always listen
to yourself.*

He rose and stood facing the streaked panes.

I left an envelope with twenty francs on the
mantelpiece. 🐵

Haruki Murakami

————

Creta Kano

translated by Gitte Hansen

MY NAME IS CRETA KANO, and I help my older sister, Malta Kano, with her work.

Of course, my real name is not Creta Kano. This is the name I use when I am working with my sister. When I am not working, I use my real name, Taki Kano. Creta is the ancient name for the island of Crete. I have never been there. I chose Creta because my sister chose the name Malta.

Occasionally I look at a map, and I see how close Crete is to Africa. The island is long with rough edges, like a dog bone with scraps of meat still stuck to it. Crete is also home to a famous ruin—the palace of Knossos. As the legend goes, a young prince fought his way through a labyrinth to rescue a princess. If I ever get to Crete, I am definitely going to see the palace of Knossos.

My older sister makes a living from listening to water, and it's my job to assist her. She listens to the sound of water in people. It goes without saying that this is not something just anyone can do. You need both ability and training. She is probably the only person in Japan who can do this. My sister acquired this skill long ago, at a place on the island of Malta where water has great meaning. She trained there for many years. Allen Ginsberg and Keith Richards were among the people who visited the place where she trained. When she came back to Japan, she called herself Malta, and began listening to water in people for a living.

The two of us rent an old house in the mountains. In the cellar my sister keeps many types of water that she has collected from all over the country. The waters are in ceramic urns. Cellars are as well suited to storing water as they are for wine. It is my role to care for the waters. I scoop out any debris that floats to the surface, and in winter I make sure the water doesn't freeze. In summer, I see to it that no larvae are hatched in the urns. It is not a difficult job. Nor does it require much time. So I end up spending a large part of the day drafting architectural plans. When clients come to see my sister, I serve them tea and snacks.

Every day my sister spends two or three hours in the cellar, pressing her ear against each of the urns. Listening to the faint sounds that emanate from the

different waters keeps her ears sharp. From each urn comes a distinct sound. My sister makes me listen too. I close my eyes and focus all my attention on my ears. But I can't hear the water. I don't have the special talent she does.

Listen to the water in the urns first, my sister says. Do this, and someday you'll be able to listen to the sound of water in people. So I listen some more, but I still can't hear a thing. There are times when I think I might be picking up a slight sound. It feels like something made a small move far, far away. Like a small insect beating its wings. It's not so much that it makes a noise—it's more like the air trembling ever so slightly. Then in an instant the sound disappears, as if playing hide-and-seek.

Malta says it's too bad I can't hear anything. "You of all people should sense the sound of body waters." She says this because I am a woman weighed down by problems. "If you could hear," she says, shaking her head, "if only you could, you wouldn't be so bad off." My sister is deeply worried about me.

I certainly have problems. No matter what I do, it's always the same. Every man who lays eyes on me wants to rape me. They grab me, knock me to the ground, and drop their trousers. I don't know why, but it's been like this for as long as I remember.

I know I'm beautiful. I've got a gorgeous body. Large breasts and slim hips. When I look in the mirror, I think I'm sexy too. When I go to town, all the men stare at me like hungry animals.

"But not all beautiful women get raped," Malta says. She's right. It's only me. I must be partly to blame. Maybe men sense my fear. And when they do, it drives them to assault me.

In any case, whatever the reason, I have been violently raped by all kinds of men. There have been teachers, classmates, tutors, an uncle on my mother's side, the gas bill collector, even firemen who came to put out a fire next door. However hard I try to avoid it, it's no good. I've had a knife held to my throat, been punched in the face, and had a hose wrapped around my neck. I've been abused every way imaginable.

Which is why I stopped leaving the house long ago. If things went on like this, I was sure I'd be killed someday. And so I've been hiding out with my sister deep in the mountains where I've been taking care of the water urns in the cellar.

Just once I killed a man who was about to rape me. Well, to be precise, it was my sister who killed him. Right here in this very cellar. A police officer. He had come by to inquire about something, but when I opened the door and he saw me standing there, he lost all self-control and pushed me down. He ripped my clothes off and dropped his trousers to his knees. His pistol made a rattling sound as it scraped against the floor. Do what you like, I cried out, just don't kill me. He slapped me across the face. Luckily Malta arrived home just then. She heard the noise and grabbed a big crowbar, which she swung at the back of the police officer's head. There was a dull thud, and the policeman was knocked out. Malta then quickly fetched a knife from the kitchen and, as if slicing the belly of a tuna, made a clean slit in the officer's throat. Neatly and without a sound. My sister keeps all her knives razor-sharp. They are never dull, always cut unbelievably well. I was stunned, watching her do all this.

"Why did you do that?" I gasped. "Why did you slice his throat open?"

"Best to play it safe. We're dealing with a cop. Got to be certain he won't come back to haunt us," Malta said. She is really pragmatic.

Blood was streaming from the policeman's throat. Malta got one of the water urns to collect it in. "Better drain it all," she said. "That way we'll avoid trouble later." We pulled up the police officer by his legs and held him upside down. This took all our strength, for he was a large man and was wearing boots. If Malta hadn't been so strong, we wouldn't have been able to manage. She's as big and as strong as a lumberjack. "It's not your fault that men come after you," my sister said, maintaining a firm grip on his legs. "It's because of the water in you. It's not right for your body. That's why everyone's drawn to it. It gets on their nerves."

"But how do I rid my body of that water?" I asked. "I can't go on like this, sneaking around and avoiding attention. I don't want to live this way. I don't want to end my days like this." I want to live in the outside world. I am, after all, a fully qualified architect. Once

I received my credentials via distance learning, I entered a series of architectural design competitions and won several prizes. My specialty is thermal power plant design.

"Don't rush it. Listen carefully to the water. If you do, sooner or later you'll hear the answer," Malta said. Then she shook the police officer by his legs until the very last drop of blood had drained into the urn.

"But we just killed a policeman. What on earth are we going to do?" I said. "Killing a police officer is a serious crime. If we get caught, we could get the death penalty."

"We'll bury him out back," Malta said.

So we buried the police officer with the slit throat in the backyard. The pistol, the handcuffs, the clipboard, and the boots too. We buried everything. Digging the hole, lugging the body, filling the hole—Malta did all that. Imitating Mick Jagger, she sang "Going to a Go-Go" while she got the job done. Once the officer had been buried, we stomped the ground flat and scattered dead leaves on top.

The local police undertook an investigation. They searched for the missing officer, leaving no stone unturned. A detective came to our house and asked a lot of questions. He looked around but didn't find anything.

"Don't worry. No way they'll find him." Malta said. "We slit the bastard's throat and squeezed him dry. And that was one deep hole we dug." So we could finally relax.

But the following week the murdered cop returned. His ghost paced back and forth in the cellar, his trousers still down around his knees. His pistol was making that rattling sound. Overall, he looked rather clumsy, but a ghost is a ghost, I thought.

"Well, that's odd, I slit the bastard's throat so he wouldn't come back," Malta said.

At first, I was afraid of the ghost. We were his killers, after all. I would crawl into my sister's bed and sleep there, trembling in fear.

"Hey, don't be so scared. He can't do a damn thing to us. We drained him good. He can't get his dick up," Malta said.

It didn't take long before I got used to having the ghost around. All he did was walk around aimlessly, gasping through his slit throat. That was it. It really wasn't a big deal. He wasn't going to try to rape me anymore. He'd lost all his blood and didn't have the strength. He couldn't even talk—when he tried to say something, it just sounded like a lot of air. Just as my sister had said, slit the throat and you have nothing to worry about. Sometimes I would get naked, twisting and turning my body to arouse the ghost. I would even spread my legs. Do dirty things. Things so filthy I surprised myself. Incredibly bold and filthy. But it seemed the ghost didn't feel anything anymore.

That gave me a lot of self-confidence.

I stopped being afraid.

"I am no longer fearful. Not afraid of anyone. I won't be taken advantage of anymore," I told Malta.

"That may be," she said. "But you've got to listen to the water in your body. It's very important that you do."

ONE DAY THE PHONE RANG. I was invited to design the plans for a large thermal power plant. This made my heart jump with joy. In my mind, I drew up several sketches for the new plant. I wanted to go out into the world and design lots of thermal power plants.

"But you know, if you go out, maybe you'll have those horrible experiences again," Malta said.

"But I want to try," I said. "I want to start over. I have a feeling that it will go well this time. Because I'm not afraid anymore. Because I can't be taken advantage of anymore."

"All right then," Malta said shaking her head. "But be careful. You hear me? Don't go letting your guard down," she said.

I went out into the world and designed many thermal power plants. I had talent. And before I knew it, I was the world's leading authority in the field. The power plants I built were innovative, and they were reliable; there wasn't a single breakdown. The plants were really popular with the people working in them too. Whenever someone was thinking of building a power plant, I would be the person they'd ask. And so I quickly became rich. I bought an entire building in the nicest part of town and lived in the penthouse. I installed every available alarm system, surrounded myself with electronic locks, and hired a gay guard built like a gorilla.

I led a happy and fulfilling life. Until *he* came along.

He was a very big man with burning green eyes. He disabled all the alarms, ripped off the locks, beat up my guard, and kicked down my door. I stood in front of him, fearless, but the man didn't care one bit. He ripped off my clothes and dropped his trousers. Then, after he raped me, he slit my throat with a knife. It was a very sharp knife. He slit open my throat as if cutting through warm butter. The knife was so sharp, I almost didn't realize that my throat had been slit open.

After that came darkness. And walking in darkness was the police officer. He kept trying to say something, but because his throat was slit, it came out like whistling. Then, I heard the sound of water in my body. That's right, I could actually hear it. It was soft, but I could hear it perfectly. I withdrew into my body, and gently put my ear to its walls, listening to the faint sound of dripping water.

Drip . . .

drip . . .

drip.

Drip . . .

drip . . .

drip.

My. Name. Is. Creta Kano. 🐵

Note from the translator: This is one of just four stories that Haruki Murakami wrote with a female narrator. All were published over a span of three years, beginning with "Nemuri" in 1989 ("Sleep," translated in 2006 by Jay Rubin), "Kanō Kureta" in 1990 ("Creta Kano," translated for the first time in this volume), and the final two in 1991: "Midori iro no kemono" and "Kōri otoko" ("The Little Green Monster" and "The Ice Man," translated in 1993 by Jay Rubin). Providing a specific female perspective that we otherwise do not have access to in Murakami's works, these four narrators are all in one way or another seeking—but by and large failing—to break free of their positions as women in Japanese society. However, unlike the narrator of "Creta Kano" who repeatedly experiences rape and then murder, the other three are not as obviously oppressed. And yet, by narrating her own murder, she manages to retain subjectivity to a degree that the other narrators cannot.

Names signify a great deal about a character's persona, and I generally try to avoid altering names. Thus, I was initially reluctant to change the narrator's name, Kanō Kureta, which also serves as the title of the story, but since Kureta has no meaning in English, both the title and the narrator's name would then lose their reference to the Greek island of Crete, which is clear in the Japanese. While this issue could have been addressed by adding a short footnote, I wanted English readers to have an unfiltered reading experience, and so I was inclined to go with Kanō Crete. This logical option, however, presented a different set of issues: the name Kanō Kureta appears not only in the less-known short story "Kanō Kureta," but also in the well-known novel *Nejimakidori kuronikuru* (1994–95), which Jay Rubin had already translated as *The Wind-Up Bird Chronicle* in 1997. Looking for a way to encourage English readers to see this connection between the two works, I consulted Rubin's translation of the novel and found that, in addition to the two changes I had expected—Western name order and the removal of the macron in Kanō—Rubin had translated Kureta as Creta rather than

Crete. Thus, for English readers this mysterious character became Creta Kano. By adding a sentence that does not exist in the Japanese novel, he was able to keep the name associated with the island of Crete: "Creta is the ancient name for the island of Crete."

I decided to echo Rubin's translation, and the name Kanō Kureta has, in my translation too, become Creta Kano. I chose as well to incorporate Rubin's explanatory sentence to make the reference to the Island of Crete clear. In this way, my translation tries to achieve the same effect that Japanese readers experienced in the mid-1990s but with one important difference. While the observant Japanese reader would have met Kanō Kureta as the narrator of her own short story in 1990 and only four years later become (re)acquainted with the mysterious women going by the same name in *Nejimakidori kuronikuru*, most English readers will already have met Creta Kano in the *The Wind-Up Bird Chronicle* in the late 1990s before reading "Creta Kano" in 2022. This means that in the English context of Murakami's works, it is not the short story that sets the premise for the novel, but the novel that works retroactively. Still, read together, "Creta Kano" will, in my view, alter our understanding of one of Murakami's most famous novels.

I am grateful to the author for allowing me to make this story available to English readers of his works. In addition to the editors of *MONKEY,* I wish to thank the translator David Karashima and Murakami's first English-language editor, Elmer Luke. Both kindly took time to read and discuss my translation in early drafts.

Mutsuo Takahashi

——————

Selections from
Only Yesterday

translated and with an introduction
by Jeffrey Angles

Socrates was around only yesterday.
—Kenneth Dover

Mutsuo Takahashi (b. 1937) is one of Japan's most
prominent living poets. Since first attracting the
attention of the Japanese literary world in the 1960s
with his bold evocations of homoerotic desire, he has
published almost fifty books of poetry and numerous
collections of essays, literary criticism, and fiction.
Ancient Greece has been another recurring theme in
his work, and he has written extensively about ancient
Greek literature in particular. The 2018 book *Tsui
kinō no koto* (*Only Yesterday*), from which these
translations come, is a book of poems about his own
physical, temporal, and literary crossings to Greece.
In these poems, he describes his own travels in
Greece, his love for ancient Greek culture and literature, and the ways that ancient Greece inspired and
shaped his own love for men.

EARLY SUMMER 1969

At the top of the stone steps of the Acropolis, I head into the Parthenon
Lean briefly against a pillar before casting off on sandaled feet
I'd been reading Kitto's *The Greeks,* and as I traced the lines,
I saw how ridiculous I was, feeling I'd turned Greek in some small way
Before I knew it, I was nodding off on sea breezes from far-off Piraeus
And in the rounds of sleep, the world was nothing but tenderness
Held in this soft world's embrace, I felt as if I could do it all
I was young, so young, though it was just yesterday, or perhaps the day before

PROPHECY

A full account of the Argo
About the days to come, only one thing is certain:
Long from now, the rash voyage to which you entrusted your youth
Will be a mere memory—your skull will split in the wreckage of a broken ship
Floating in the wide, open sea, bringing you death, sudden and miserable
But still, if you stop to think, isn't that far better than the alternative?
Even if they speak in hushed voices of the evil deeds of your youth
And their merciless outcomes, wouldn't that be preferable
To a life in which nothing happens, a life in which you grow weak
With old age and no one knows of your death at all?

THE SHIPWRECKED

On the Aegean Sea
Headed beyond these great waves, towards Ithaca and Zakynthos where forests stir
So many nameless men went down with their ships and drowned between the swells
Only one man with a name was delivered safely to his home, so even now
Three thousand years later, the ship of history continues to spill the nameless overboard
The ugly eagerness of so many well-known men for influence and fame is the sole reason
The ship will shatter one day into splinters and sink, leaving not the slightest trace behind
Grieve, oh, grieve for them! Grieve with heavy heart for the nameless, faceless ones,
For they are the ones who row history's ship, as the famous seat themselves
In the commander's chair, cross their arms, and look down on them in contempt

THE LOSER'S EXCUSE
An alternative account of the Odyssey

Why is he the one always in the right? Why must we be the scoundrels?
It was he who stole strapping lads from all over and set them to sail for twenty years
But who in the meantime brought peace and security to this land?
Isn't it to our credit that we congregated in his manor and raised such a racket?
For over a decade no one occupied the throne as the surrounding countries poised to attack
The king's father grew old, his son was useless, so their assault was just a matter of time
Who knew if our lord was dead or alive? Of course, we'd choose a new one in his place—
Shouldn't he have safely escorted home all the young men he had taken away
Rather than censure us for squandering his fortune with food and drink?
For ten years, his clever wife deceived us, not until she finished weaving a burial shroud
For her father-in-law, she said, but what she wove during the day, she unraveled at night
Meaning that what she wove during those years was, in fact, our funeral shrouds
After twenty years, he returned disguised as a beggar, showed himself to son and servant
And as the archery contest ended, he tricked us, shot us all, slaying us to the last man
If justice exists, I pray your wife and the Lord of Hades will judge us fairly—
Mumbling these things to ourselves, our blood-soaked souls gather and shuffle
Downward into the fog spilling from the underworld's open maw

CHOICES
Thermopylae

All of you have a Thermopylae in your life, several even—
Spirited soldiers guarding a narrow pass against an attacking swarm
Even if you fight to the last man in its defense, you hope never to join
The onslaught of attackers who feel so safe in numbers, or worse still,
Never to turn traitor, guiding the enemy along a mountain trail—
This possibility is within you, whether you stay on the defense,
Defect to the attackers, or get down and dirty simply to survive

THE RIGHTS OF THE ORDINARY MAN

To be a hero one must fall in the prime of youth in the most tragic way imaginable
Heroes who survive are sure to devolve into ugly despots,
Achilles, slayer of so many soldiers, would have ended up
Like Agamemnon, slain by an unfaithful wife—yes, even Alexander
Barely managed to become a hero, thanks only to a sudden death
From fever at age thirty-three, at the height of his glory
Meanwhile, the joy of arguing at age eighty over which one was best
Belongs to us, the masses destined never become neither hero nor tyrant

WHAT IS GREECE?

The Greeks existed, but the country of Greece did not
The Greeks traveled forth, and where they settled became Greece
One day, a small Greek ship drifted ashore on my heart's headland
Before I knew it, the island that is myself had become Greece
And once I acknowledged that, I too became Greek
I breathed Greece, in other words, I breathed freedom—
The airless freedom of a vacuum, which exists nowhere at all

RUIN

Long ago, the Greeks built cities and colonies
Dotting mountainsides and coastal shores
Sparks flew from there to this city in what is now the Far East
But these tiny colonies grow full with just ten people
Shinjuku, Shibuya, Shinbashi, Ueno, Asakusa—each night hopping
From place to place, I drifted through my youth
Tethering my line to the bar's footrest, I encountered
Many eyes, lips, thighs before setting off again
I learned many aspects of Greek love before I forgot
Now, decades later, the bow of desire's boat
Rarely points toward such pleasure-filled harbors
But when I close my eyes, they come alive again
Countless burning gazes, feverishly whispered words
After so much time, I find that I've become
The misshapen ruin left by those colonies of love

NAVIGATION BY NIGHT

The boat is the symbol of desire—
Fleets of Achaean ruffians off to conquer Troy,
The Argo off to steal the Golden Fleece,
Rogue ships searching for the New World
During my youth, the nightly navigations
Of the bow between my thighs was no exception
Now I am moored to the pier—my small boat rows
Secretly at night toward poems on my desk
As my only guide, I rely upon the unreliable ars poetica
Learned during days adrift on a licentious sea

THE MEDITERRANEAN

They say the Greeks, conquered by the Romans, conquered Rome in the end
But long before that, the Greeks were conquered by the Mediterranean Sea
The fascination we feel for Greece is really the enchantment of the Mediterranean
Our powerful attraction to the gods, the wisdom, the poetry,
And to all things Greek, born of its glittering swirls of ultramarine

DO A SKETCH!

The master artist berates his students: Do a sketch! Sketch it out!

He's right, that is an option, I say to spur myself on,

But as I reflect, I see that sketches aren't just made by artists working with lines

Indeed, the poet's business of grappling with words is also sketching

But going back further, isn't the act of living day to day sketching too?

For instance, opening a window and letting the new morning in

For instance, sipping hot water and waking the darkness in one's mouth

All these things are sketches for the artwork that is our lives

To tell the truth, isn't every one of our lives a sketch by some faceless artist

For the infinitely enormous masterpiece of the completed cosmos?

ON DIALECTICS

Start with a familiar subject, repeat through trial and error,

And little by little, one reaches the true essence of the subject—

Isn't that kind of a dialectic, conducted in roadside dialogues,

The starting point for the sketch as well?

To put it another way, the sketch is also a dialectic dialogue

With the torso, with fruits and dishes, with flowers and birds,

So too the endless dialogues conducted in solitude by those who seek poetry

Sketches of formless things, those things invisible to the eye, are always new

AT THE GRAVE OF MOZART

The poets of Greece were men and women who spun words

And placed them on the strings of lyres, transposing them to sound

That makes you the direct descendant of those men and women

Just as their words descended from snow-white mountaintops

Your sounds came calling from the invisible depths of the cerulean sky

Morning, day, and night—they came calling so often

You had no time to sleep nor even to properly wake

Your scores, written in an almost automatic hand, still sound even now

Even if we search through labyrinths of graves, we won't find yours

We find your true grave only in your still reverberating scores

Just as the poet's grave lies only in fragments of words left behind

FOR P.B. SHELLEY

I won't laugh at you for calling yourself a follower of Pythagoras
Because you ate no meat, the reason: I know of your premature death on the Italian seas
And of the terrifying, quick end that befell Pythagoras's followers in Italy too
If it was possible to conduct an autopsy two centuries later
And open the stomach of your corpse washed to shore after the storm
I wonder if we'd find fava beans, or their chewed-up remains
As religious leader, Pythagoras strictly forbade the consumption of fava beans
The notion that favas belonged to the dead is one of his mysteries
But in later eras, Italians came to enjoy drinking white wine with fresh favas
Could you have had some on your yacht and been beckoned to the world of the dead?
This is one of the wild fantasies that spins freely through my imagination
As I wash my fava beans down with a glass of white wine

FOR THE SAPPHO OF AMHERST

Dare you see a Soul at the White Heat? —Emily Dickinson
In a dusty cemetery in town, I was taken to your grave but you were not there
Not just you—nowhere could I detect a trace of anyone you once held dear
Where did your carriage carry you, accompanied by eternity and death?
Where was the neighbor who spoke across dirt, covered to mouth and nose in cold moss?
Since your garden was where you wrote your poems, that place has become your eternal abode
For eight days, I returned to rest, then went home with mind full of memories
Home again, I pulled a chair into my garden, where I recited your poems again and again
And now my garden, too, has become your grave, a continuation of yours so far away

Mutsuo Takahashi

119

Eli K.P. William

Lost and Found Babies

"I'VE COME TO PICK UP SOMETHING I left here," I said to the clerk behind the counter. I was at the lost and found office in Nishi Nakano Station.

"Could you tell me what it is that you forgot, please?" asked the clerk. Wearing the train company uniform, he looked to be about fifty. Lingering strands of hair from the sides and back of his head had been rallied to form a crosshatch on top.

"A book," I replied.

"And the title?"

"*Coin Locker Babies,* by Ryū Murakami."

"And when did you misplace it?"

"Yesterday afternoon. It was around four."

I'd ended up at this counter the previous day after forgetting my drawing tablet on a special express. When I noticed it was missing and called the train company's central lost and found for the Tokyo region, they informed me that someone had turned it in at their Nishi Nakano office. It was this clerk who had attended to me, though he showed no sign of remembering now.

After retrieving the tablet, I spent the ride home sketching on it to make sure everything still worked. It wasn't until I stepped in the door of our apartment and was taking off my coat that I reached into my pocket for the novel I'd been reading all day and discovered it wasn't there. I recalled last seeing it at the lost and found, but by the time I was finished making dinner for my wife, it was too late to go back, so I'd just returned first thing in the morning.

"And where did you leave it?" the clerk asked.

"On the counter," I said.

"The counter where, sir?"

"Right here."

I pointed down at the counter between us. The man's gaze followed my finger. It took another moment for my meaning to register with him.

"You're absolutely sure?" he asked gravely. "You mean to say that you left it in this office?"

"Yes, here, like I said from the start."

The clerk frowned, pulling forward the bare skin of his scalp but leaving the crosshatch in place. "Then I'm afraid we don't have it."

"Really? But I remember leaving it here very clearly. I was reading while waiting in line. You were

talking to an elderly lady in front of me about her umbrella. She had these big glasses. I only put it down for a moment to fill out the form."

"Yes, sir. I believe you, sir. But if you left it here, then I can tell you with certainty that it's somewhere else."

"You're not telling me that someone took it? I just—"

"Nothing like that, sir. It's simply that we don't keep items that get lost here here."

"Then where do you keep them?"

"In the lost and found lost and found."

"The—excuse me?"

"By protocol it should have been sent there this morning, though I didn't personally sign off on it. I apologize for the inconvenience." The clerk gave a curt bow.

I rubbed my fingers against my wedding ring, a habit when I'm stressed.

"If the book has been sent somewhere else, I'd like to call them to confirm," I said, taking out my phone. "The number, please."

"I'm afraid it isn't listed."

"Well, could you look it up internally then?" I gestured with my chin to a display on a desk behind him, beginning to feel annoyed.

"I wish I could be of assistance, sir. Unfortunately, it no longer shows up in our database."

"Uh-huh," I said, finding it hard to believe that a company couldn't access the phone number of one of its own offices but not in the mood to press him. "Give me the address then. I can take the train there right now."

"I'm afraid that isn't listed either at the moment."

"You won't even tell me the address?"

"We don't know the address."

"What are you saying? But you—"

"It's been lost, sir," the clerk interrupted, speaking more loudly and with a pained look in his eyes, as though I'd forced him to admit something shameful. Then more calmly, he added, "For months now."

"What has?" I asked. "The address?"

"No. The lost and found lost and found."

"Has been lost?"

The clerk gave a quick nod, making his crosshatch rear up for a moment when his chin returned to neutral.

I shook my head in bafflement. "How can I find it then?"

"If we knew that . . ." the clerk trailed off, as though the rest of the sentence were so obvious it would be rude to finish.

"Then what am I supposed to do about my book?" I said with exasperation, pointing again to the spot on the desk where I had set it down.

"I'm very sorry, sir," said the clerk with a deeper bow. His crown had gone bald in the pattern of a perfect spiral. "But if you don't mind, there's another customer."

Turning, I saw in line behind me a woman who could have been a model. She had frosted curls and was wearing jeans and a silver lamé blouse, the sort of look you'd expect to trend in the future as imagined in the 1980s. Suddenly I felt bad for keeping her waiting. Why get so upset over a paperback that I could buy used for almost nothing?

ONCE OUT OF THE ARRESTING PRESENCE of the woman and riding the train home without a book to read, I thought back on what had just transpired and found myself becoming increasingly irritated. I'd been inconvenienced by arbitrary rules many times in my life. A manufacturer had refused to fix a defective computer still under warranty because I'd moved to another city. A real estate agency had made me rewrite a lengthy form by hand because I'd crossed out a mistake with three lines instead of two. Usually I shrugged off such annoyances as inevitable, but I'd been enjoying that novel—I could sense it building toward something. Try as I might, I couldn't imagine any justification for transferring an item left in the lost and found to a separate facility. It was like having a second sewage treatment plant for the toilets in a sewage treatment plant or a second bank for the salaries of bankers. The thought made me lightheaded.

It was 11:00 a.m. when I stepped into the apartment, plenty of time before my wife would return from work, so instead of doing the laundry and dishes, I sat at the dinner table and searched on my phone for "lost and found lost and found." I was excited to see hundreds of thousands of hits, and my eyes went immediately to the top result: "Lost and Found Lost and Found." The

domain name was lostandfoundlostandfound.co.jp. But when I clicked it, all that appeared was a blank page with the lone sentence: "The homepage you are looking for has been lost. You can find its homepage here." Odd. I'm no expert, but if a link was broken, I thought it should say something like the page "could not be found." I clicked the hyperlink anyway. This brought me to lostandfoundlostandfound.co.jp/hp, another blank page that read: "This homepage homepage has been lost. You can find its homepage here." Weirded out and afraid I'd soon stumble upon an infectious website, I clicked back to my search results. For the first time, I read the hits below the initial listing:

The Lost and Found Lost and Found Homepage Homepage
lostandfoundlostandfound.co.jp/hp
This homepage homepage has been lost. You can find its homepage here

The Lost and Found Lost and Found Homepage Homepage Homepage
lostandfoundlostandfound.co.jp/hp/hp
This homepage homepage homepage has been lost. You can find its homepage here

The Lost and Found Lost and Found Homepage Homepage Homepage Homepage
lostandfoundlostandfound.co.jp/hp/hp/hp
This homepage homepage homepage homepage has been lost. You can find its homepage here

THIS SERIES CONTINUED to the bottom of the page, set to display twenty results. I didn't bother jumping to the next one. All I could do was stare, shaking my head at the display. Who'd ever heard of a homepage having a homepage? Obviously, I wasn't going to find anything this way.

I was about to put in another call to the lost and found central office when a strange noise began to resonate through the room. It started as staccato bursts of humming akin to birdsong, then shifted to an almost atonal melody, like a choir of phones ringing in the distance. The sound gave me goosebumps.

It wasn't especially loud, but it seemed to coat the air like a membrane and enter my consciousness through my pores rather than my ears.

As though summoned by the melody, a vision came to me, a memory from childhood. My mother stood looming over me, her big black eyes peering down into mine from what seemed like a stratospheric distance as she told me something I didn't want to hear. My real father was my second grade teacher, who I hated, and not the professional swimmer who took me out to play catch on Sunday afternoons. A year or so earlier, she had told me that my real father was the swimmer, rather than the man who had lived with us and died of cancer when I was a toddler. Now she was telling me that this confession of her lie had actually been a lie. The location she'd chosen to deliver this news to seven-year-old me was the lost and found office I'd just visited, except that the walls and furnishings were much newer and there was a long lineup. Someone kept saying *psst* as though trying to get my attention, but I resisted the urge to look away from my mother to see who it was.

"Are you listening?" she demanded, noticing my distraction.

I nodded as I looked up at her stern face, my eyes brimming with tears, unsure why she was telling me this right here, right now. Compulsively, I reached up to pick my nose (a habit replaced since marriage by rubbing my ring).

"Don't!" my mother snapped, and I stopped my arm midair. It wasn't my nose picking per se that bothered her. It was that I'd reached with my left hand, and she'd been trying for years to train my left-handedness out of me. (The result was a partial success: I'm nearly ambidextrous and feel shame to this day when doing illustrations or other work that requires my slightly stronger hand.)

"Good." She nodded approvingly. "Now wait here. I'm going to the restroom."

When she left the office, I hung my head and let out faint choking sounds as I struggled to hold in my sobs.

Psst, I heard again and looked up. Blurred by tears was the clerk, some twenty years younger, with a big puffy wasp's nest of hair in place of his crosshatch. I watched his lips move but couldn't quite process the

words that came out because, at that very moment, my mind drifted back to the apartment, where these long-buried feelings were erupting like some toxic geyser. I realized that I was lying on the floor, crying. Seeking to stop the melody that was trapping me in this all-too-vivid memory, I got up and staggered toward its source, following my ears across the room. The sound seemed to emanate from just outside the front door, which I hastily opened without checking the peephole.

There in the hall stood a young man. Short and scrawny, he wore tight faded jeans and a bright plaid shirt. His mouth was wide open, his chest and throat vibrating, and I realized that the sound was his singing. He narrowed his eyes at me standing in the doorway, as though irritated by the interruption.

"Stop that singing," I pleaded breathlessly. "Please."

Just then I heard the crash of shattering glass behind me and a *thud* that shook the floor. Turning, I saw another young man lying prone amid the shards of my now broken window.

"What are you—" I rushed toward him, clenching my fists, until I saw that he was bleeding. "Are you alright?"

"I'm here to give you some advice," he said as he did a pushup to his feet, the glass that had settled on his back showering to the floor.

I was speechless.

"I'm here to give you some advice," the man repeated. Tall and well muscled, he wore a tight training suit, torn by the numerous shards of glass embedded in his skin. He gave me a cool under-the-eyebrow stare as he casually plucked the shards from his forearms, dripping blood onto the floor.

"You're insane!" I exclaimed. "How did you reach my window?" My apartment was on the third floor.

"Pole-vaulted," the man replied.

It was then that I noticed the singing had stopped. Afraid to turn away from this powerful intruder, I glanced over my shoulder and saw that the door was closed, the singer now standing beside me.

"Okay. You two have got to get out of my apartment."

"*We* are here to give you some advice," said the singer. He glanced at the pole-vaulter when emphasizing the word "we" as if to chastise him for forgetting that they were together.

"Yeah, we," the pole-vaulter acknowledged.

"I didn't ask for any advice. What—"

"Just forget about the lost and found," crooned the singer.

"But—"

"You'll pay," said the pole-vaulter.

"Yes," the singer agreed. "You'll definitely pay unless you give up."

"What's that supposed to mean? Are you threatening me?" I was ready to scream if they made any sudden movements.

But the pole-vaulter just dusted the remaining glass particles from his shoulders and sauntered past me to the door, which the singer was already opening. The singer sighed and shook his head as they both stepped into the hall. "That was no threat. Only a warning for your own good," he said, as the pole-vaulter closed the door gently behind them.

I went immediately to lock it. Then I put my eye to the peephole and watched them stand silently in the hallway, waiting for the elevator. It was as the doors slid open and they stepped in that I realized something even more baffling than anything else that had happened that day. The two men reminded me of people that I knew in a certain sort of way: the main characters in the novel I had left at the lost and found.

I KNEW I HAD TO REPORT THE BREAK-IN to the authorities, but I was pretty shaken up, and I didn't feel like answering any questions just then. So I found myself sitting on a chair in the middle of a room littered with blood-flecked glass, my hands trembling, a fall wind chilling the back of my neck through the broken window as my mind cycled through the events of the day. Occasionally I'd glance at my drawing tablet in the corner, yearning for some activity to distract me, but knowing that this was no time for work. Those two men simply could not have been the coin locker babies, Hashi and Kiku. And yet, everything about them reminded me of how the characters were described. As I was going over the incident with my mother brought back by the song, I finally recalled what the young clerk had said.

"Go to 63. Nishi Nakano Station."

It was as though he'd decided to tell me in memory what he'd been unwilling to tell me in person, and I began to wonder, *Could that be the location of the lost and found lost and found?*

Soon I was on the train for Nishi Nakano Station, wishing again that I had something to read on the ride. As I rubbed my wedding ring, I thought of the mess back home and was glad that my wife had texted earlier to tell me that her court proceedings were dragging on. Before I'd been searching for the novel because I was indignant about a good story being interrupted for no good reason. Now this task had taken on much greater importance. Despite the so-called advice of the two men, I had no intention of giving up. They'd left peaceably enough, but what if they came back? What if someone more threatening showed up? What if my wife was there? Finding that book was all I could think of to ward off such dangers. Whatever happened, I was going to read my way to the end of the story.

But when my train arrived at Nishi Nakano and I began searching around the station, I realized that I had no idea what the clerk might have meant by 63. While there were several doors leading to off-limits staff rooms, none of these were numbered, and while the passing trains all had serial numbers, too many contained the pair of numerals in question for it to seem relevant. I considered asking the clerk, but the lost and found office was now closed, and it didn't seem worth the effort to explain my situation to the station attendants.

I reflected again on the memory, and began to wonder if it could have been some sort of hallucination, with no genuine connection to my lost book. It wasn't as if my mom would have ever revealed the truth about my father in the lost and found office at this station. I couldn't recall where else we might have been when she made that particular announcement about the swimmer, but over the years she'd continued to tell me that each new man who appeared in her life was in fact my real father, and thankfully she always chose a discreet location for her confessions. I wasn't sure if Nishi Nakano Station even existed back then. And how could the clerk have given me a clue about something that wouldn't happen for more than two decades?

I was beginning to second-guess whether those two men had actually looked like the coin locker babies, when an idea hit me: what if 63 were the number of a coin locker? I did another pass around the station and immediately spotted a locker room directly beside the lost and found, that I did not remember being there. From the open doorway, I could see the room was filled wall to wall with coin-operated lockers. All had their keys in place except for numbers 63 and 62. This struck me as an auspicious sign, though I would need to find some way to open locker 63.

The square door was only two small lockers above the floor, so I crouched in front of it. I tried tugging on the lock, I pried the jambs with my fingers, and then in a surge of frustration I banged the door with my palm—all to no avail. I was going over my options when I heard a faint noise. It seemed to be coming from the locker. Just to be sure, I opened the doors of all the lockers around 62 and 63 but found them empty. Then I waited, ear tilted to 63. Sure enough, I soon heard the softest metallic scraping.

"Hello?" I said, as though someone might be inside, but of course that was madness. *Or could a baby have been abandoned in there?* I thought suddenly. *Had my memory or daydream or whatever it was led me here to save a human life?* Such a fortunate turn of events struck me as strangely fitting after my wife's abortion the previous summer. The reason she'd given for her decision was that raising a child would disrupt her career, but I was certain that my behavior had been the biggest factor and had felt bad about it ever since. While I'd said that I would support her in whatever choice she made, I'd also asked her repeatedly whether I was the actual father. When I insisted that I didn't doubt her faithfulness and reminded her of the trust issues I had around fatherhood—dating back to my mother's endlessly provisional confessions—she was willing to forgive me for implying that she was having an affair. Liberating an abandoned baby now might soothe my guilt for making her think twice about having a child with me. I even began to muse on the prospect of making it up to her by adopting it.

This was especially appealing since there would be no question about who the father—

The return of the sound interrupted my ruminations. My attention had been elsewhere, so I wasn't certain, but the scraping seemed to follow a pattern. Once again, I made an effort to listen, steering my focus from the whirlpool of thoughts stirred up by my apprehension about what might be in the locker.

Less than a minute later, the scraping returned once more. It had a distinctive rhythm that reminded me of scratching on a turntable. I imitated it with my fingernails on the metal door, picturing myself as a DJ. Immediately I heard the click of a lock, and the door of number 62, not the locker I was scraping, swung open.

Inside the small chamber was a tiny man wearing a white suit, a red bowtie, and tortoiseshell glasses. He looked just as I'd imagined Mr. D from *Coin Locker Babies* except that he was about two inches tall. Behind him was a black leather wallet with a red heart on it, a silver bracelet, a flip-phone, a key chain attached to various keys and a green plastic possum, and a neon-orange toy handgun. I was feeling disappointed that there was no baby, until I spotted, wedged into the slat of the door to keep it open, a copy of the novel. I knew instantly it was mine from the tear in the cover at the base of the spine.

The man was sitting on a wine cork at a miniature tinted display case divided into square cubbies, each containing the severed tip of a finger. They varied slightly in size, but all had clearly belonged to an adult, and I cringed at the sight. The minuscule stature of the man was somehow intimidating. Once I'd worked up the nerve to speak to him, I said, "This must be the lost and found lost and found."

"Could be," he said in the Osaka dialect. "Have you been lost and found?"

"Yes. No. Not me. It's my book," I said, glancing at the cover to draw his attention to it.

"This book?" he asked, pointing at the flip-phone.

"No, the *book*," I said pointing to my book.

Still pointing at the phone he nodded. "You can have it, but you'll pay," and he tapped the display case in front of him, causing the severed fingertips to jiggle as though made of jelly.

"Look. I'd like to have my book back, and I'm not paying a thing."

"You can say what you want, but you'll pay."

"No, I will not," I insisted. "I only left it on the counter next door for less than 24 hours."

The tiny man crossed his arms and glared at me. "Your move," he said.

I frowned, trying to make sense of this. "So I can take it?"

The man continued to glare.

"Okay then. So I'm taking it." I reached cautiously into the locker as though into a scorpion's nest, afraid that this living effigy of Mr. D might do something to my arm as it passed little more than an inch over his head. Once I got hold of the book, I snatched it out so quickly that my hand banged painfully against the top of the locker. But at last I had the book!

I'd expected the door to swing shut the moment I removed its doorstopper, but the man had hurdled over the display case and was holding the door open, sneering up at me.

"Did anyone else lose you?" he asked.

"No?" I said, so he promptly closed the door, and I watched the key in 62 click back into place.

EXHILARATED TO HAVE MY BOOK BACK, I boarded the first train that came, hardly caring which direction it was going. In spite of everything, I'd found the lost lost and found lost and found! And as the doors of the train closed I decided that tomorrow I'd go inform the clerk of its whereabouts, to spare the next person who left something on his counter the trouble I'd endured. Then, taking a seat, I eagerly opened my book and was flipping through to where I'd left off when a lizard leapt out from the blur of pages and bit into the thumb of my right hand.

Shrieking, I swiped instinctively at the creature with my left hand and batted it across the car. It hit the glass panel in one of the doors and fell to the floor. I saw that it had dropped something from its mouth: the tip of my thumb. With blood spurting from my hand, I sprang to my feet and stumbled toward the stunned lizard. It quickly roused itself and began to scramble for its prize, until it saw me raise

my foot to stomp on it and fled, squeezing between the doors and out of sight. As I retrieved the tip of my thumb and held the base of my wounded finger to staunch the flow of blood, the other passengers stared at me, looking more appalled than concerned, as though I'd got what I deserved for walking around with a vicious reptile on my person.

AFTER MY THUMB had been stitched back together, I was sitting in the hospital lobby, waiting for my medical bill to be tallied. I couldn't stop staring at the copy of *Coin Locker Babies* on my lap, afraid to open it. I kept seeing the cover fly open and that creature lunging for my hand. A repeat attack would have been bad enough wherever I happened to be, but I especially dreaded the thought of sustaining an injury here, in a hospital. Would I then be carted off to a hospital hospital?

At some point, the green blur linked in my mind to an image of a crocodile, and I realized that what had bitten me probably wasn't a lizard. Anemone, Kiku's girlfriend in the novel, had a pet crocodile named Gulliver. This reminded me of the Lilliputians in *Gulliver's Travels,* which I'd been reading a few months ago, and, come to think of it, lost before I'd finished. I hoped that that tiny version of the crocodile would be the final parallel between my life and fiction now that I had the book back.

I felt my phone vibrate. It was a video call from my wife. I got up, put in my earbuds, and went to a far corner of the lobby.

"Hey, is something wrong?" I asked, worried because she almost never called me from work.

"No, I'm fine. There's something I want to tell you," she said. Then she frowned at the screen. "Where are you?"

The resolution on the feed was worse than I'd ever seen. Her face was awash in pixels while her every syllable crackled and buzzed. This distraction made it even harder for me to decide how to respond.

"I'm . . . at the big hospital near the stadium. My finger started to hurt, so I came to get it looked at."

"Are you alright?"

"Yeah, they say I'm good to go now. So what did you want to talk about?"

"Right, so um, I called the fertility clinic again."

"The fertility clinic."

"Uh-huh. I'm representing the defendant for this one case. It's pretty run-of-the-mill. A woman accused by her sister of misappropriating property from their maternal inheritance—a few antique chairs, a decorative umbrella, some other family treasures. Anyway, we were interrupted today while I was questioning a witness. Someone got pickpocketed."

"Pickpocketed? In court?"

"Right? It was a college student there as an observer. Her wallet had been replaced in her purse with a dummy wallet. When the police searched everyone in the public gallery, they found her actual wallet in the bag of a middle-aged man. But the young woman swears it wasn't the man who was the *thief.*"

The video ground to an abrupt crawl, stretching out the word "thief" and turning her voice so deep it sounded almost demonic, as the image of her face warped into an inhuman splatter. Then just as abruptly it sped back up and stabilized.

"Apparently, the man never approached her and by coincidence she knows him from her neighborhood. She refused to believe that he would steal from her. I doubt we'll ever hear anything more about it because the incident fell under the jurisdiction of the court court, but it made me realize something."

Though I was struck by the phrase "court court," I was eager to hear more and too tired to interrupt.

"Whether or not the young woman *believed* that the man was a criminal, if he had stolen her wallet, then he was a criminal *in fact.* So it's not really important whether you believe that you're the father of our child."

"What?"

"I mean, if the child is really ours in fact, and we love each other as a family, isn't that enough?"

I was too busy puzzling out the implications for our relationship to even attempt an answer. "So . . . what you're saying is that you contacted the fertility clinic because you're thinking you might want to start a family with me after all, is that right?"

"Exactly. That's what I called to tell you."

"Thank you," I said softly, feeling true gratitude. "I'm so glad you've come around to seeing me as a viable father."

She laughed. "You're way better than viable. I'm sorry for not realizing this sooner. We should talk more."

"Let's."

"Yup. Okay. I'd better get back to work."

AFTER WE SAID GOODBYE, I returned to my seat, buoyant with relief. The pall that had settled over our relationship finally lifted, and I had a clear prospect of the future for the first time in ages. There we were—me, my wife, and our kid—living together in a condo with a great view of the city.

Then I recalled the eerie moment when she had said "thief," and something about our conversation began to feel off. I was reminded of the dissonance I'd experienced after the two men broke into my apartment. It wasn't merely the terrible resolution, was it? That had just obscured a more disturbing problem. Yes, the more I thought about it, the more I was certain that the woman on the display of my phone had been identical to the striking woman lined up behind me at the lost and found that morning. In retrospect, her voice now also seemed too high, her manner of speech too scattered. How could I have mistaken a complete stranger for my wife?

Spooked, I glanced at the cover of the book, remembered the tiny version of the crocodile Gulliver biting my thumb again, and hit upon something like an answer. The 1980s future outfit. That woman was just as I had imagined Anemone! But of course that wasn't my wife's name, nor was Anemone a lawyer. . . . I thought of the student's wallet being switched for a decoy and suddenly the word "thief" took on a new meaning.

Doing my best not to panic in front of the other seated patients, I unlocked my phone and reopened the messaging app. My wife's profile pic was now a washed-out hint of a face engulfed in white, but I clicked "call" anyway.

Five attempts later, she still hadn't picked up.

HURRYING ALONG the cold dark streets, I held out my bandaged thumb in front of me as though it were lighting the way. It was my last source of consolation at the end of this horrible day. I may have ended up paying—as Kiku and Hashi and Mr. D, if those were really their names, had warned me—but I had not parted with that gruesome currency I'd seen in the display case. At least my body was intact, and I held out my other hand to compare it with the injured one. That was when I noticed something that stopped me on the sidewalk: my wedding ring was gone. It must have fallen off when I pulled my hand out of the locker. But that meant . . . Could it have already been sent to the lost and found lost and found lost and found? What might I have to lose to find it this time?

Immediately I felt ashamed for using my left hand to reach into the locker. My mother had been right. I should have made more effort to become right-handed. Was there any way to explain this to my wife, whoever she might have become? I only wished I had a baby to offer her, from the locker or anywhere else. If I could have been the father that she wanted me to be, real or otherwise, it would have been so much easier to make her understand.

Maybe if I finish the story, I can break the cycle, I thought, and I ducked into an alley to flip frantically but awkwardly with one thumb and one index finger to the now bloodstained page where I had left off. Under the faint glow of the streetlights, I read the last few remaining sentences and turned to the next page, but it was blank, as were all the pages that followed. 🐵

© Sara Wong / TOOGL

Aoko Matsuda

———

A Father
and His Back

translated by Polly Barton

THERE'S AN OLD SAYING in Japan that goes, "A child grows up watching his father's back," but this particular father didn't want his back to be watched by his child. The thought of being observed like that left the father with a sense of pressure, and the idea that his own back might be pushing his son in a certain direction seemed a burden too heavy to bear. He wanted to avoid his back communicating with his son out of his own line of sight.

The son grew into a healthy young boy, and the father took meticulous care not to reveal his back to him. Hiding his back from a baby had been simple enough, but once the boy started walking, the father had to respond to his son's movements, constantly turning this way or that to evade his gaze. He became very adept at walking backwards and sideways. The sight of his father doing all this was so funny that it often had the boy in stitches.

At home, the father took up position at the side of the room wherever possible, living his life with his back pressed flat against the walls. In their household, the idea of father and son taking a bath together and scrubbing each other's backs was entirely out of the question.

In primary school the boy made a clay model of his father that was just like one of Giacometti's cat or dog sculptures. Giacometti never properly observed a cat or dog except head-on, so his sculptures of these creatures have heads that are fully fleshed out, while the rest of their bodies are thin as wire. On a middle-school excursion to a rusting old theme park, the boy saw a row of panels designed to look like a street of houses from some foreign country. The fronts of the panels had been painted with illustrations of colorful houses, but their backs were just the exposed wooden frames holding them up. Asked about them upon returning home, the boy commented, "They were just like Dad." Whenever the boy saw crabs, he was reminded of his father. When the boy encountered the *nurikabe,* a spirit that manifests as a plaster wall and blocks passersby, he was reminded of his father.

The father was perpetually on the run from his son, inwardly entreating the boy not to look at his back and doing everything he could to avoid showing it to him,

and yet relations between the two were not particularly bad. In fact, it was only when the father was
hugging his son that he was freed from the worry of
having his back seen by him, and so the boy grew up
being constantly embraced by his father. 🐵

Note from the editors: In September 2017 the novelist
and translator Aoko Matsuda visited Pittsburgh to
help launch the new issue of *Monkey Business,* where
she was on a panel with transplanted New Yorker
Adam Ehrlich Sachs. After returning to Tokyo, Aoko
translated five of Adam's stories from *Inherited
Disorders,* his collection about fathers and sons, for
the Japanese *MONKEY* (Spring 2018). For the
same issue, she wrote a story in response to Adam's
work, which we are publishing here in Polly Barton's
translation. In "How do you convey voice? Remarks
from twelve translators" (page 162), Aoko discusses
her experience translating Adam's work.

© Akino Kondoh

Keijirō Suga

With the Archaeopteryx

translated by Chris Corker

It felt like I was looking at a terrain
Through the eyes of a bird, or those of an insect
From the sky, or perhaps peering through a droplet of water
I saw it from the height of an orbiting satellite
The delta of a colossal river, the rippling desert
Charmed by a seed fallen from a tree
I wandered into the ancient forest
The canyon with its hexagonal basalt pillars
Carved by rushing waters
As sunrises and sunsets beyond the telling passed
Contrast grew, encouraged by the murmurs of orbiting stars
And the mere glow, the light and the shadow
Interpreted the dark gradation
From which all color began
In the Dutch workshop once a chicken coop
By rope and pulley to the third-floor studio
The slate was raised
And work commenced
Lithography's secret is in the liquid's whims, the surface's tension
But how can we mediate a dialogue between ink and stone?
Yet before the drama unfolds, we must polish the slate
Smooth the surface
This limestone was found in Solnhofen
In South Germany where the Archaeopteryx was first unearthed
archaeopteryx lithographica
The Lithographic Bird
Described on the stone was the Jurassic sky
Under which this first bird roamed
Carrying with it the flora and fauna
Of that age
We do not know the color of a species turned to stone
In that flurry of silence
We take up their many remains
And attempt to retrace what once was
There is no "I" to call myself
As in a dream, the shape forms behind the eyelids
More distinct than a cave painting, it divides up the world
Water and liquid linseed forever distinct
In that aversion the nascent form of will arrives
Something is flowing
Is it the current of protoplasm that separates water from life?
Are the lines I draw yet another network of canals?

For a while I soared through the sky in my sleep
Returning finally to the city of this island nation
Here Archaeopteryx is missing, but the archetype remains
Circles, the essence of all life
Not the soul, but the physical shape of autonomy
Or does the soul too, as if aspiring to the corporeal
Assume the guise of the sphere, of the circle?
There are always innumerable circles before our eyes
And the moment we realize
Yet more are born from that realization
This very world is formed from spheres of light
So you must forgive the planed circle that stands in for that sphere
Before the light of the world, our pupils are windows
The most perfect circle on this earth
The black hole surrounded by the iris
Only when we awoke did the true experiment of color begin
The light seen while submerged in the water
And the light of the depths glimpsed from above
Imbued with a blue-green, it undulates and glimmers
Disturbing the indigo and turquoise that blanket the ocean
Ultramarine, in which sunrises and sunsets reside
A wavelength that cannot be calmed
Fluctuates once more
Aquamarine, cyan, lapis lazuli
Putting aside these colors we know
From a time before time
The Earth has been etched in every kind of blue
These are colors born from the union of minerals and optics
And just so the first colors of life
Are those that emerge when protein absorbs the light
The colors of antioxidants, the colors assumed by flowering plants
The spectrum visible to our eye is finite
But wherever there is light we sense color
And through that intuition come to understand the world
Within the limits of my own understanding
I will embrace each and every hue
The split fruit and the broken bodies
Sunlight filtering through the trees and showers from a cloudless sky
Those things seen only by fish
Eggs like grains and the coming night
The world
That is the true experience of color

Note from the author: This poem was inspired by
the lithographs of Yuki Hasegawa.

Hiromi Kawakami

———

Mysterious Deaths,
The Formula,
Electricians, Prohibitions

translated by Ted Goossen

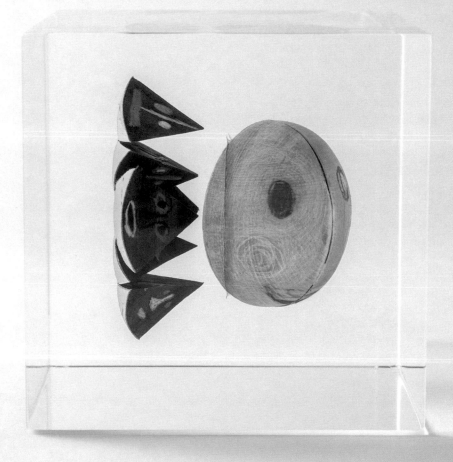

MYSTERIOUS DEATHS

OUR SCHOOL ASSIGNMENT was to find people who had lived in our neighborhood the longest and record their memories of what it was like "back in the old days." So that weekend, we each went out and found a local old person to talk to.

Kanae's choice was the old lady who sold pigeon food at the local shrine. "What was this neighborhood like back when you were young? Please fill me in," she asked, in what was for Kanae the politest of tones. All she received in return, however, was a disclaimer: "I moved here only fifteen years ago, so I know nothing of the old days."

Akai chose to interview the president of our local bank. It was an independent stand-alone bank, not a branch or affiliated with any of the banks in the city. It was also family-run—the president, vice-president, and employees were related, and all lived in the area. Yet the bank president too brushed aside Akai's question, saying, "I moved here only thirty years ago, so I know nothing of the old days."

All our other classmates encountered the same problem. As if in unison, those who they assumed were born and raised in our neighborhood—the farm wife, the lady who ran the Love, the dog school principal, the grandparents of the Shikishima family, the old taxi driver who lived in the tenement, the Yoko who survived—all said that they knew nothing of the old days. Some of our classmates interviewed members of their own families, including grandfathers and great-grandmothers, but they also demurred, saying, "We really haven't been here all that long, so we don't know anything."

When classes resumed the next week, our teacher encouraged us to present the fruits of our labors. She was met with dead silence. Even Akai, who always cracked a stupid joke at such times, looked as if he wanted to sink into the ground as he sat shivering in his chair as if he were cold.

"Won't someone volunteer?" the teacher asked. "Alright then, let's start with Miss Kawamata."

Our teacher pointed at Dolly. But Dolly wasn't her usual self: she seemed to have reverted to her original name (Midori), and a cloud of doom clung to her as she rose listlessly from her seat. It was like she'd been turned into a twisting curl of ash left by one of those black-snake fireworks.

"I don't get it," she mumbled. "I really don't understand."

It didn't take long to figure out that not one of us had been able to come up with anything about the history of our neighborhood. Assembling the evidence, we reached the conclusion that the lady who ran the Love and the old taxi driver had arrived first, and that was only forty or so years ago.

"You mean there's no one who's been living here any longer than that?" our teacher asked, clearly surprised.

Our teacher had been posted to our school from far away the previous year, so she knew almost nothing about our local history. When the bell rang ending class, we had tentatively concluded that a dividing line could be drawn at the forty-year mark. Anything before that was unknowable. That didn't sit well with Kanae.

"There's some kind of secret being kept from us," she said. "A big secret."

Kanae spent the rest of that day lost in thought, shaking her head from time to time. Thereupon, Kanae, Michio, Kanae's sister, and I launched a long-term, secret investigation into our neighborhood's hidden history, dividing the tasks into four. Big secrets were involved, so we knew it would be no easy job to uncover them. It was also clear that if it became known that we were sniffing around, our very lives could be in danger. Our investigation therefore had to be discreet, meticulous, and unhurried.

One year passed. Five years passed. Ten years passed. After ten years, it came to light that it was not the lady from the Love or the old taxi driver who had lived here the longest but rather a Mr. Arashimura from the six-person apartments on the edge of town. After twenty years, we discovered that Mr. Arashimura's mother had been a double agent during the war. After thirty years, our research revealed that a century earlier our neighborhood had been under Portuguese rule. After eighty years, we learned that people from the prehistoric Jomon era had survived in our area until the 1800s. Not long after, however, both Kanae's

sister and Michio met with a mysterious death. The word on the street was that old age was the cause, but we knew better. Our investigation was the real reason.

Finally, Kanae and I, the two survivors, were able to pin down the biggest secret of all: our neighborhood was built on a fissure that intersected space and time, and was connected somehow to the constellation Cygnus, otherwise known as "the Swan." We take great satisfaction in our discovery. However, at this moment neither we nor anyone else are aware that, mere months from now, we will both die a mysterious death. Everyone will say we died of old age, but we know better.

THE FORMULA

ON THE FAR SHORE of Lake Neighbor sits a settlement called Neighboring Town, and it was from there that representatives came to discuss the planning for this year's joint festival.

Until thirty years ago, relations between our neighborhood and Neighboring Town were marked by constant strife. The bad blood began with a dispute over sharing water to irrigate the rice paddies, and then spread to other conflicts—over fishing rights in Lake Neighbor, or where to situate a highway, or businesses being enticed to relocate to the other side—so that the animosity deepened over the years, until finally, thanks to one particular incident, ordinary people began clamoring for peace. It was then that the festival was devised as a means to bury the hatchet.

That "particular incident" followed the dramatic formula set by Romeo and Juliet.

"Is that what they call Romeo and Juliet—a formula?" Kanae, sitting beside me, complains, but I ignore her for the moment and continue my explanation.

Back then, there was almost no contact between our neighborhood and Neighboring Town. People from the two communities came together only at official meetings to hash out their internecine battles, and there was no socializing afterwards, no convivial drinking party, not even informal chatting.

"Yeah, but common people found the whole thing ridiculous," Kanae puts in. And who were those common people? Everyone except the mayor and deputy mayor, the bank president, and the dog school principal.

"How the hell did the dog school principal get to sit at the table? I can't buy that," Kanae grouses.

The role of Juliet was filled by the lady from the Love, while Romeo was Mitsuru, a young man from Neighboring Town.

The lady from the Love was thirty at the time. She had already divorced her husband and was raising their daughter as a single mother. Mitsuru was eighteen. Fresh out of high school, he had just started working at Neighboring Town City Hall. The two first met on Mt. Neighbor. Both had ventured far into the mountains, the lady who ran the Love intent on picking shoots from Japanese angelica trees, Mitsuru on gathering morels. In keeping with the formula, both had lost their way when, also following the formula, it began to thunder, and rain poured down. Forced to take shelter, they both happened upon a natural hollow on the mountain's slope where, despite it being their first meeting, they huddled together for warmth. The upshot, also consistent with the formula, was that they fell in love.

Given the animosity that divided our neighborhood from Neighboring Town, the lovers always met in the mountains. For their trysts they chose the natural hollow where their affair began. At each encounter the lady from the Love would fidget bashfully, eyes downcast, while Mitsuru would gaze at her and blush to his ears. Then they would walk through the mountains hand in hand. Occasionally accidents occurred —she slipped off a cliff and fell, he was bitten by a poisonous snake—but these only served to deepen their love, as per the formula. In the end, they reached a decision: they would come out to their warring communities, whatever the result.

Their confession of love caused a huge uproar in our neighborhood and in Neighboring Town. For one thing, the lady from the Love was our neighborhood's "number one divorcee," the woman men dreamed of marrying; for another, the handsome Mitsuru was the reigning "idol" at Neighboring Town's City Hall. Almost everyone gave their blessing to the couple and followed developments in their relationship with great

interest. The exceptions were, in our neighborhood, the mayor, deputy mayor, the bank president, and the principal of the dog school; on Neighboring Town's side, it was their mayor, the head of their chamber of commerce, and the town's president who were the holdouts. Their president's opposition was so extreme that he took the step of imprisoning Mitsuru in his official residence.

It did not take long for an underground movement to develop, aimed at protecting the lovers. Following the formula, they helped Mitsuru escape the president's residence. But the lady from the Love believed the wild rumor that Mitsuru had gone on a hunger strike and starved to death, driving her, again following the formula, to take her own life by drinking poison.

"But the lady from the Love is as healthy as they come," Kanae protests. "And Romeo's the one who jumps to a hasty conclusion and offs himself, right?"

Kanae's partially right—the lady from the Love is still with us today, and in great shape. You see, she almost died but managed to pull through, after which she found that her love for Mitsuru had utterly vanished.

"Let's go find out what kind of near-death experience she really had," Kanae says. So, we head off to the Love to ask its proprietress. Her answer is simple and straightforward.

"My near-death experience took me to the obligatory field of flowers," she said, "and it was there that I met the true, honest-to-god Romeo face to face. But he turned out to be a disgusting man, a real turn-off. To make matters worse, he was the spitting image of Mitsuru."

Today Mitsuru is the president of Neighboring Town. He plans to invite Beyoncé to perform at next year's festival, but with neither funding nor connections, nor anything else for that matter, it's hard to see how that could possibly happen.

"At any rate, girls," the lady from the Love warned Kanae and me, knitting her eyebrows, "be careful what formula you get mixed up in."

ELECTRICIANS

THE LIGHT ABOVE the toilet keeps going out, Michio said. I thought it was the bulb, so I stuck in a new one, but it went out after being turned on just two or three times. The same thing happens no matter how many times I change the bulb. You've got to call an electrician, Kanae said, and for once Michio didn't argue with her, just nodded his assent.

The next day the light above the toilet at Kanae's house blew out as well.

"I really hate when it happens on dark and rainy days like this," she said.

Unable to see what she was doing, Kanae commandeered the toilet until the very last minute that morning, forcing her older sister to use their neighbor's, which made her late for school. The following day it was the Kawamata toilet light, and the day after that it was the one at the Akais' house that bit the dust.

The electrician's van was parked in front of someone's home all week. It was an orange van with "Electrician" written on it in big black kanji. The electricians always worked in pairs, but the makeup of the pairs varied: one day it would be a boy whose voice hadn't broken accompanied by a girl of similar age; then it was two boys in high school uniforms; another time it was two middle-aged women; and still another time it was an old man and a monkey.

"Our electrician was an otter," Dolly boasted.

"Was he cute?"

"He was a giant otter from the Amazon River, so he was more fierce-looking than cute."

"Was the other electrician human?"

"No, it was an anteater."

"Could either of them speak?"

"Yeah, they could handle both Japanese and English really well. The anteater said he was raised in New York."

Our neighborhood's struggles with toilet lights went on and on. Electricians visited almost all of our homes, briskly fixing each problem as it emerged. When we asked the cause, they would cock their heads and say, "wiring issues," and leave it at that, without going into further detail.

Six months passed, and the electrician's orange van was still a constant presence, sure to be parked in front of someone's house. It was the old farmer who first noticed that some sort of image had been added right below the black "Electrician" on the side of the van.

"It's round and white," he said, trembling all over. "It looks like something alive, but it ain't got no nose or eyes. When the repairmen enter the house," he went on, "that white thing peels off the side of the van and follows 'em in."

The white thing was about 20 centimeters in diameter. It hovered in the air like a piece of fluff while the repairmen worked, and returned when they were finished, so that by the time they got back to their van it was somehow back in its place under the black lettering, as though it had never left.

Michio and Akai were bound and determined to solve the mystery, so they started by tracking down the van after class. This wasn't difficult, since its orange color made it stand out. They stuck to the van like glue, trying to somehow catch that precise moment when the round white whatever-it-was reattached itself to the side. Yet that moment always eluded them. Just when the thing returned, there would be a clap of thunder, or the lady from the Love would show up to ask directions, or the dog that the dog school principal was walking would start barking and lunging at them, and they'd be distracted. How many times would they have to watch the repairmen breezily climb back into their van after finishing the job? It drove them absolutely nuts!

Michio and Akai finally decided that, to solve the mystery, they would have to get jobs at the electricians' company. Kanae laughed at the idea that two kids their age could get work like that, but the company was a generous employer, as one might have guessed from the anteater and the giant otter, and the boys were hired, albeit on a temporary basis.

The outages continued for three years, during which Michio and Akai became thoroughly trained in the skills required for the job. In fact, by the time they entered junior high school, they were the company's most skilled employees. Around then, the anteater went back to New York, and the giant otter returned to the Amazon. Not long after the anteater's departure, Michio and Akai made their discovery: the fluffy white thing was actually their boss, the head of the company. He was following his crews around to make sure they weren't goofing off on the job. This strategy, though, ultimately backfired. The constant surveil-lance made working conditions so stressful that the workers, led by one of the company's directors, rebelled and forced the boss out. The new boss, the director who led the revolt, was a green three-sided triangular prism about a foot in height. Like his predecessor he enshrined himself on the side of the van just beneath the "Electrician" sign, but he didn't follow his workers when they went inside. Instead, he would fly off with flapping wings to a nearby park or empty lot where he would chase down mosquitoes and gnats and eat them with great relish.

PROHIBITIONS

ONE DAY, SUDDENLY, a ban on taking walks was announced.

No major highways pass through our neighborhood, and the streets are mainly single lane with narrow sidewalks. The logic was that if a pedestrian strayed into the street by even an inch, then they were likely to be struck by a bicycle or speeding car (accidents have been increasing every year).

Needless to say, the people in our neighborhood didn't accept this new law quietly. For a start, walking had always been encouraged, whether it be a morning, afternoon, or late-night stroll—there was even an annual contest for the best essay on the topic. Moreover, if you were ranked in the top ten for total walking distance over the course of the year, you were entered into a raffle that offered fancy prizes to the winner.

Reaction to the ban was therefore swift, and people began gathering in front of Town Hall each Sunday carrying placards with phrases like STOP THE WALK-ING BAN written on them. The demonstrators met at ten in the morning to chant their demands in a rousing chorus before setting off on their march, circling the downtown area. The demonstration ended at noon, giving those with free time a chance to repair to our neighborhood park for a shared barbeque. The sun would still be high in the sky, and a dense smoke would fill the park, while demonstrators belted out raunchy songs, or drunkenly sprawled across benches, or else accosted other park-goers, demanding that they share in the grilled meat. No surprise, then, that barbeques were quickly banned as well.

The dog school principal played a central role in the demonstrations.

"Why the hell," he sputtered, "would they steamroll a stupid law like this through town council?" In response, a new law was enacted the following week that banned sputtering.

"This is the height of stupidity," declared the five members of the town's Greetings Club, speaking as one. They soon put this line to music, allowing soprano, alto, tenor, and bass voices to join in perfect harmony. This caught on, which led to the next ban, on harmonizing in public.

Over the next year, our neighborhood had over a hundred bans imposed on it in this fashion. Bans on using heavy stones to make better pickles, on wearing berets, on cultivating cauliflowers, on dream diaries, on the use of backscratchers. Even the signature song of the lady who ran the Love, "Hardly Worth Confessing," was banned.

Although the dog school principal led the movement at the outset, when it was thriving, he had to step down after six months due to ill health. The farmwife who replaced him similarly had to quit after two months when she fell victim to a severe depression that left her compulsively chasing her chickens around the yard from morning till night. Michio and Akai teamed up to run things after that, and for a time the movement regained its momentum, but they became so engrossed that their grades at school plummeted and they were forced to walk away.

Enter Kanae, the last person to take on the leadership role.

The first thing she did was call a halt to the demonstrations. Instead, she headed off to Town Hall by herself after class every day, where she spent her time not protesting but just walking the halls.

One by one, Kanae fixed those big eyes of hers on the people working there. The power of her gaze was so great that it burned holes in the uniforms of the civil servants it targeted, while those who happened to meet her eyes were briefly turned to stone. The duration of their petrification was so short—a minute or so—that no one was aware of what had happened, but victims were sure to suffer excruciating muscular pain the following day.

Within two weeks of her first visit, therefore, all those who worked at Town Hall were eating out of Kanae's hand, willing to do whatever she asked. Once she had turned you to stone, it seemed, it was simply impossible to stand against her.

Then, finally, Kanae discovered the headquarters of the Prohibitions Department, located five levels down in the basement.

This is what she encountered when she opened the door.

Wet earth covered the entire floor, and a number of *kunugi* and *konara* oaks grew here and there. Giant horned beetles clustered in these trees, sipping on the sweet sap. They held meetings as they sipped. The horned beetles were discussing, cautiously and deliberately, what new prohibitions they might come up with. This was their entire purpose in life—to promulgate bans certain to subtly aggravate human beings. Once they made their decision, one of the smaller beetles would buzz up to the top-floor office of the mayor, alight on his neck, and presto, the new ban would be enacted. This was the system that Kanae was able to bring to light.

The mayor, who had been "beetle-ized" (somewhat similar to being turned into a zombie), was quickly recalled and a new mayor appointed, who moved immediately to disband the Prohibitions Department on the fifth basement level of Town Hall. On that day, Kanae recorded with her camera the western migration of the horned beetles, so numerous that they covered the entire sky, in a series of shots that won her the gold medal in our local photographic competition. From time to time afterward, Town Hall employees who had succumbed to beetle-ization were discovered. We knew who they were because their faces reverted to horned beetle form when they came into close contact with *kunugi* or *konara* oaks. Since that was the only change that took place, a number of them have continued as beetle-ized employees at our Town Hall. 🐵

Tomoka Shibasaki

———————

One summer during a long
rainy spell, student number
one from class one and student
number one from class two
discover mushrooms growing
in a flower bed next to a covered
walkway at their school;
two years after leaving school
they bump into each other,
but after that, ten years pass,
twenty years pass, and they
don't meet again

translated by Polly Barton

Catching sight of something, student number one from class one in the first year of high school went over to the flower bed to discover a round white growth.

It's times like these, she thought, *that you use the word "unheralded."*

Large raindrops struck her vinyl umbrella, making a pattering noise. Student number one from class one loved that sound. When it rained, the weed-riddled patches of grass around the flower beds would soak up water, and when you stepped on the grass, the water would come oozing out, as if you were walking through swampland.

The mushroom was perfectly white. The grass and the fallen leaves around it were spattered with reddish-brown earth and steeped in muddy water, but on the mushroom's round white surface there was not so much as a single grain of dirt. Presumably because it was growing under a bush, there were no droplets of water on it either. Student number one from class one wondered if someone had brought the mushroom from somewhere else and put it here. That explanation made more sense to her. *Put it here so that somebody would find it.* If that were the case, then she, as the person who had found the mushroom, needed to scope out the situation.

Student number one from class one looked around but saw no one. Today she was seriously late. In ten minutes' time, second period would end, and it would be morning break. Kids were expected to spend the break in their classrooms for a homeroom meeting.

The flower bed lay next to a covered walkway that connected the gym with the old school building. Student number one from class one had entered through the back gate, passing round the back of the gym. From inside, she had heard children shouting. It sounded like a practice match for some kind of ball game.

Student number one from class one stepped onto the grass, which was marked "KEEP OFF." The rain seeped out from the ground and the fallen leaves, soaking through the canvas of her gym shoes in an instant, and a cold sensation spread across her feet.

Crouching down to look, she found another white mushroom further back in the bed than the first one. Then, further back still, another one. The mushrooms were identical, but grew progressively smaller. She couldn't see any further than the third, for the ground was obscured by the azalea bush. Student number one from class one moved forward to peer underneath it.

"What're you doing?"

The sound of a voice addressing her made student number one from class one's shoulders tense up reflexively. Turning around, she found student number one from class two standing there. Student number one from class two was holding the exact same kind of transparent vinyl umbrella, on which the raindrops were pattering. The rainfall grew stronger, and the sound grew louder.

Student number one from class one was Yōko Aoki, and student number one from class two was Yūko Asai. As of last year, their high school had started merging the genders in their class registers, and both girls were still unused to their newfound status as "student number one." In kindergarten and middle school, the boys had always been listed first in the register, as though that was just the way things were done in this world. Entering this school and discovering that it had been no more than a matter of convention was all well and good, but always having their names read out first and all the attention that came with it left them a bit uneasy. The two had spoken about it just once, during gym class.

"Mushrooms," student number one from class one answered. She pointed with her index finger directly at the largest mushroom growing at the front.

"Did you plant them?" student number one from class two asked, frowning uncomprehendingly. She seemed to want to ask, *Why would you do something like that?*

"No, no, no. They were just growing here."

"Ah, phew!" student number one from class two said, visibly breathing a sigh of relief.

"There was no sign of them yesterday."

"I know! Amazing."

It had been raining for two weeks. It was a cool summer, and there'd even been a typhoon, which was a rarity for July.

Stepping a bit further in and looking closely, they spotted a mushroom that looked exactly like a shiitake. Its size, however, was nothing like that of a shiitake.

The cap was at least thirty centimeters in diameter. Its shape was so perfect that it looked fake. Maybe someone had planted them here, after all.

Just then, something small and blue moved through the edge of the girls' vision.

A small—creature?

The two looked at one another.

"Did you see something?"

"Something whizzing past?"

Patter patter patter, went the rain on their umbrellas. Its rhythm shifted. *I know a song that goes like this—what is it again?* student number one from class one thought, but she couldn't bring it to mind.

The bell rang, and the two girls hurried off to their respective classrooms.

In neither their second nor their third year were they in the same class, and they left school without ever having much opportunity to speak to one another. Throughout their three years of high school, each of them was "student number one."

In the summer of her second year at university, student number one from class one went to see a rock band playing an outdoor concert in Kyoto. In front of the concert venue, the pedestrian crossing heaved with people. As she crossed the road, wiping the sweat dripping from her face while she rushed not to lose sight of the friends she'd come with, she thought she heard someone calling her name.

When she reached the other side, she stopped and looked around, and there was student number one from class two's face, popping out from the crowd.

"What're you doing?"

"I'm going to the concert."

"Me too."

"You like their stuff?"

"Hmm, not so much."

Student number one from class two laughed. Then their friends called their names.

"Okay, well, see you around!"

They waved to each other and parted ways. Inside the venue, they didn't see one another again.

Three years later, student number one from class one saw student number one from class two on the television that she'd left on. The program, screened late at night, was a documentary about one of the remote islands on the Inland Sea. The island had once had a thriving fishing industry, but now its population was declining as more and more people moved away. Among those who did remain, however, there were lots of personalities, and the documentary covered, over the course of a year, the various bars, restaurants, and events on the island. There, among the customers of an udon restaurant, was student number one from class two. In the evening, she played guitar at the restaurant. The program featured an interview with her. She explained how, after leaving high school, she'd moved between various part-time jobs, finally arriving six months earlier on the island, where she was helping out at the udon restaurant. She also spoke of a project to convert an empty seafront building into a guesthouse, which would open the following month. The program showed her playing guitar and singing on the beach, too. Student number one from class one hadn't known that student number one from class two could play the guitar. The song she sang was great. It was a shame that they showed only a short clip.

Student number one from class one wanted to speak to student number one from class two, but she didn't have her contact details nor any friends in common, so nothing came of it.

The following year, student number one from class one moved to Tokyo and started working at a real estate agency. She wrote a film blog that after a while became popular, and she transitioned to writing articles for a magazine and review sites. Four years after taking up magazine work, she was asked by someone she'd met there to start up a "life advice" feature on late-night radio. They called it "life advice," but the problems they featured were nothing serious—rather they were the sort of niche queries that you might hesitate to seek advice about elsewhere. The feature was popular enough, though, and a good number of people wrote in with their questions. One day, while reading through the messages sent in to the show on social media, she found one that read:

"Ms. Aoki, you're doing a great job! I was actually at the same high school as you."

Wondering who the message was from, student number one from class one checked the sender's user

account only to discover that, apparently, it was student number one from class two. Her account used a nickname she'd had at school rather than her real name. It wasn't clear where exactly she lived, but it wasn't the island where student number one from class one had seen her on TV ten years earlier. Posted on her account were photos of her with her two children at a shopping mall and a theme park.

Student number one from class one contemplated sending student number one from class two a message, but the woman in those photos, in which the faces of both the mother and the children had been artfully blurred, somehow seemed to her a different person from the one she knew, and so she held back. Student number one from class two never directly contacted either student number one from class one or the program. Student number one from class one had the feeling that she would run across student number one from class two somewhere. Sometime, somewhere, just like when student number one from class two had called out to her on the street that summer all those years ago.

The radio feature went on for three years. After quitting the program, student number one from class one released three essay collections.

Years later, she was asked by a friend to take up a teaching post at a university. At the end of her first lesson, one of the students came up to talk to her. He was a pale-skinned boy.

"My mom said she went to the same high school as you."

The boy was student number one from class two's elder son. Their features were similar.

"Is your mom well?"

"She's living in Dalian now. For my stepdad's work."

The boy took out his smartphone and showed her a photo. Student number one from class two stood, for some reason wearing a cherry-red sweatsuit, on the deck of a boat moored in a harbor.

"My mom said that you two saw an alien while you were together. A small silver one."

It seemed that student number one from class two's son was very eager to hear the story. 🐵

Hiroko Oyamada

———

Turtles

translated by David Boyd

© Johnny Wales

MY AUNT SAID she had some takenoko she'd cooked for me, so I went over to her house. I brought my daughter along. On the phone, my aunt told me that the girls were visiting. "The girls" were my aunt's granddaughters—my cousin's children, which I think makes them my daughter's second cousins. When we got there, Aunt K was at the dining table, pen in hand. "Hana-chan, come in!" My aunt looked at me and stretched. "Where's Naa-chan?" "Mei-chan and Mami-chan were outside, so she went to play with them." My aunt made a face. "Those two have been in the mud all day. Naa-chan isn't wearing white, is she? If she is, I can give her something else to wear." "It's fine. I think they're done with the mud for now. They said they were looking for gold." Finding gold-colored bits in the soil and pretending they're real gold. We did the same thing when I was a kid, with sparkling pieces of white quartz. Maybe this one's a diamond? One little voice in my head would say, "Yeah right," while another would whisper, "But what if . . . ?" Either way, I thought I could make it shine if I kept rubbing it. "Yeah, gold . . ." My aunt was wearing a long dress with what could have been a William Morris print on it; she had her graying hair up in a bun, neat as always. I once asked her if she had some special way of doing it, some secret, but she just said, "All you need's a hairpin—shove it in from the side, like this." "Mimi-chan's at work?" "Mhm," Aunt K nodded as she got up and went into the kitchen. I sat down in the chair diagonally across from hers. It's nice out today, so the back door is open. From where I'm sitting, I can't see the girls through the screen door, but I can hear their voices. Beyond the fence, I can see the neighbor's cherry blossom tree. It's tall enough for us to enjoy the flowers from here, but that means the falling petals and caterpillars and leaves get into my aunt's yard. Bees are buzzing by the white deutzia. I heard one of the children laughing, but it wasn't my daughter. I couldn't tell if it was Mei or Mami. "Here ya go," my aunt said, setting a cup of coffee in front of me, no saucer. "Thanks," I said. My aunt placed a second cup in front of herself and made a sound as if to say *Time to get started,* then cracked open a thick album bound in pearl-colored cloth. Inside was a slightly yellowed black-and-white photo of a man and a woman, sitting in a pair of Western chairs, wearing Japanese clothes. The man was holding a cane, its tip resting on the floor, and the woman was holding a folded parasol in the same way. He was probably in his forties, and she had to be about ten years younger. The man's hair was cropped short, and the woman's hair was up in a plain-looking chignon. "Kozo-san and Tane-san. Mom's parents." "These are your grandparents?" "Mhm. Grandma and Grandpa to me, Kyoko and Katsuyori. Which I guess makes them your great-grandparents." "Wow." Neither of them looked anything like my aunt, my mom, or my uncle. I didn't look like them, either. To think it had only been two generations since people did their hair like that and photos were black and white. "My mom's fiftieth anniversary is coming up, you know?" My own mother had mentioned that a little while ago. I nodded as I drank some coffee. "In the fall, right?" "November. I was talking with your uncle, and we were saying how we don't know how many more times we'll be in the same place while we're all still alive and kicking . . . So we thought it'd be nice to have something to give you guys and your kids—not just a family tree, but something pretty simple with who did what written on it . . ." "Oh yeah?" "Yeah. That's what I'm working on. Well, your uncle kind of pushed it on me, saying, 'You don't have anything else going on, do you?' It's kind of a lot, though." "Hmm." There were a few sheets of white printer paper on the table in front of her with all kinds of things written on them. One sheet really did look like a family tree, with names connected by horizontal and vertical lines. The other sheets were covered in writing, but they were facing the other way and written in tiny cursive script, so I couldn't read anything. I could tell it was Japanese. There were years written in some places. Showa 20. Showa 25. Heisei 5 = Showa 68. "There's a lot of stuff you guys wouldn't know. Like how Kozo-san had three wives before Tane-san," my aunt said as she ran a finger over the man's kimono. I don't know that much about kimonos, but what they were wearing looked expensive and well made to me. The woman seemed to be showing a lot of nape for someone having her portrait taken in a studio, and that also struck me

as part of some bygone era. But they probably wore kimono every day, I told myself, and picked up the tree. There were two large names—my grandparents'—surrounded by lines stretching out toward other names. As the names moved farther away from the center, they got smaller and smaller. Crossed-out names and marriage lines, circles in red pen, question marks, even my name. My husband's name was written next to mine in small script (misspelled, too), my daughter's name under ours. Mei and Mami's names were there too. Right under Mimiko and Kotaro: Meiko and Mamiko. "That's Kozo-san and Tane-san up here." My aunt pointed at the K and J near the top of the page. "What's the J for?" "Oh, that's a T, for Tane. I guess it'd be easier to read if I spelled her name out." There were three other horizontal lines next to the big K, each connected to a number. Wife 1, Wife 2, Wife 3. "His first wife was a really sweet person, but she died young. Then his next wife was his first wife's sister." "He married sisters?" "Well, that would have been pretty normal back then. Even in my day, it wasn't that unusual. Anyway, his second marriage didn't last long, and for whatever reason, neither did the one after that. That's when Tane-san came along. She was divorced too, and it seemed like a good match, so they got married and had my mom right away. I mean, after three wives and no children, Kozo-san was worried that the problem was on his side." "Right." "When my mom was born, he was so happy that he started to hiccup and couldn't stop." "Couldn't stop?" "Yeah, he kept going, all day and night. You know how they say you'll die after a hundred hiccups? Well, it turns out that isn't true." "Who knew…" I drank some more of my coffee. My aunt had hers too. "Oh, and then there's Granny, who was in Manchuria…" "Manchuria? What was she doing in Manchuria?" "I mean, you know… the war and all. She said there were girls over there who still had bound feet. They were as tall as girls over here, except with feet just like dolls. Seriously. Grandma said she saw them when she was a kid." "Grandma? You mean Tane-san?" "No, no, that was Nobu-san." "Nobu-san?" I looked at the top of the family tree for an N, the name Nobu, or any kanji that could be read that way, but found nothing. "Where

is she?" "Yeah, see what I mean?" My aunt laughed. "That's why Katsuyori asked me to write everything down. It'd go right over his head if I just told him, he said. You know how men are with these things. They never take it in, even when they're right there. I've got a decent memory for things I heard when I was a kid, the things Mom told us. But seriously, this is a lot harder than you'd think. When you try writing it down, when and where everything happened, it all falls apart." "What if you asked a pro? I'm sure there are companies out there that can help with family histories. People who will make a book out of everything you tell them. We could even chip in to cover the cost." My aunt shook her head. A stray hair curled over her ear, turning dull yellow as it caught the light. "If I could tell it in a way that some stranger could understand, then there wouldn't be any problem. I can write just fine. The thing is, no one was born anybody's aunt or grandma, you know?" Yeah. Everybody in our family who's dead and didn't die young is "Grandma" (or "Grandpa"), and to the girls playing outside, Aunt K's "Grandma," and I'm "Aunt H." When you go around calling everyone Aunt or Grandma, it's hard to keep track of who's who. "Katsuyori said he'd type it up if I wrote it out, but I don't know if I'm going to make it on time." "You'll make it." "Time's not on my side. It's only because Mom died so young that we're all still here fifty years later…" It's true, that's why my grandmother on my mother's side, my mom's mom, will never be Grandma. She's only ever Mom, or Auntie at most— and when she died at forty, when my mom was eight, it was Aunt K, her older sister, who was there to comfort her. She'd come home after school with my mom's favorite tamago-senbei, which she'd bought with what little allowance she had (there was a rice cracker shop by my aunt's school that sold what were locally known as "schoolgirl senbei," branded with the wisteria flowers that were on the school crest). I knew the whole story. How amazing the senbei were, how happy they made my mom, and how they also made her feel so guilty and even more alone; how one time she folded up the wisteria-covered paper they came wrapped in and kept it safe until it got chewed up by a mouse, probably because it still smelled like

senbei, and how she'd had to throw the paper away; how a classmate of hers later married into the family that ran the senbei shop, but they eventually tore the place down and built an office building where it had been . . . My mom had told us those stories from time to time, but thinking about it now, I wonder if my little brother remembers any of that stuff. Maybe he doesn't. I heard shouts from out back. At first, I thought the girls were just playing, but there was a note of urgency in their voices, so I went over to the screen to see. The sisters were standing side by side, jumping and screaming. My daughter was a couple of steps away, looking up at them in confusion. "What's going on?" I asked as I stepped into the sandals by the back door that my aunt probably used when she hung up the laundry or had to go into the yard. The plastic sandals were almost hot on the soles of my feet, but the wind on my face was chilly. "What's going on?" "Where's Turteyyy?" the older sister shrieked, then looked up at me, posing like Munch's *The Scream*. Turtey . . . right, there are turtles here. In the yard, there's a shallow plastic storage box with three Mississippi red-eared sliders inside: a big one, a small one, and a medium one. It was my cousin—the girls' mom, my aunt's daughter—who brought turtles home when she was a kid and even in college, and she may have looked after them at first, but before long, as always happens in such situations, it fell to my cousin's mom, Aunt K, to take care of them. "Hey, when I die, these guys are gonna be yours." Whenever my aunt said that to the girls, they'd answer in unison: "Kaaay." "I just hope they don't outlive you. Maybe they won't get to be as old as Lonesome George, but you never know." She was always talking about Lonesome George, as if they were the best of friends. Nobody knew how old the turtles were when Mimiko found them, so they could have been over a hundred already. "They're not a native species, so you can't just let them out. You've gotta take good care of them, up until they die." Mississippi red-eared sliders. Sure, they weren't from around here originally, but this place had better be home to them by the time my aunt's dead and the girls are all grown up. I took a look inside the box. There's a metal grille over it so that the turtles can't get out, held down by bricks on either end. I could see two dark shells inside. One turtle sat on a brick island, and the other in the shallow water. "Yeah, where's Turtey?" "There," my daughter said. "Turtey's in there." "See how there's two of them, sweetie? There's supposed to be one more." "One more?" My daughter was still trying to catch up. She'd never paid much attention to these turtles. Even the sisters had just noticed one was missing, and they'd been playing in the yard all day. Of the two turtles still in the box, the one on the island was smaller than the one in the water, but which ones were they? The big one and the small one? The big one and the middle one? The middle one and the small one? "One of them got out!" "He ran away!" "Where's Grandma?" The girls ran up to the back door. "Grandma! Turtey's gone!" But wait—what if he didn't run away? What if he was dead? Even turtles die sometime. How do you tell the difference between a dead turtle and one that's just hibernating? "Hey! Grandma!" My daughter was still staring at the turtles in a daze. When I squatted down next to her, I could smell the garden in her hair. "Turtey! Turtey!" "Okay, okay . . ." My aunt opened the screen door to come outside, took a good look around for her missing sandals, saw them on my feet, then, as if to say *I'll be right back,* shut the screen door and went back inside. A second or two later, the front door opened, and my aunt came out in a different pair of sandals, not made of plastic. "Sorry I took your sandals." "No, no, don't worry about it." "Grandma! We can't find Turtey!" "I know, the thing is . . ." My aunt let out a huge sigh, then kept going. "Turtey's gone. He ran away." "Didn't you have the cover on?" "Mhm. I just let them out so they could get some sun, now that it's getting warmer." My aunt said she'd let the turtles wander around the garden in the past, and they'd never gone far—there was a big step all around the garden, and the gate was shut. But this time, when she thought it was about time to put them back in their box, she couldn't find the third turtle. "I thought he'd come back when he got hungry, but you know, turtles will eat pretty much anything, so . . ." "When was that?" "Last Wednesday. I've been keeping an eye out for him ever since." "Noooo!" the girls started screaming again. "What if he's lost?" "What if

he got hit by a car?" "If he did, that car would have taken some serious damage. And I haven't heard anybody say anything about hitting a turtle, or seeing anything like that." "You're so mean, Grandma!" the little one yelled as she started punching my aunt's fleshy belly. "You gotta put up posters that say HAVE YOU SEEN THIS TURTLE?" "I don't think so. This isn't a dog we're talking about . . ." "So what?" "You gotta do something!" "You're so mean!" My aunt took another deep sigh. "Hey, it was your mom who brought the turtles home in the first place. When she got married and bought a house, I told her to take the turtles. Do you have any idea how many times I asked? Thirty, at least . . . But no—she left them here. Over the years, I've had to clean up after them, keep them fed, make sure their shells stay dry! If you've got a problem, you should call your mom right now and take them home with you!" As I listened, I couldn't help but feel that my aunt was right—and wrong at the same time. "Hey, Aunt K," I said. "Which turtey was it that escaped? The big one, the middle one, or the small one?" "The middle one. Kamekichi. That's Kameko and Kametaro in there." "They have names?" "Sure. Your cousin came up with them, not that she tried too hard. All the turtles are male, by the way, even Kameko. And yeah, I'm the one who's had to call them by those names this whole time. Geez, I'm the one who should be complaining!" Aunt K snorted, then suddenly muttered in a different tone of voice: "You hear that? They're cutting down another tree." "Tree?" "Yeah, I could have sworn I just heard someone cutting down a tree . . ." I listened, but heard nothing. "They've been tearing down a lot of the old houses recently . . . It could be a tree outside one of those houses. Too bad . . . If I'd known, I would have asked them if I could take it. There was one house a little while ago that had this beautiful white wisteria that bloomed every year, but they turned the whole place into an empty lot before I heard anything about it. I'm sure there are people who would pay good money for a tree like that, but whoever inherited that house probably had no idea what it was worth, and just chopped it down or ripped it out. It breaks my heart." "Grandma, you're crazy! Feeling bad for flowers when you don't feel bad about Turtey!" "Enough,

you two! All your screaming's gonna drive me crazy!" my aunt said as she left her front-door sandals by the screen door and went back into the house.

AFTER THAT, the kids went around Aunt K's garden—which was by no means small, but not that large either—searching for the missing turtle. I kept an eye on them without really watching. The sisters went into bushes, looked under rocks, picked up pots and planters, and chanted "Here, Turtey" as they dug and stomped and rummaged around. My daughter was more interested in the turtles in the box. They were black-green with yellow and red patterns on their faces. Both were still in the same positions —the big one (Kametaro) was in the water, and the little one (Kameko) was on the island—making quick movements with their feet. There was something comical about their perfectly round nostrils, and as I wondered if they'd always looked like this, my daughter said, "They have pretty eyes." "Pretty eyes . . . uh-huh." Their eyes looked more human than I remembered. It was scary to think that they'd had eyes like this ever since they were baby turtles—but maybe it was even scarier to imagine that their eyes had become more human with time. "Mom, what's that?" I followed my daughter's finger and spotted something at the bottom of the tank. It was transparent, or almost transparent—triangular, with black markings on it. I couldn't tell if it was something that had once been alive or just some old piece of plastic. "Maybe it's trash." "Trash?" "That's a bit of shell," my aunt said through the screen door. "Hana-chan, are you coming inside?" "Yeah, in a second. This came from one of the turtles?" "Yeah, look at Kametaro's shell. By the tail? Hey, Mei-chan! Don't dig up that part of the garden! That's where the ginger comes up in the summer!" Part of the big turtle's dark shell was turning white. I thought it was just changing color, but looking closer I could see a thin layer was coming loose. "Want a better look?" Aunt K asked as she stepped outside in sandals, removed the bricks over the box, and took off the grille. The turtles suddenly looked much greener, as if there'd been a layer of glass between us. The pinstripes on their necks and limbs looked so vivid now. "They

come off in pieces. What you see there, it's just a piece of shell." My daughter reached down to grab it. Kametaro instantly craned his neck and looked up. "Naa-chan!" my aunt shouted. My daughter jerked her hand back. "Anything that moves looks like food to them. And they're stronger than they look. It'll hurt if they bite you. Don't ever put your fingers in there, okay? Never!" My daughter trembled, then burst into tears. "Honey, I'm not mad at you. Naa-chan, Naa-chan . . . your auntie's not mad!" "Sorry, Aunt K. It doesn't take much to make her cry . . ." I picked her up. "It's okay . . . you didn't know . . . Aunt K was just looking out for you." "Hey, she's a sensitive one, isn't she? Just like her mom." "What do you mean?" "You used to cry and cry . . . Remember that time at New Year's, back when Great-Aunt K was still alive, with the kazunoko . . ." "Gran-maaaa!" the sisters cried, cutting her off. "We found Turtey!" "Where?" my aunt asked as she headed toward them. "They found him," I said to my daughter. "Let's go see." Still crying, she shook her head. The shoulder of my shirt was completely wet. It felt warm for a moment or two, then started to chill. Ever since I started getting cried on regularly by my own daughter, I've gained a different understanding of evaporative cooling. "Where?" "In the parsley!" "Look!" "Hey! There he is!" "I wanna see," my daughter said in a tiny voice. "I wanna see Turtey." "Okay, let's go, let's go." My daughter switched her wet face over to my other shoulder and wiped her cheek on it. "Over here, Naa-chan! Come and see! Here he is!" In the corner of the garden was a wild clump of dark-green parsley, out of which shot stiff stalks with buds that had yet to bloom. Under the buds that my aunt brushed aside, her wedding band glinting on her left hand, was a black-green turtle. "Wow!" "Right?" "You really found him!" Aunt K clapped. "Great job, guys!" "I can't believe you, Grandma! This was the most obvious place to check!" "I looked! He wasn't here before. Anyway, I'm glad you found him! Thanks!" My aunt reached in to pick up the turtle. I could feel my daughter tense up in my arms. I gave her a few pats on the back. "When you pick up a turtle, there's a secret to it. You've got to get the right spot. Spot, or like, you know . . ." Aunt K put one hand over

the turtle's shell, then lifted him up. "There you go, Kamekichi . . . Good boy," she said as she took the turtle back to the box with the others. "Look at that! Now Kameko's trying to make a run for it." Taking advantage of the opening, Kameko had gotten his front legs up on the rim of the box as if he was about to crawl out. "Never a dull moment with you guys." My aunt dropped the turtle into the water with a little plop, then returned the would-be runaway to his brick island. "Wait . . ." Now that all three were back in the box, the one that the girls had found looked small—definitely smaller than the one that just tried to run away. "Aunt K, was it the small turtle that was missing? It had to be Kameko, right?" "Huh?" My aunt looked down at the three turtles in the box. "I don't even know which is which anymore," she said, then burst out laughing. Even though she'd just been crying at the thought of getting her finger bitten, my daughter started to reach out for the big turtle's back to peel off the shedding part of his shell. After that, we went inside for snacks. Then the kids went back into the garden to play until evening. When it was time for us to go home, my daughter whined about how badly she wanted to stay. I did what I could to console her, and then we left. When we got home, I realized I'd forgotten about the take-noko. Later that night, the intercom buzzed. It was my aunt with a platter full of harumaki. "Freshly fried, with takenoko inside," she said. "Wow, they look amazing. Thank you!" "Oh, and keep the plate. It's Royal Copenhagen. Consider it part of your inheritance." "Huh? It's too early for that!" She headed back to the elevator with a gleeful cackle. The rolls were still warm, and stuffed with pork, takenoko, and wild parsley. After eating two (my daughter had one), I felt full, but telling myself they tasted best when they were fresh, I decided to have one more. 🐵

Natsuko Kuroda

———

The City Bird

translated by Asa Yoneda

THE NOTEBOOKS GIVEN to the child who had only just started writing perfectly suited their owner's hands in size and lightness, and being prized for this reason quickly stacked up until they numbered twenty-two, but the four-year-old's letters were so large that some pages held just two lines of four or five and sometimes half the spread would be given over to drawing so the writing simply named the thing depicted; nonetheless, once all the pages were filled, the child satisfied that a book had been created would conclude each one with a closing flourish and a triumphant signature.

Nearly all of the notebooks were from the same shop and made in the same way: twenty-five sheets of two-fold lightweight paper tucked between covers of slightly thicker paper further doubled and bound with bright silk thread that was passed through the stack, back up around to the front and through again before moving on to the next of the four awl holes along the right-hand side; but their covers were each different in design though mostly printed in four-color woodblock and busy with the festive colors of the title labels affixed in the upper left-hand corners and the colors of the binding threads, and their suppleness also sweetly comforted the fingers of the child who would line them up in order of preference or lay them out in rows and columns to try out different color combinations.

The one who looked upon the notebooks after many years during which their threads had all faded to an indistinguishable straw color only then noticed that around half the covers depicted items relating to dance plays dating back to the Edo period, and making the assumption that such objects could only have been riddles for the four-year-old who was yet to have been to the theater felt even more suspicious of the fact that no memory of that mystery accompanied them, but on turning the pages to find multiple if rudimentary drawings of dancers clearly holding or wearing these objects reached a kind of realization that brought both reassurance and a sort of disappointment. In clay, wood, cloth, and paper, large and small, the objects had been around the home in the form of dolls, while many of the same items quilted in relief also adorned the flight of a dozen or so miniature battledores on display

throughout the year in the room of the child's ancestor two generations removed, and as the ancestor had by habit referred to many of these after the characters in the stories, the child had also called them by those names while still being hazy on whether they indicated the character or the object itself—for instance, the sedge hat, the yoke and buckets, or the design of the crest—and was in fact already acquainted with the handholds to these images that would go on to be supplemented and shaped by things that were observed later—or so it seemed the child was mocking gently from beyond the years during which this had been forgotten.

There were also several notebooks that had been assigned to the ancestor or the caregiver and which they had filled or started filling and left half-blank. On some of the pages they had at the direction of the child reproduced a specific part of a picture book or copied out verses one to five of a certain song, while on others were meticulous renderings by the adult who perhaps since it pleased the child for them to sit at the same table and busy themself reaching for and handling the same color pencils had started drawing familiar flowers or birds from memory or sketching toys that were nearby, and finding after a long estrangement from making such images that their adult eye and hand could create something quite passable had gradually become engrossed, or perhaps seeing the other's unexpectedly accomplished efforts became invested in spite of themself in winning the four-year-old's approbation.

Clustering in the hundred or so days before the child started writing longer pieces, the notebooks' contents offered little in the way of clues as to sequence, but the recollection of which of them was the first to be brought home had remained clear and untangled, and in the end the child may have always liked that one best.

Irregular pale blue lines evidently indicating the flow of a large river tilt gently across the cover from right to left. Upon it floats a white waterfowl stylized in the shape of a teardrop with only its beak red and the tip of its tail black, surrounded by fallen petals. Perhaps the elder in search of a small notebook that the child might like had picked out a design that would stand apart of any storyline, and as such the cover is appealing in its simplicity and abundant use of white.

Having brought the notebook home and handed it to the child, the elder who was asked gave the names of the bird and the river by reflex, not having invoked them until then, and the child likewise took them into memory as given, but on encountering one of them in a classroom almost ten years later the transposition of a faraway remembered capital to the East for another in the West caused the child to stumble; too, the existence according to a note left in commentary of alternate theories regarding the identity of the river; there was also a widely known popular song about tree blossoms along the river that the child knew, but the passage from the Heian period laid out on the school desk took place judging from what followed and came before not during that flower's season but at some point after that of the perennials whose deep violet flowers bloomed by the water in droves, leaving all these scenes confused in the imagination.

The one who overlaid and pictured both of these times from a point when the silk had faded to the color of straw also belatedly noticed that of the pictures on the covers the bird was the only thing that was alive, but it too was just a part of the landscape, and what was missing was the figure of the traveler who asked the ferryman for the bird's name and called to it for news from back home; which was to say that all the covers supposed an absent character and that even prior to knowing anything of them it had been those absences that were so fascinating, at which point they were greeted by the child's apparent amusement that it certainly took them long enough to get there.

EVEN AT A SCALE to fit in the palm of the child's hand and as such almost divorced from any expectation of being sat on, how precarious was a chair made of glass; whereas a vase or a dish was practical, and taking color well and being washable the material was perhaps suited for ornaments no matter the shape; still, a piece of furniture that should bear the weight of a person seemed like a whimsical impulse on the part of the glassmaker.

There were other models of things for sitting on, including copies of armchairs in wood and cloth whose introduction in a set of six positioned around a round table prompted the display of an unsuspected interest in arraying the multitude of identical shapes and sizes, and which the store was therefore bought out of at the next opportunity so they numbered fifteen in total. They were simply made, from painted quarter-inch-thick pieces of coffee-colored wood fitted together and a piece of fabric glued over the seat and the backrest, but since the designs outlined in black on the rose cloth were of string and wind instruments, they inspired the laying out of seating for audiences of yet-to-be experienced recitals. When the notion of curved rows was hit upon, the sequence of three, five, and seven fanning out from the front and neatly arranged into three rows was repeated and remained in favor for some time. To serve as the source of the sound that was the point of the whole scene there was only a keyboard instrument even smaller than one of the armchairs, but this was apparently to be explained by its distance from the rows of seats, as in some picture or photograph that must have been glimpsed and absorbed in passing.

A smaller, cream-colored pair went with a small box-shaped table of the same color, and their backs which extended vertically out of the likewise box-shaped base did not seem restful at all, but at least the stuffed seat where goldenrod and peach and a small amount of leaf green melded and mixed was soft and gently mounded. Another was larger, velvet-upholstered in tea green and going by its proportions and height from the floor would fit three people side by side or one lying down, and from the hem of the cloth ornate chestnut-colored legs peeked out at each corner and a neat ivory fringe hung silkily, and matching carved cylinders wrapped in velvet lay at each end that could serve as an elbow rest or a pillow, only being too narrow to be a bed and lacking in a backrest to be a sofa it was most often used up on the shelf as a shelf on which to rest or prop small stuffed animals.

Although the blue glass chair did not match any of these it immediately became a favorite and was often placed on the periphery of scenes it had little to do with. Care was always taken that it should be placed where nothing should lean or fall on it, as even without a specific warning from the adults it was known to be of a material both very prone to breaking and very dangerous when broken. Four long, thin legs supported a circular seat frame, and the inside of it and the curved horseshoe-shaped frame of the chair back were filled in with a fine interleaving pattern that was still too large in proportion to the chair as a whole—presumably an attempt to model in glass an exemplar woven in cane.

The six-year-old whose admittance to group education overlapped the death of the ancestor also then joined in with the games that took place in the street outside the home. Some of the child's coevals had already been part of that group for a year or so, but the caregiver of the elder and the child had found it weighed less on the mind and made lighter work on the hands to have them both within the house, and the child finding nothing wanting in the way things had been had considered the mass of voices coming through the hedge immaterial, but once invitations were naturally extended by those the child walked home with to meet back here later then the development was only to be expected. Even then, the child was initially seen looking on at their play without stepping too far from the plantings, or clutching without playing with it one plaything or another from inside the house.

Was the chair of blue glass taken outside at a point when there was no longer a need to be holding onto something familiar but the lingering habit was still regarded without suspicion, or perhaps it was out of a simple desire to be praised. There had already been several things which though commonplace to their owner had been treated as objects of wonder, in fact this one too had been passed around between the older ones and held up to the sun this way and that and made to sparkle, and once that aim was satisfied and the next game started it was placed atop the stone wall of the neighboring house for later, when on the child's return it was found to have disappeared. Thinking the location had been misremembered or it might have been picked up and moved the child looked around for it discreetly, and in vain. But would

speaking up cause someone else distress, or what if someone who had reached for it without meaning to take it had knocked it over on the stone and chipped it and not wanting to own up to it had hidden it away—so the various possibilities meant the six-year-old stayed silent as the sun went down.

If only the child had asked, someone might have called out helpfully to say over there and the chair might have been returned just like that, unscathed, and to do so might have relieved another conscience, too, but the hesitation, if also influenced by a reticence toward those of whom most were older, was perhaps largely out of not wanting to be seen to be attached to a toy, or wanting to maintain the appearance of possessing an object so beautiful quite casually, and thus the day when the child had to let the thing go knowing it never would have been lost had it not been shown off in the first place, so in any case the root of the matter was the child's own self-regard—was another day that ended amid the sweet scent of being on the verge of summer.

A STAND OF EVERGREEN CONIFERS by itself might give off an air of celebration, or perhaps the austere chill of the holiday when the count of the year's days is renewed, but despite the simplistic use of color once a staggered line of trunks and boughs twisted in the sea wind faces the color of water in the foreground on the right and the small flat-topped form of mountains appears against the distant sky, then immediately the scent of the shore rises and the sound of waves comes rushing back, and the gentle presence of the one who flew away and the bewilderment of the one who was left behind reflect off the blankness of the white sand.

While a row of flowering trees in full bloom might do no more than indicate a season, with the addition of a giant bell that a grown person might hide inside and a lightweight golden headpiece with a colorful strip of cloth around the brim, or instead of a great bell a small drum and in place of the golden headpiece a traveler's hat and walking stick, instantly their beguiling dreams are raveled.

By the time the twenty-two small notebooks with covers showing deserted scenes had been bought and given to the child the elder's strength was starting to dwindle, and the days left in which to teach and prepare the child likely ran out more quickly than was hoped. That said there were already some seeds sown that could be nurtured by later learning, and some stakes planted when it came to books that would continue to provide support for some time.

The stockpile that the elder alarmed by the sudden waning of their ability to walk out into the city and comb through store after store had acquired ahead of time for the child who was then still mainly reading picture books, and which was remembered by the caregiver and moved to the shelves dedicated for the child's use some time after the household had settled from the upheaval caused by the elder's passing, included a hundred or so tales of a characteristic style that were embellishments of abridgments of retellings in a different tongue of folk stories from foreign lands. Being a regathering in five volumes of individual issues published for young readers, the books' pages of packed print were somewhat heavy going for the seven- or eight-year-old, so the flock of stories was not read in order from the beginning but chosen starting with the ones that were most within reach, and perhaps this way of reading only underlined the impression they made, drawing the child in with unexpected characters or customs from their originating cultures at the same time as they drew attention to their likewise unexpected likenesses.

An only child or just one of a set of siblings had to set off on a treacherous journey. Mysterious helpers joined along the way, but these talking birds and beasts were wise or brave souls who had been transformed by magic, and after guiding the inexperienced adventurer to success were themselves freed from their curses and restored to their rightful positions. Thus was engrained the principle that it was in sets of three that challenges and tests would arise on the route.

A golden feather rests upon the path. About to pick it up, the adventurer is stopped by a talking horse. A little farther along there is another feather, and another forestalling. Picking it up will mean trouble, the child is told, but the third and most splendid feather is irresistible, and once in hand seems like reason enough to go back and retrieve the other two. By themselves, the feathers are just feathers, but as

soon as the three are reunited an enchanting vision appears, and the adventurer must undergo three trials for the magnificent golden bird to whom the feathers belong.

Likely it was only an impulsive naiveté rather than true courage to feel that now the glass chair was lost the only hope was to set out and find the golden feathers, but of that group of stories many were read as a quiet provocation left to the child by the one who had departed. 🐵

How do you convey voice?
Remarks from twelve translators

———

Translators are forever talking about conveying voice. We discuss
various approaches with glee, at the same time lamenting
how difficult it is to reproduce levels of formality, to do justice to
the music of dialect, or more broadly, to capture an author's
unique voice. In the following pages, a dozen translators weigh in,
including three Japanese authors who are also translators
(Hideo Furukawa, Hiromi Kawakami, and Aoko Matsuda).

JEFFREY ANGLES
on finding the author's voice in English

Translating the content of a text into another language is always far easier than rendering the *voice* of a text—the particular literary style an author uses to convey that content. Imagine, for instance, an original so funny that a native reader guffaws out loud. Explaining the joke in another language is usually possible, but that isn't the same as telling it in a way that evokes laughter. A similar thing goes for poetry. Conveying the contents of a poem often isn't hard, but unless one also reproduces the unique ways in which the poem is told, the translation, while not necessarily wrong, won't feel even remotely similar.

That being said, if we sit down and think about voice in our native languages, it isn't always easy to identify what exactly makes one writer's voice distinct from another's. Certain discursive aspects might be immediately noticeable—slanginess, politeness, dialect, non-standard diction, etc.—but beyond those surface features, an author's voice is hard to pin down.

So what should the poor translator do? Every translator needs to think about what makes each author (or perhaps even each character in a particular writer's work) sound distinct, then think about how to evoke similar impressions in the new language.

One crutch might involve thinking about authors in the target language whom the original author resembles. I remember that before ever starting his masterly translations of Ishikawa Jun, William Tyler spent a year reading Ishikawa's experimental English-language contemporaries (William Faulkner and Djuna Barnes, among others), mastering the turns-of-phrase and tone of the 1930s avant-garde. When I expressed my amazement, he told me he was trying to find Ishikawa's voice in English. This may seem like an ad hoc solution, but after all, translation is as much an art as a science.

POLLY BARTON
on voice boxes

There are almost infinite amounts to be said about the translator's task of grasping a specific voice, but I'm interested, too, in the question of what happens to a voice after that initial capture. Where, exactly, does it go?

I'm saying this because all three authors whose work I've translated in this volume of *MONKEY* are writers I've been lucky enough to work with several times. Each, I would say, has a very particular authorial voice (which is partly what drew me to their work in the first place), and when first translating their prose, I performed all kinds of textual contortions in the quest to find an English voice that felt like a twin of their voice in Japanese. Eventually I managed it to an extent I was satisfied with—and that satisfaction expressed itself as a visceral sense that the voice in that particular novel or story had assumed its own shape and capacity. It felt almost like a garment I could take on and off. And then, of course, I moved on. I started new projects, forgot about the garment.

The funny thing is, though, that when I sit down and translate something else by one of these three authors now, the garment is magically there before me again. The best way I can think to describe it is that, quite subconsciously, I go and open up the box where, unbeknownst to me, it has been stored all that time. That's not to say that these (or any) writers maintain the same voice across all their works; sometimes the garment will need major or minor adjustments, or sometimes a new voice will be so different that I don't even think to put it on. A lot of the time, though, it's not only useful but somehow comforting to be reminded of the existence of those voice boxes, stored away in my inner attic.

DAVID BOYD
on good vibrations

ANNA ZIELINSKA-ELLIOTT
on discerning a voice

In 2011, I translated a two-part story by Akio Nakamori called "The Day the World Ends, We . . ." The first part was written in 1987, and the second part was added twenty-four years later, after the nuclear disaster in Tohoku. Nakamori opens both parts with a song title: the first is "Tokei-jikake no setsuna" (A Clockwork Moment) by ZELDA (1987); the second is "Rock 'n' roll wa nariyamanai" (Rock 'n' Roll Will Never Die) by Shinsei Kamattechan (2009). Two songs doing very different things. While the halves of the story create a whole, each part is essentially its own, rooted in its own time and built around a distinct voice. To keep that in mind as I translated, I had ZELDA on repeat when I was working on the first part, then switched over to Kamattechan to work on the second. With the right song playing, it was so much easier to stay in the pocket. The music kept the voice for me.

Ever since working on "The Day the World Ends, We . . .," I've used music to find the voice for everything I translate. With notable exceptions, such as sci-fi writer and music lover Izumi Suzuki, authors don't typically provide their own soundtracks. That being the case, tracking down the right song or album is up to me—and it's one of my first tasks as translator. At this point, it feels like a necessity: a second source text.

How to translate the author's voice? First and foremost, one hopes to be able to discern a voice and have some idea of how to render it in translation. This doesn't always happen easily. Even when it does, a problem may arise if one is *too* sure that one can hear it and know how it should sound in translation.

Years ago, I was asked to translate the second half of Haruki Murakami's *Norwegian Wood* into Polish. A friend of mine had translated the first half but became ill and was unable to finish. The publisher asked me to edit the first part and ensure that the two halves fit together in terms of voice. Therein lay the problem. The voice my friend heard differed considerably from what I heard. Reading some of the dialogue that featured the character Midori in my friend's translation, I found myself thinking, "Midori would never ever have said that! She would never have used that word!"

The problem with this way of thinking is that it is completely arbitrary. Not only did Midori not speak Polish, she didn't even exist. . . . And yet I *knew* she would not have used that word. *Never ever*.

This conviction—arbitrary though it may be—comes from the confidence (or is it arrogance?) necessary to undertake a translation in the first place: to create a new Midori in a new language and make her speak a certain way. What often works for me is to keep in mind either somebody I know or a fictional character that Midori (or the character I am working on) reminds me of, and then give my Polish Midori some of the personality and linguistic habits of that person, without overdoing it. When it works, it is truly satisfying.

HIDEO FURUKAWA
on voice in *The Tale of the Heike*
translated by Sam Bett

For my modern Japanese translation of *The Tale of the Heike,* I used the Kakuichi edition as my source text. This edition was compiled in the late fourteenth century by the blind itinerant biwa player Akashi Kakuichi in an effort to record vocal recitations of the tale by lutists of his day.

I was inspired by Royall Tyler's translation of *Heike* into English. After researching notations that stipulated how *Heike* was to be performed, Tyler rendered sections in verse in what was widely considered a prose work. This was an excellent strategy for introducing *Heike* to the West, where epic poetry has long been revered.

Tyler's approach transcends space, as he uses translation to shift the work "horizontally" into a new cultural context. The nature of my task was "vertical," transcending time by going from medieval Japanese into the Japanese spoken today. I focused my attention on the *plasticity* of lyric that was lost when these poems and performances were codified in Kakuichi's text. Hoping to return the tale to a state where it could shake, rattle, and roll, I sought to highlight fleeting traces of the performers left in the original. One might say that I asked the performers to bring the biwa back into the telling of the tale.

In my effort to translate basically every element of text in the Kakuichi edition (all twelve standard chapters, plus the extra thirteenth), I worked to the strengths of modern Japanese to give the story dramatically more room to breathe, granting the narration a greater expansiveness. My strategy, then, was to rescue the medieval lyricality of the poem—all but stifled when it was forced to fit the written word—and to unleash its spirit on the modern world.

TED GOOSSEN
on love and danger

What is that voice that speaks to us when we read certain foreign texts, seducing us to render them in our native language? Is it a siren's song, luring us towards the reef, or the soothing rhythm of our mother's voice reading to us as a child? Love or danger, the lady or the tiger?

Naoya Shiga, the first writer I translated, was presented to me as a reef. His style was said to be untranslatable, built as it was on words like "ki" (気), which have no direct English equivalent. For years I worked to find that voice; now, to borrow Polly Barton's phrase, it is a well-worn garment hanging in my closet, awaiting its season to roll around again. It even smells like me!

Haruki Murakami's voice was not my mother's, but still had something warm and reassuring about it. If translating Shiga sent me back to Hemingway, another writer with a deceptively simple style, working on Murakami directed me to Chandler, Brautigan, and Fitzgerald—the literature of my youth. David Boyd writes here of the role music can play in finding the right voice. Ditto for me when it comes to Murakami's early works. I don't need to listen to the CD, though. The music is already playing in my head.

Hiromi Kawakami, the writer I am currently translating, calls to me in a voice that is at once perilous and eerily close to home. Her literature is so sonically rich, so full of onomatopoeia, that I wrack my brains to find a language that even approaches hers. But I persist. I must be getting used to being flung upon the rocks. Yet there is also something intensely familiar about Kawakami's voice, for it speaks of that nebulous realm where dream and reality overlap. It comes to me from my childhood, from the dream world, a siren's song perhaps.

HIROMI KAWAKAMI
on the impact of translating *Tales of Ise*
translated by Ted Goossen

Seven years ago, I translated *Tales of Ise* from classical into modern Japanese. This masterpiece of poetic prose and 31-syllable waka poems was written during the Heian period (784–1185). Each short chapter is based on an episode in the life of the nobleman Ariwara no Narihira. Although the work describes events, we cannot be sure what is fact and what is fiction, when it was written, or even who composed it (possibly more than one person). Given that *Tales of Ise* is mentioned in *The Tale of Genji,* written around 1000 CE, it was likely already circulating a century earlier, though with fewer than the 125 chapters of the version we know today.

Classics deepen and grow over time, as generations of readers experience them in what is an endless and dynamic process. Values change. Norms evolve. A tree, initially slender, expands its girth, putting out one new branch after another.

My challenge was to find a voice that would allow me to take values accumulated over a millennium and drop them into the narrow sliver of time and space that is the present. You might say *Tales of Ise* is an expression of the collective unconscious of generations of readers, which makes finding and sustaining a singular voice extremely difficult for the translator. Steering away from my own voice as much as possible, I fashioned instead a mode of expression that attempts to incorporate the countless voices of those living in Japan today. In the process, I found I had to suppress some of the values of ages past while adding some new, very different values. I was translating from an earlier form of Japanese, yet I found the contrast to be even starker than with a foreign text.

The translation was beneficial to my own work: four years later, I published the novel *The Third Love,* which takes up, among other things, the task of comparing the vast differences between Heian and modern ways of thinking.

SAM MALISSA
on finding the voice through voicing

For me, one of the keys to finding the voice in a text is to actually voice the text—by reading it out loud.

What do we mean by voice? What do we look for to help describe it? Voice is in the language markers you'd expect—such as the formality of register and connotations of words, as well as the content of the story and turns of phrase—but as these come together, they reveal something aggregate and complex, and terribly difficult to quantify. We might also think about voice as affect, character, vibe. In trying to grasp it, I find that some essential aspect is revealed when I read the text aloud. It's like compelling the words and the world they weave to perform, and then feeling my way through any clues that surface during that performance.

I always try multiple takes. This helps me to find the different voices in the text, or the different shades of a single narrator's voice. By different takes, I don't mean dressing up the story in other genres and styles—it's not "read a tragedy but make it a comedy." Rather, through repeated readings in the same general style, different notes emerge, different emphases and flows start to feel more right. This helps me decide what to give weight to, what to watch out for, what not to miss.

I also read aloud because it's fun. It gets me into the story. It takes the participatory element of literary voice, the part that happens in the reader's reading, and manifests it in the physical world. I read aloud in the original to try to find what I'm after, and then I do it with the translation, to see if I've found a good match.

(Process note: I always read short stories out loud, but usually not an entire novel. It might be too much for my family.)

AOKO MATSUDA
on retaining humor
translated by Sam Bett

In translating Adam Ehrlich Sachs's stories about fathers and sons into Japanese, what I found most challenging was conveying the humor in each piece. Adam's stories are very funny. But unless you focus on the funny elements, the humor can very easily get lost in translation. Whenever I started to feel that excessive faithfulness to the original might result in a net loss of funniness, or in a breakdown in the rhythms of the work, I knew it was time to shift the emphasis, at the word or sentence level, and adjust the spirit of the original.

As much as I love reading translated literature, I often find that if the translation prizes fidelity to the original above all else, it risks missing the point and becomes hard to read, which deprives us of the joys of reading. If there's one thing that I've learned from having my own work translated into other languages, it's that I'd rather have the translator devote their energies to the creation of a genuinely enjoyable reading experience, even if that means departing here and there from the original (without going too far)—something I'm always grateful to detect in a translator's work.

This is all to say that I've done my best to relay the humor in Adam's writing in the Japanese translation—a process that has brought me no small amount of pleasure. I am indebted to Adam for trusting me with his work.

MOTOYUKI SHIBATA
on first person singular

Take first-person narrative. Singular, and male (sorry, but that's the voice I've done most often). As you may know, when translating from English into Japanese, there are several options for the pronoun "I": the standard *watashi,* which beginners are advised to stick to; the youngish *boku,* favored by Haruki Murakami narrators; and the more roguish *ore,* a good word to use in front of your boss if you want to lose your job, but quite okay among friends. The opening sentence of Sōseki Natsume's *I Am a Cat* became immortal in part because the cat uses the extremely pompous *wagahai* to refer to himself.

I would say that the choice of pronoun determines 60 percent of the character of the first-person voice in Japanese. The remaining 40 mostly depends on the handling of sentence endings—relentlessly tinkered with by translators—which are important too, but the pronoun is crucial. Sometimes the choice is almost automatic. You'd never let Holden Caulfield use *watashi,* which represents what the boy rebels against, and he's too middle class to use *ore,* so the obvious choice would be *boku.*

For Steve Erickson's novel *Tours of the Black Clock,* I thought *ore* was best for the narrator, but my editor argued for *watashi.* (Choosing between *boku* and *ore* is a much more common debate—for example, either would work for Huck Finn.) We discussed it for hours. Finally, we made a radical decision: use *ore* in the first half of the novel and *boku* in the second half. It sounds crazy, but right in the middle of the book is the line "1945. I can see the smoke," and with this mushroom cloud a subtly but wholly different world appears: one in which World War II is still being fought into the 1980s. The first-person narrator changes too, slightly but crucially, and so our decision had some organic logic to it.

ROYALL TYLER
on finding the right idiom

ASA YONEDA
on talking voice to voice

Kazuo Ishiguro's characters (an English butler, say, or a delicately programmed robot) speak exactly as they should. In Proust's *Recherche,* a single sentence can identify or confirm a character's background and standing in the world. One imagines such writers simply transcribing speech supplied autonomously by their imagination and, of course, in their own language. A translator lacks the latter advantage, especially when the original work is a thousand years old. For better or worse one must then invent diction of one's own.

With the prospect of translating *Genji* before me, I vaguely imagined some startlingly contemporary idiom—one far beyond me even to attempt in practice, since nothing about my native mid-Atlantic English is regional or localized. I also regretted not knowing British court language and terminology, which might certainly have been useful. So I looked back, more in flavor than in detail, to the speech and ways of my distinguished grandparents on my father's side: a British-educated Yankee European and a perfectly trilingual descendant of late Franco-Italian aristocracy.

The memory heartened me, but developing it into a functioning idiom was difficult. I translated several chapters several times, in search of a voice at once suitable and alive. Murasaki-no-ue's silent protest *ware wa ware,* in "The Pilgrimage to Sumiyoshi," made a tidy challenge. The familiar "I'm *me*," being ungrammatical, demeaned her, so after verifying the literary validity of the expression I gave her "I am I." Then there was marriage, an endlessly absorbing topic for which the tale has no single word. *Kekkon,* even if known to the author with her Chinese learning, would have been too grossly explicit for a *Genji* courtier to use. I still treasure the moment when "see her advantageously settled" floated from somewhere into my mind.

"Voice" seems to be an idea that we refer to without precisely defining. Does it belong to the author, the piece, or the character? How does it relate to things like race, time period, or punctuation? Why do we find it useful? My best theory currently is that it's a way of acknowledging the identity or personhood of others through the medium of text—of relating to one another through writing.

Thought of this way, as the imagining of an entity that has the right to say what it does (and also reasons for doing so), the recognition of voice is an act on the part of the reader. You need only look at two different translations of a text to see how individual two translator-readers' impressions of the same piece can be, and to understand that the voice you're reading really is the translator's. (Only the reader of both a translation and its original is in a position to observe the voice that comprises both.)

Voice conveys things like tone and rhythm, but also elements we usually take for granted, like description, theme, and plot. Just as the what and the how are irrevocably intertwined in literature, translating is for me about establishing a mutual relationship between my text and the original. This isn't about language-to-language correspondence. I'm talking voice to voice. I'm trying to understand where the decisions that went into the original are coming from using a model that's incomplete and constantly being adjusted. People can always surprise you, and writing is even better at that.

As I'm working, there's an ongoing invisible exchange that asks: Why did this voice say this? What could it have chosen to say instead? Or, put another way: If this voice were to translate what mine is saying, would it come back different, or the same?

Contributors

JEFFREY ANGLES (b. 1971) is a professor of Japanese language and literature at Western Michigan University. His translation of Hiromi Itō's novel *The Thorn Puller* will be published under the new Monkey imprint with Stone Bridge Press in 2022. He has also translated two poetry collections by Hiromi Itō: *Killing Kanoko* and *Wild Grass on the Riverbank* (Tilted Axis, 2020). His translation of the modernist classic *The Book of the Dead* by Shinobu Orikuchi (University of Minnesota Press, 2017) won both the Miyoshi Prize and the Scaglione Prize for translation. He is the author of *Writing the Love of Boys: Origins of Bishōnen Culture in Modernist Japanese Literature.* Angles is also a poet; his book of Japanese-language poems *Watashi no hizukehenkōsen* (My International Date Line) won the 68th Yomiuri Prize for Literature. His essay "Finding Mother" appeared in vol. 1 of *MONKEY,* and excerpts from *Thorn Puller* appear in vols. 1 and 2. His translations of poems by Mutsuo Takahashi are featured in vol. 3 of *MONKEY.*

POLLY BARTON (b. 1984) is a translator of Japanese literature and nonfiction, based in the UK. Recent translations include *Spring Garden* by Tomoka Shibasaki (Pushkin Press, 2017), *Where the Wild Ladies Are* by Aoko Matsuda (Tilted Axis / Soft Skull Press, 2020), *There's No Such Thing as an Easy Job* by Kikuko Tsumura (Bloomsbury, 2021), and *So We Look to the Sky* by Misumi Kubo (Arcade, 2021). After being awarded the 2019 Fitzcarraldo Editions Essay Prize, in 2021 she published *Fifty Sounds,* her reflections on the Japanese language. Her translations of stories by Aoko Matsuda and Tomoka Shibasaki appear in vols. 1–3 of *MONKEY,* and her translations of stories by Kikuko Tsumura appear in vols. 2 and 3.

SAM BETT (b. 1986) writes and translates fiction. In 2016 he was awarded Grand Prize by the Japanese government in the 2nd JLPP International Translation Competition for his translation of "A Peddler of Tears" by Yōko Ogawa, which appeared in vol. 7 of *Monkey Business.* He translated "Every Reading, Every Sound, Every Sight" by Jun'ichi Konuma for *MONKEY,* vol. 2. He is also a founder and host of Us&Them, the quarterly

Brooklyn-based reading series devoted to showcasing the work of writers who also translate. His translation of Yukio Mishima's *Star* (New Directions) won the 2019 Japan-U.S. Friendship Commission Prize for the Translation of Japanese Literature. With David Boyd, he co-translated the novels of Mieko Kawakami for Europa Editions.

DAVID BOYD (b. 1981) is an assistant professor of Japanese at the University of North Carolina at Charlotte. His translation of Hideo Furukawa's *Slow Boat* (Pushkin Press, 2017) won the Japan-U.S. Friendship Commission Prize for the Translation of Japanese Literature. He has translated three novellas by Hiroko Oyamada: *The Factory* (2019), *The Hole* (2020), and *Weasels in the Attic* (2022). He won the Japan-U.S. Friendship Commission Prize for the second time for his translation of *The Hole.* His translations of Kuniko Mukōda's "Nori and Eggs for Breakfast," Hiroko Oyamada's "Something Sweet," and Kanoko Okamoto's "Sushi" appear in vol. 1 of *MONKEY.* For vol. 2, he translated Oyamada's "Along the Embankment" and an excerpt from the novel *Takaoka's Travels* by Tatsuhiko Shibusawa. His translation of Oyamada's "Turtles" appears in vol. 3. With Sam Bett, he has co-translated three novels by Mieko Kawakami: *Breasts and Eggs* (2020), *Heaven* (2021), and *All the Lovers in the Night* (2022).

ANDREW CAMPANA (b. 1989) is an assistant professor of Japanese literature at Cornell University. He has been published widely as a translator and as a poet in both English and Japanese. His forthcoming monograph, tentatively titled *Expanding Verse: Japanese Poetry at Media's Edge,* explores how poets have engaged with new technologies such as cinema, tape recording, the internet, and augmented reality. His collection "Seven Modern Poets on Food" was published in vol. 1 of *MONKEY,* "Five Modern Poets on Travel" in vol. 2, and "Four Modern Poets on Encounters with Nature" in vol. 3.

CHRIS CORKER (b. 1985) is a British-Canadian writer and translator of Japanese fiction and nonfiction. He is currently pursuing doctoral research on the

relationship between nostalgia and natural disaster in Japanese literature and film at York University. His translation of an essay by Kengo Kuma is included in *Touch Wood: Material, Architecture, Future,* edited by Carla Ferrer et al. (Zurich: Lars Müller, 2022). His translation of poetry by Keijirō Suga appears in vol. 3 of *MONKEY.*

STUART DYBEK (b. 1942) is one of the most important short story writers in the United States today and is also much loved and respected in Japan. His poem "Nowhere" appeared in vol. 2 of *Monkey Business,* the short story "Naked" in vol. 4, and "The Crullers" in vol. 5. "Lessons," a poem and a story, appears in vol. 3 of *MONKEY.*

ANNA ELLIOTT (b. 1963) is the director of the MFA in Literary Translation at Boston University. She is a translator of modern Japanese literature into Polish. Best known for her translations of Haruki Murakami, she has also translated Yukio Mishima, Banana Yoshimoto, and Junichirō Tanizaki. She is the author of a Polish-language monograph on gender in Murakami's writing, a literary guidebook to Murakami's Tokyo, and several articles on Murakami and European translation practices relating to contemporary Japanese fiction.

MICHAEL EMMERICH (b. 1975) teaches Japanese literature at the University of California, Los Angeles. An award-winning translator, he has translated books by Gen'ichirō Takahashi, Hiromi Kawakami, and Hideo Furukawa, among others. He is the author of *The Tale of Genji: Translation, Canonization, and World Literature* (Columbia University Press, 2013) and *Tentekomai: bungaku wa hi kurete michi tōshi* (Goryū Shoin, 2018) and the editor of *Read Real Japanese Fiction* (Kodansha) and *Short Stories in Japanese: New Penguin Parallel Text.* His translations of Masatsugu Ono, Makoto Takayanagi, and others are featured in *Monkey Business* and *MONKEY.*

KAORI FUJINO (b. 1980) is an award-winning author. Her debut work of fiction, "Greedy Birds," was awarded the Bungakukai Newcomers Prize in 2006, and

her novel *Nails and Eyes* won the Akutagawa Prize in 2013. In 2017 she was a resident at the University of Iowa's International Writing Program. Her story "You Okay for Time?" was translated by Ginny Tapley Takemori and appeared in *Granta* in 2017. "Someday with the One, the Perfect Bag," translated by Laurel Taylor, is featured in vol. 3 of *MONKEY.*

HIDEO FURUKAWA (b. 1966) is one of the most innovative writers in Japan today. His novel *Belka, Why Don't You Bark?* was translated by Michael Emmerich; his partly fictional reportage *Horses, Horses, in the End the Light Remains Pure: A Tale That Begins with Fukushima* was translated by Doug Slaymaker with Akiko Takenaka; and his short novel *Slow Boat* was translated by David Boyd. His stories appear in every issue of *Monkey Business* and now *MONKEY*; vol. 1 of *Monkey Business* features an interview with Haruki Murakami by Hideo Furukawa.

TED GOOSSEN (b. 1948) teaches Japanese literature and film at York University in Toronto. He is the editor of *The Oxford Book of Japanese Short Stories.* He translated Haruki Murakami's *Wind/Pinball* and *The Strange Library,* and co-translated (with Philip Gabriel) *Men Without Women* and *Killing Commendatore.* His translations of Hiromi Kawakami's *People from My Neighbourhood* (Granta Books and Soft Skull Press) and Naoya Shiga's *Reconciliation* (Canongate) were published in 2020. His translations of Sachiko Kishimoto, Kawakami, Shiga, and others are featured in every issue of *Monkey Business* and in *MONKEY,* vols. 1–3.

GITTE MARIANNE HANSEN (b. 1974) teaches Japanese literature, popular culture, and translation at Newcastle University. She works on character construction and narrative strategies in relation to gender and transmedial production. In 2018 she led the project *Eyes on Murakami* (https://research.ncl.ac.uk/murakami/), which brought together translators, artists, filmmakers, and researchers of Japanese literature. She has written *Femininity, Self-harm and Eating Disorders in Japan* (Routledge, 2017) and co-edited *Murakami Haruki and Our*

Years of Pilgrimage (Routledge, 2021, with Michael Tsang) and *The Work of Gender: Service, Performance and Fantasy in Contemporary Japan* (NIAS Press, 2022, with Fabio Gygi). Her translation of "Kid Sister" by Yūko Tsushima appears in the 2012 issue of *Words Without Borders.* Her translation of "Creta Kano" by Haruki Murakami is featured in *MONKEY,* vol. 3.

KENDALL HEITZMAN (b. 1973) is an associate professor of Japanese literature and culture at the University of Iowa. He has translated stories and essays by Kaori Fujino, Nori Nakagami, Tomoka Shibasaki, and Yūshō Takiguchi. He is the author of *Enduring Postwar: Yasuoka Shōtarō and Literary Memory in Japan* (Vanderbilt University Press, 2019). His translation of "The Little Woods in Fukushima" by Hideo Furukawa appears in *MONKEY,* vol. 3. His translation of Kaori Fujino's *Nails and Eyes* is forthcoming from Pushkin Press.

SEIKŌ ITŌ (b. 1961) is a writer, performer, and one of the pioneers of Japanese rap. His novel *Imagination Radio* (2013) reflects on the March 2011 earthquake and nuclear disaster through the eyes of a deejay. He also writes nonfiction, including a 2017 book on Doctors Without Borders. Itō has long been interested in Noh, and he and Jay Rubin have collaborated with Grand Master Kazufusa Hōshō in a contemporary performance of the traditional Noh play *Hagoromo.* Rubin's translation of Itō's *Fujito* appears in vol. 1 of *MONKEY, Kurozuka* in vol. 2, and *Tudanori* in vol. 3.

HIROMI KAWAKAMI (b. 1958) is one of Japan's leading novelists. Many of her books have been published in English, including *Manazuru,* translated by Michael Emmerich; *Record of a Night Too Brief,* translated by Lucy North; and *The Nakano Thrift Shop, Parade: A Folktale, Strange Weather in Tokyo* (shortlisted for the Man Asian Literary Prize in 2013), and *The Ten Loves of Nishino,* translated by Allison Markin Powell. "The Dragon Palace" appeared in vol. 3 of *Monkey Business* and "Hazuki and Me" in vol. 5. "Banana" appeared in vol. 4 and was included in *The Best Small Fictions 2015* (Queen's

Ferry Press). "Sea Horse" appears in *MONKEY,* vol. 2. *People from My Neighborhood,* translated by Ted Goossen, was published by Granta Books in 2020 and Soft Skull Press in 2021. The series continues to be featured in both the Japanese and English editions of *MONKEY.*

MIEKO KAWAKAMI (b. 1976) is an award-winning novelist, poet, singer, and actress. Her novel *Breasts and Eggs,* translated by Sam Bett and David Boyd, was published by Europa Editions in 2020 to great acclaim. *Heaven,* also co-translated by Bett and Boyd, was published in 2021, and *All the Lovers in the Night* was released in 2022. Her short novel *Ms Ice Sandwich* (Pushkin Press, 2018) was translated by Louise Heal Kawai. Her stories and prose poems, translated by Hitomi Yoshio, appear in vols. 1–7 of *Monkey Business.* "Good Stories Originate in the Caves of Antiquity," a conversation with Haruki Murakami, was published in *MONKEY,* vol. 1; "Seeing," a poem, appears in *MONKEY,* vol. 2; and "Upon Seeing the Evening Sky," an essay, in vol. 3.

SACHIKO KISHIMOTO (b. 1960) is known for her translations of Nicholson Baker, Lucia Berlin, Judy Budnitz, Lydia Davis, Thom Jones, and Miranda July. She is also a popular essayist; her latest collection, *The Sea I'd Like to Visit Before I Die,* appeared in 2020. Excerpts from *The Forbidden Diary,* a fictional diary, translated by Ted Goossen, are featured in vols. 1–7 of *Monkey Business.* "Misaki" appears in vol. 1 of *MONKEY,* and "I Don't Remember" in vol. 3.

SATOSHI KITAMURA (b. 1956) is an award-winning picture-book author and illustrator. His own books include *Stone Age Boy, Millie's Marvellous Hat,* and *The Smile Shop.* He has worked with numerous authors and poets. His graphic narratives appear in vols. 5–7 of *Monkey Business*: "Mr. Quote" in vol. 7, "Igor Nocturnov" in vol. 6, and "Variation and Theme," inspired by a Charles Simic poem, in vol. 5. In vol. 1 of *MONKEY,* he published "The Heart of the Lunchbox"; "The Overcoat" appears in vol. 2, and "The Cave" in vol. 3.

NATSUKO KURODA (b. 1937) is a writer whose uncompromising style is distinctive for its evocative power as well as its grammatical and visual strangeness. Kuroda founded the literary journal *Sajō* while at Waseda University and won the Yomiuri Shimbun debut short story prize in 1963 for "Ball." In 2012 she published the novella *a b sango,* which was selected for the journal *Waseda Bungaku* and subsequently won the Akutagawa Prize. Her story "The City Bird," translated by Asa Yoneda, appears in *MONKEY,* vol. 3.

SAM MALISSA (b. 1981) holds a PhD in Japanese literature from Yale University. His translations include *Bullet Train* by Kōtaro Isaka (Harvill Secker, 2021), *The End of the Moment We Had* by Toshiki Okada (Pushkin Press, 2018), and short fiction by Shun Medoruma, Hideo Furukawa, and Masatsugu Ono. His translations of stories by Kyōhei Sakaguchi appear in vols. 1–3 of *MONKEY.*

AOKO MATSUDA (b. 1979) is a writer and translator. *Where the Wild Ladies Are* (Soft Skull, 2020), translated by Polly Barton, won a World Fantasy Award in the best collection category. In 2013 her debut *Stackable* was nominated for the Mishima Yukio Prize and the Noma Literary New Face Prize. In 2019 her short story "The Woman Dies" (from the collection *The Year of No Wild Flowers*), translated by Polly Barton and published by Granta online, was shortlisted for a Shirley Jackson Award. Her short novel *The Girl Who Is Getting Married* was published by Strangers Press in 2016. She has translated work by Karen Russell, Amelia Gray, and Carmen Maria Machado into Japanese. Her stories appear in vols. 5–7 of *Monkey Business,* translated by Jeffrey Angles. "Dissecting Misogyny," "The Most Boring Red on Earth," and "A Father and His Back," translated by Polly Barton, appear in vols. 1–3 of *MONKEY.*

HARUKI MURAKAMI (b. 1949) is one of the world's best-known and best-loved novelists. All his major novels—including *Hardboiled Wonderland and the End of the World, The Wind-Up Bird Chronicle,* and *1Q84*—have been translated into dozens of languages. "On Writing Short Stories" in vol. 7 of *Monkey*

Business is the second half of his conversation with Motoyuki Shibata, published in vol. 9 (Summer/Fall 2016) of the Japanese *MONKEY*. An interview by Hideo Furukawa appears in vol. 1 of *Monkey Business*. His essays "The Great Cycle of Storytelling" and "So What Shall I Write About?" appear in vol. 2 and vol. 5 of *Monkey Business*. Vol. 4 of *Monkey Business* includes an essay by Richard Powers on Murakami's fiction. "Good Stories Originate in the Caves of Antiquity," a conversation with Mieko Kawakami, appears in vol. 1 of *MONKEY,* the essay "Jogging in Southern Europe" in vol. 2, and the story "Creta Kano," translated by Gitte Hansen, in vol. 3.

MIDORI OSAKI (1896–1971) was a film critic and modernist writer. Born in Tottori prefecture, she was most active in the 1930s. Her best-known work, *Dainana kankai hōkō,* published in 1931, has been translated into English by Kyoko Selden and Alisa Freedman as *Wandering in the Realm of the Seventh Sense.* "Walking" (Hokō), which appears in vol. 3 of *MONKEY,* was also published in 1931. Her life was the subject of the 1998 film *Wandering in the Realm of the Seventh Sense: In Search of Midori Osaki* by pink film director Sachi Hamano.

HIROKO OYAMADA (b. 1983) is one of Japan's most promising young writers. Her short novels *The Factory, The Hole,* and *Weasels in the Attic* were translated by David Boyd and published by New Directions. Her story "Spider Lily" was translated by Juliet Winters Carpenter and published in the Japan issue of *Granta* (Spring 2014). "Lost in the Zoo" and "Extra Innings," translated by David Boyd, appear in vols. 6 and 7 of *Monkey Business.* "Something Sweet," "Along the Embankment," and "Turtles," also translated by David Boyd, are featured in *MONKEY,* vols. 1–3.

JAY RUBIN (b. 1941) is professor emeritus of Japanese literature at Harvard University. One of the principal translators of Haruki Murakami, he translated *The Wind-Up Bird Chronicle, Norwegian Wood, After Dark, 1Q84* (co-translated with Philip Gabriel), *After the Quake: Stories,* and *Absolutely on Music:*

Conversations with Seiji Ozawa. Among his many other translations are *Rashōmon and Seventeen Other Stories* by Ryūnosuke Akutagawa and *The Miner* and *Sanshirō* by Sōseki Natsume. He is the author of *Haruki Murakami and the Music of Words* and the editor of *The Penguin Book of Japanese Short Stories.* His translations into English of Seikō Itō's modern Japanese translations of Noh plays appear in every issue of *MONKEY.*

KYŌHEI SAKAGUCHI (b. 1978) is a writer, artist, and architect. His work explores alternative ways of being, as in his books *Zero Yen House* and *Build Your Own Independent Nation.* His novel *Haikai Taxi* was nominated for the Yukio Mishima Prize in 2014. "Forest of the Ronpa" appears in vol. 1 of *MONKEY,* "The Lake" in vol. 2, and "The Tale of Malig the Navigator" in vol. 3—all translated by Sam Malissa.

MATTHEW SHARPE (b. 1962) is a writer highly regarded for his versatile and innovative style. He has published four novels, including *The Sleeping Father* and *Jamestown* (both Soft Skull Press), as well as a collection of short stories. "In Another Time and Place" appears in vol. 5 of *Monkey Business.* "2020 Triptych" is featured in *MONKEY,* vol. 3.

TOMOKA SHIBASAKI (b. 1973) is a novelist, short story writer, and essayist. Her books include *Awake or Asleep, Viridian,* and *In the City Where I Wasn't.* She won the Akutagawa Prize in 2014 with *Spring Garden,* which has been translated by Polly Barton (Pushkin Press). "The Seaside Road" appears in vol. 2 of *Monkey Business,* "The Glasses Thief" in vol. 3, "Background Music" in vol. 6, translated by Ted Goossen, and "Peter and Janis" in vol. 7, translated by Christopher Lowy. Her stories, translated by Polly Barton, are featured in vols. 1–3 of *MONKEY.*

MOTOYUKI SHIBATA (b. 1954) translates American literature and runs the Japanese literary journal *MONKEY.* He has translated Paul Auster, Rebecca Brown, Stuart Dybek, Steve Erickson, Brian Evenson, Laird Hunt, Kelly Link, Steven Millhauser, and

Richard Powers, among others. His translation of Mark Twain's *Adventures of Huckleberry Finn* was a bestseller in Japan in 2018. Among his recent translations is Eric McCormack's *Cloud*.

KEIJIRŌ SUGA (b. 1958) is a noted poet and critic. His *Agend'Ars* poetry series was released in four separate volumes from 2010 to 2013. Ten collections of critical essays have also been published, including *Shasen no Tabi* (*Off the Beaten Path*), which was awarded the Yomiuri Prize for Literature in 2011. His Japanese translations from French, Spanish, and English include works by Isabel Allende, Aimee Bender, J.M.G. Le Clézio, Maryse Condé, Édouard Glissant, and Jamaica Kincaid. He teaches critical theory at Meiji University, Tokyo. His poem "With the Archaeopteryx," translated by Chris Corker, appears in vol. 3 of *MONKEY*.

MUTSUO TAKAHASHI (b. 1937) is one of Japan's most prominent and prolific living poets. Since first attracting the attention of the Japanese literary world in the 1960s with his bold evocations of homo-erotic desire, he has published forty-eight books of poetry and numerous collections of essays, literary criticism, and fiction. These include his magnum opus *Tsui kinō no koto* (*Only Yesterday*), which describes travels in Greece and his interest in Ancient Greece. Several collections of Takahashi's poetry are available in English translation including *On Two Shores* (Dedalus, 2006) and *Poems of a Penisist* (University of Minnesota Press, 2012). His memoir *Twelve Views from the Distance* (University of Minnesota Press, 2012), translated by Jeffrey Angles, was shortlisted for a Lambda Literary Award. "Only Yesterday" appears in vol. 3 of *MONKEY*.

MAKOTO TAKAYANAGI (b. 1950) has published numerous books of poetry. His collected works appeared in two volumes in 2016. A third volume was published in 2019. *Aliceland* was his first publication, in 1980; a translation by Michael Emmerich appears in vol. 7 of *Monkey Business*. "Five Prose Poems" is featured in vol. 1 of *MONKEY*, and "The Graffiti" in vol. 3.

LAUREL TAYLOR (b. 1989) is a translator, writer, and PhD student in Japanese and comparative literature at Washington University in St. Louis. She holds an MFA in literary translation from the University of Iowa and currently works as an assistant managing editor for *Asymptote*. Her translations include fiction and poetry by Yaeko Batchelor, Aoko Matsuda, Noriko Mizuta, and Tomoka Shibasaki. Her translation of "Someday with the One, the Perfect Bag" by Kaori Fujino appears in vol. 3 of *MONKEY*.

KIKUKO TSUMURA (b. 1978) is a writer from Osaka, and she often uses Osaka dialect in her work. She has won numerous Japanese literary awards, including the Akutagawa Prize and the Noma Literary New Face Prize. Her first short story translated into English, "The Water Tower and the Turtle," won a PEN/Robert J. Dau Short Story Prize for Emerging Writers. Her novel *There's No Such Thing as an Easy Job*, translated by Polly Barton, was published by Bloomsbury in 2020. Her stories appear in *MONKEY*, vols. 2 and 3.

ROYALL TYLER (b. 1936), now long retired to a rural property in New South Wales, taught Japanese language and literature in the U.S., Canada, Norway, and Australia. Among his translations are *Japanese Tales* (1987), *Japanese Nō Dramas* (1990), *The Tale of Genji* (2001), and *The Tale of the Heike* (2012). He has received the Japan-U.S. Friendship Commission Prize, the Japan Foundation Award, the MLA-Roth Translation Award, the NSW Premier's Translation Prize, and the Order of the Rising Sun.

ELI K.P. WILLIAM (b. 1984) is the author of The Jubilee Cycle, a trilogy set in a dystopian future Tokyo: *Cash Crash Jubilee* (2015), *The Naked World* (2017), and *A Diamond Dream* (2022). A Canadian, he has been a resident of Japan since 2009. He has published in the *Japan Times, Cha,* and *Writer's Digest,* among other publications. His essays and book reviews have appeared in the literary journal *Subaru*. His translation of *A Man* by Keiichiro Hirano was published in 2020, and his short story translations have appeared in *Granta, The Southern Review,* and

Kyoto Journal. His story "Lost and Found Babies" is featured in vol. 3 of *MONKEY.*

ASA YONEDA (b. 198Q) is the translator of *The Lonesome Bodybuilder* (Soft Skull Press, 2018) by Yukiko Motoya and *Idol, Burning* (HarperVia/ Canongate, 2022) by Rin Usami. With David Boyd, Yoneda is co-editing *KANATA,* a collection of Japanese fiction chapbooks of Japanese for Strangers Press. "Walking" by Midori Osaki, co-translated with David Boyd, appears in vol. 3 of *MONKEY.* Yoneda's translation of "The City Bird" by Natsuko Kuroda is also featured in vol. 3.

HITOMI YOSHIO (b. 1979) is an associate professor at Waseda University. She specializes in modern and contemporary Japanese literature, with a focus on women's writing. Her translations of Mieko Kawakami's works appear in *Denver Quarterly, Freeman's, Granta, MONKEY, Monkey Business, Words Without Borders,* and *The Penguin Book of Japanese Short Stories.*

Credits

Page 5: Illustration © Akino Kondoh.

Page 6: Illustration © Jillian Tamaki.

Page 12: Photograph © Yoshiaki Kanda.

Page 20: *People,* 2021 © yasuo-range.

Page 30: *Painting for Painting's Sake 010,* oil on panel, 2016 © Teppei Takeda.

Pages 34–35: Illustration © Akino Kondoh.

Page 36: Still of Machiko, played by Eri Yu © Tantansha. From the 1998 film *In Search of a Lost Writer: Wandering in the World of the Seventh Sense.*

Pages 43, 45, 50: Photographs © Kunikazu Furukawa.

Pages 56–57: *The Shiranui Sea,* pastel on paper, 2022 © Kyōhei Sakaguchi.

Pages 82–105: Graphic narrative © Satoshi Kitamura.

Page 106: Illustration © Alina Skyson / TOOGL.

Page 108: Wood-fired stoneware with ash glazes, height: 26 inches, 2009 © Willi Singleton. Photograph © Ken Ek.

Page 128: Illustration © Sara Wong / TOOGL.

Page 131: Illustration © Akino Kondoh.

Page 132: *Floating Time Purplish Blue,* lithograph, 2020 © Yuki Hasegawa.

Page 136: Artwork © Seitarō Kuroda. Photograph © Kanji Yoshima.

Page 146: Illustration © Johnny Wales.

Page 157: Illustration © Alina Skyson / TOOGL.

MONKEY

CONTEMPORARY JAPANESE FICTION IN TRANSLATION

The MONKEY imprint at Stone Bridge Press is proud to announce the publication of **THE THORN PULLER**, a novel by Hiromi Ito, translated by Jeffrey Angles.

Ito may have written this book in prose, but we never forget that she's a poet. There is a special music even in the complaints, scolding, arguments, phone conversations, and gossipy moments.

—YOKO TAWADA, **AUTHOR OF** *MEMOIRS OF A POLAR BEAR* **AND** *THE EMISSARY*

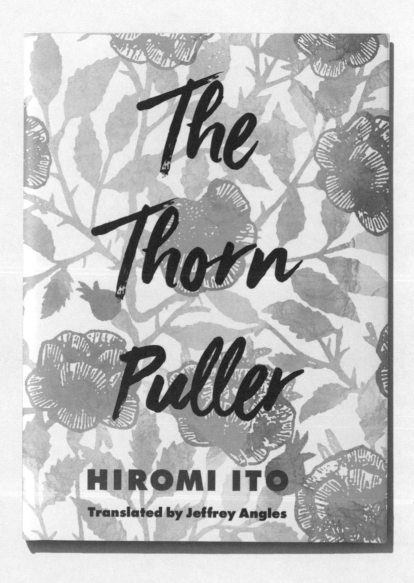

PRINT 978-1-7376253-0-8   EBOOK 978-1-7376253-1-5

The FOOD & TRAVEL issues

MONKEY

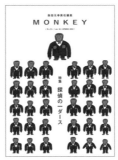

MONKEY CELEBRATES
MONKEY New Writing from Japan

SWITCH PUBLISHING   *www.switch-store.net*

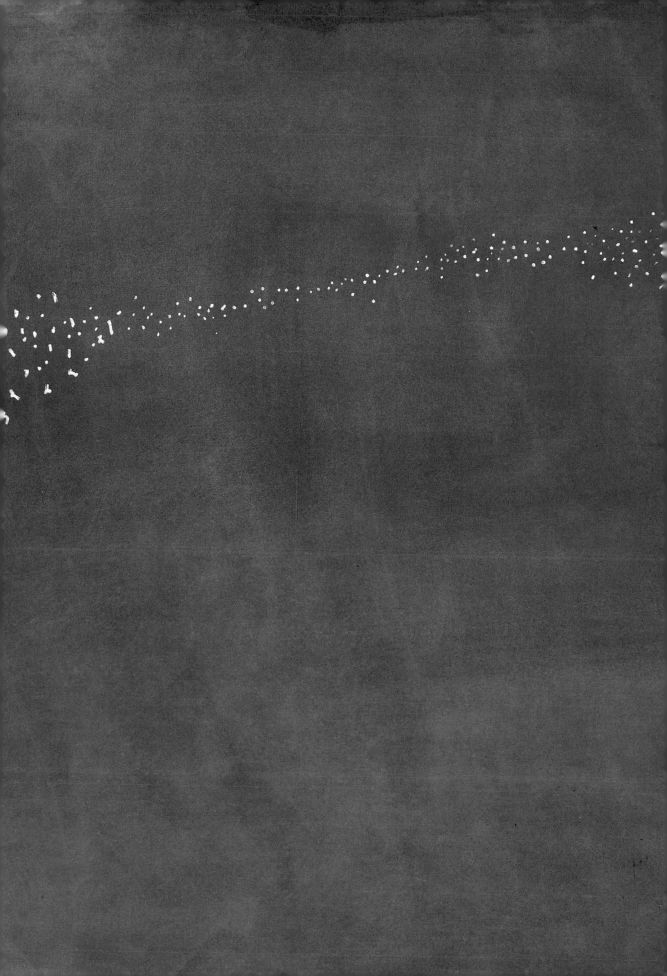

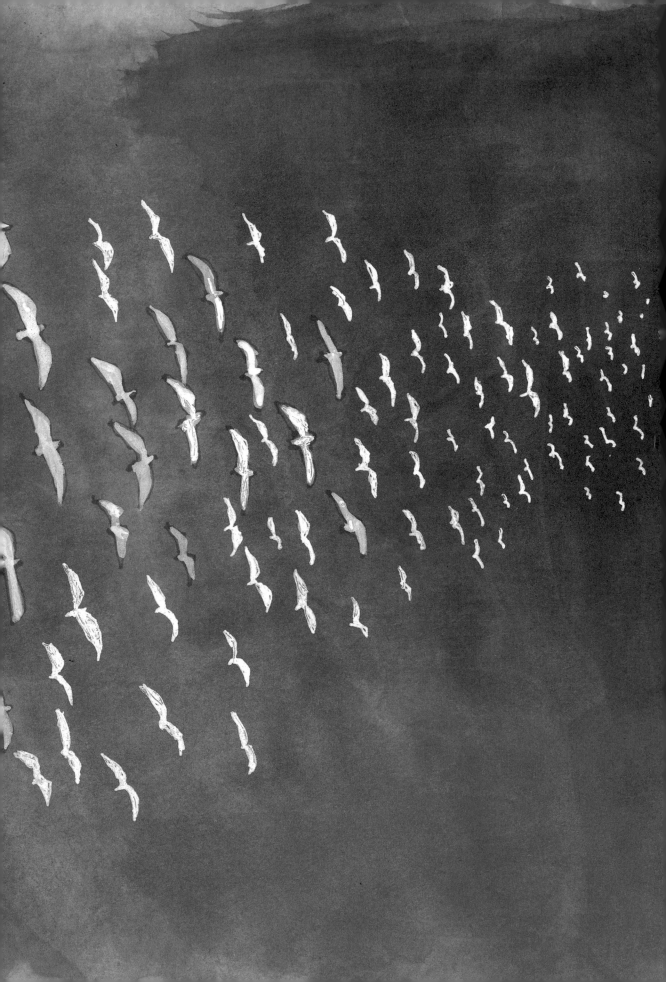

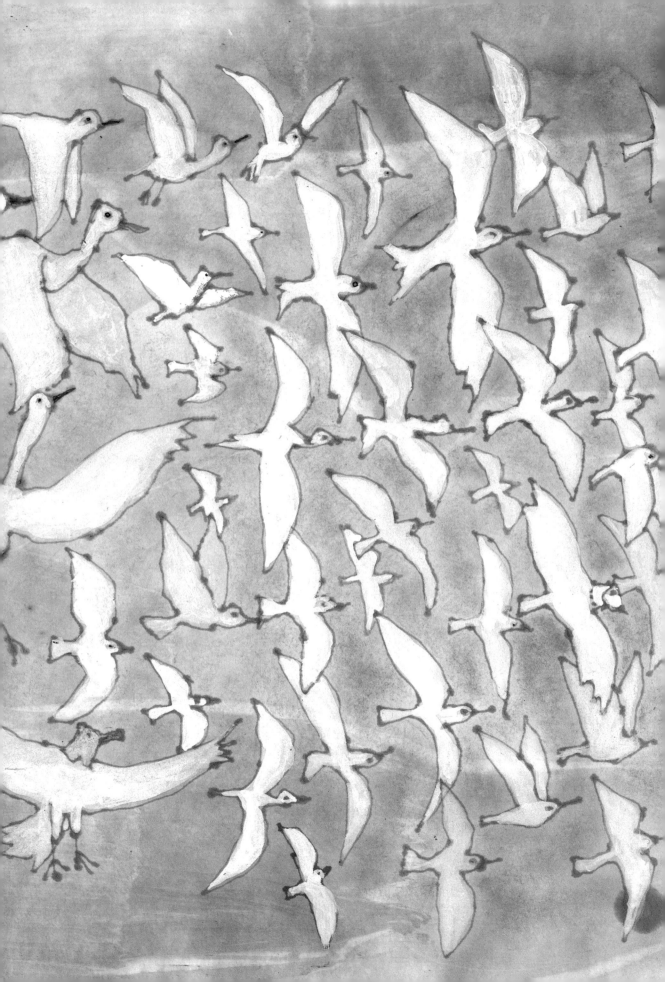

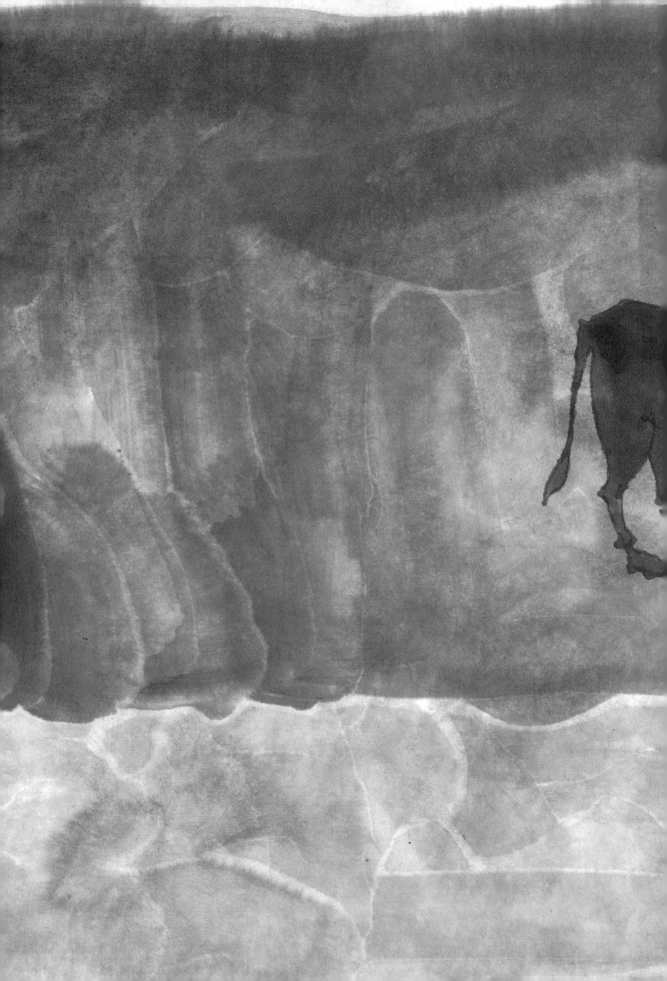

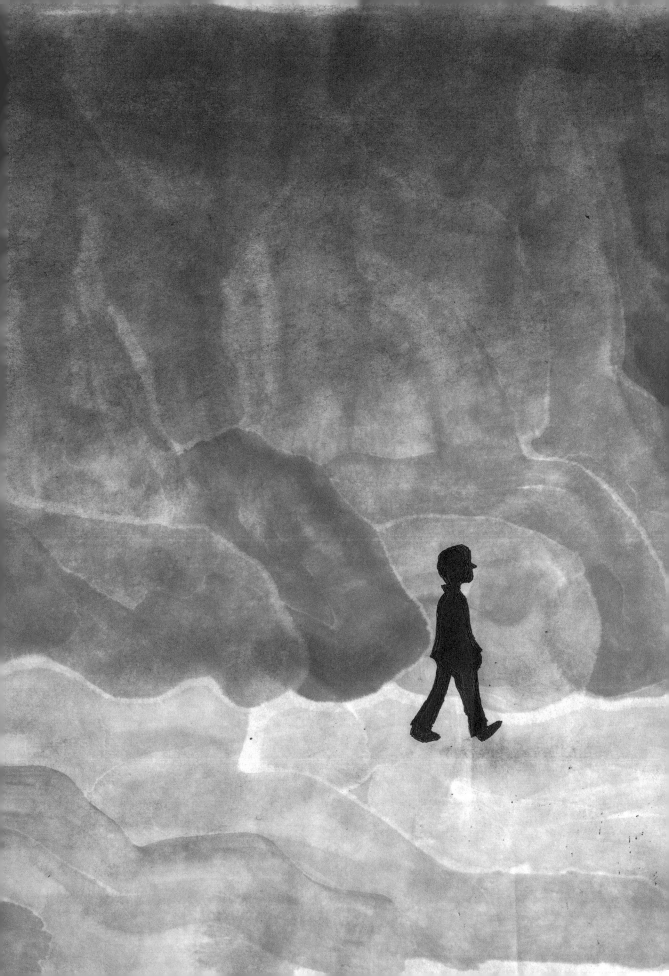

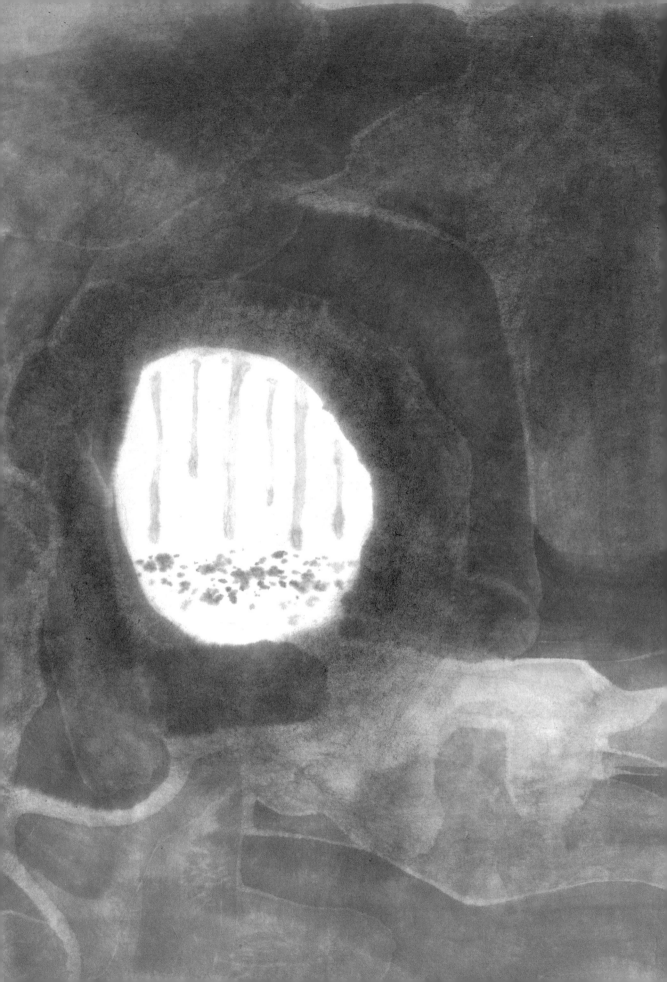

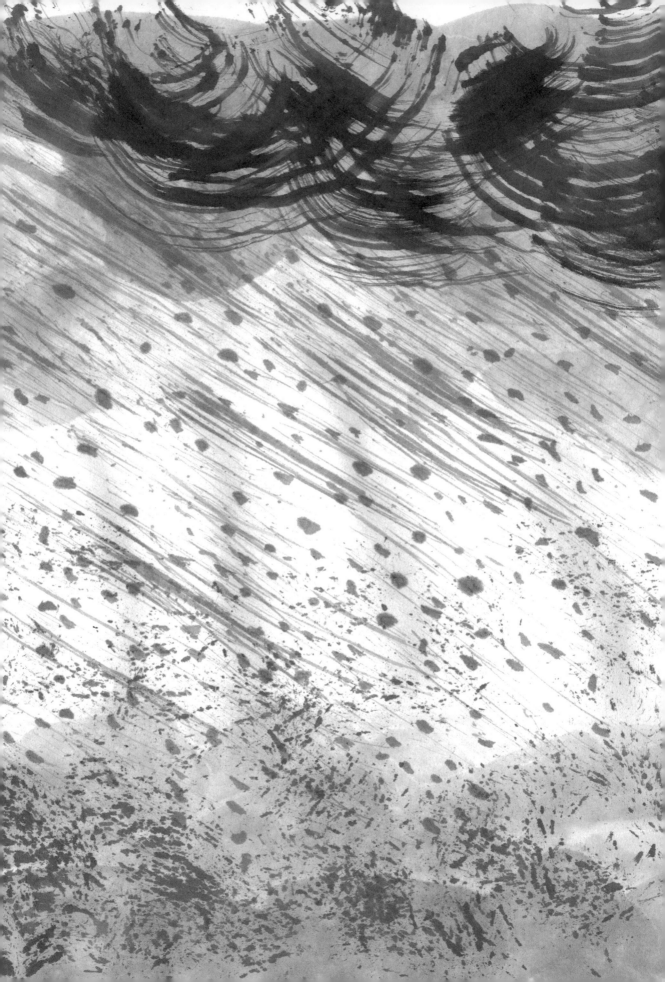